LOST
FREQUENCY

LOST FREQUENCY

a novel of

Sound, Speed, Power, and Greed

by BARRY SWANSON

Lost Frequency

A Novel of
Sound, Speed, Power, and Greed

Barry Swanson

FIRST EDITION

ISBN: 978-1-7327025-0-9
eBook ISBN: 978-1-7327025-1-6

Library of Congress Control Number: 2018955211

Cover Design by Melissa K. Harris

Pendrell Sound Press

For Elio,
For Michael,
For Chumley

"If you talk to the animals they will talk with you and you will know each other. If you do not talk to them you will not know them and what you do not know, you will fear. What one fears, one destroys."

—CHIEF DAN GEORGE

ONE

September 1964

The mother turned to look back at her young son who, in typical form, had become distracted, wandering slightly off the meandering path the family had taken that morning. Fortunately, the young one's aunt was keeping an eye and she gently nudged him forward, giving a quick knowing look up ahead to her sister, who nodded a silent thanks.

The sun was just starting to pierce the eastern sky over the San Juan Islands of the Pacific Northwest and light was beginning to glisten off the calm, black water of what's now known as the Salish Sea. A light fog had formed over the water, reflecting the orange-purple glow of the nascent sunrise. It was a few hundred yards off of the rocky sandstone shore and the air was still and the water serene, and all that could be heard was the caws of a nearby flock of gulls feeding off of a school of eulachon.

From below the water, a dark shape, darker than the water, rose quickly towards the surface, breaking the calm and rising more, revealing the massive dorsal fin of an orca. From the orca's blowhole came a puff of mist, like steam, spraying ten feet into the air. Had one been watching from a distance, through the dissipating fog, the sound of his expelled breath would have been heard an instant later. Then the orca took in a giant breath and was gone, down below. Shortly the entire family of orcas was breaking the water, including the mother and her son.

The sky was lightening as the sun rose higher and some of the more curious whales spyhopped to make a visual inspection of the environment above the waterline. Spyhopping is common among orcas and consists of a whale rising straight up and holding itself vertically, keeping its head and pectoral fins above the surface by kicking its strong tail flukes. Some of the orcas swam inverted and slapped their tails on the water. The area, so somnolent and still just moments before, was now alive with movement and otherworldly sounds.

The son became engrossed in a game of hide and seek with his juvenile cousins, the sunlight now streaming below the surface casting shadows through the bull kelp, creating good hiding places. The young whales reveled in the game, making whistling and clicking noises to register their delight. But soon the mother came along and the son followed her. He didn't always. As an eighteen-month-old youngster, he was gaining confidence and beginning to test the limits of his independence. He was becoming curious and inquisitive about the world around him, often going off on his own for short periods, albeit within the general confines of the pod. But now, he followed his mother; it was breakfast time.

In short order the mother echolocated something thirty yards away and, from the echolocation feedback, she knew it to be a salmon. Moreover, through her sensitive sonar, she could also discern from the salmon's elevated heart rate that it had become aware it was being preyed on. She moved in quickly for the kill, her son in pursuit. Fifteen feet below the surface, she pinned the salmon to the volcanic rock wall then manipulated it into her strong jaws where she cradled it, turning then to present the meal to her son. He took what he needed and left the rest for her.

The salmon was a Chinook salmon—the preferred meal of the family for its nutritive benefits and oil. But the next salmon the mother seized was a keta or chum salmon. Chum salmon have fewer nutrients; however, they're smaller, making this species of salmon perfect for the mother's purpose of teaching her son. It was her own unique approach. In fact, for the first few years of her own life, the mother preferred chum salmon. She found it milder and more palatable than the heavier tasting Chinook.

Quickly, she released the salmon from her jaws, allowing the wounded fish to swim away. The son wasted no time in going after it, taking it in his own jaws and then proudly returning to his mother who signaled her approval. Now, it was her who took the first bite. No longer on mother's milk, the son was learning the rules of the community. Food was shared.

The morning ritual and the hunting techniques of the whales had been passed down from the generations that had come before them. Like all groups of orcas, this one was matrilineal, the line of descent coming from the female side. The male offspring of orcas stay with their mothers their whole lives, leaving only to hunt or mate, and even then only for a few hours at a time. As many as four generations might travel together at any given time.

The particular matriline that this mother and son belonged to was part of several matrilines that were closely related by blood. Such an assemblage is known as a pod and pods can reach up to forty members or more, all traveling together—a socially-cohesive community. Pods can sometimes join other pods in "clans," the defining characteristic being a shared language. It's a complex and orderly structure, more ordered and unified than perhaps any community on earth. But of course none of this was known at the time.

Eight miles away in Friday Harbor, the scene was chaotic. At one end of the marina, men in windbreakers and canvas shoes were hurriedly loading gear into two large fishing trawlers and four runabouts, motors all running, the salt air thick with the smell of exhaust. "Get 'er loaded up, boys!" someone yelled. "Careful with that equipment!" someone else shouted. "No, no, no...stow the netting on the *starboard* side! Ain't you listenin'?!"

Young Dr. James Parker looked on at the frenzied activity from the flying bridge of the larger of the two trawlers. His childhood home was nearby, a mile south. Friday Harbor was on the eastern shore of San Juan Island, the main island of the San Juan Islands archipelago that sits off the northwest coast of the State of Washington. Parker's boyhood had been spent on the islands, a boyhood full of fishing and boating and hiking along the jagged shoreline of the isles. By the age of eleven, he was running his father's old Chris-Craft seemingly everywhere, his curiosity about the ocean in which his island home was situated never-ending. It was hardly a surprise that he became a marine biologist, a doctor of marine biology, at that.

But his career path had taken him from his beloved home and he vowed to one day return. And it wouldn't be to live in the cramped, three-room, clapboard house that was all his fisherman father could afford. Not that his father hadn't worked hard. As a teenager, he'd found employment in the lime quarries and kilns for which San Juan Island was famous. Lime was used as the primary mortar for masonry buildings and there was a time when the lime business was booming. The majority of the lime used to rebuild San Francisco after the 1906 earthquake came from San Juan Island. But the local industry suffered during the Great Depression and most of the kilns went under. This was the time James's father had worked in the lime business. By necessity, he changed careers and did what seemingly every other able-bodied young man did around the San Juan Islands at the time: he fished, working as a mate on a trawler, harvesting salmon in which the Salish Sea was rich. But rich would never be a word anybody would use to describe James's father. For James, it would be different. No low-wage labor jobs for him. No little clapboard house. He'd own a big modern house right on the water with a big boat to match, probably across the channel from San Juan Island on Orcas Island, the largest of the San Juan Islands.

That dream seemed far away, though; as far away as San Juan Island was from Los Angeles, the home of the growing marine park he was operating. The park was originally a glorified aquarium in Santa Monica that James had initially been hired to manage, but his expertise and forward-thinking had earned him a piece of the action. The original ownership had envisioned more of a carnival type park, with nautically themed rides that James found insipid at best and tacky at worst. He'd convinced them to expand on the aquarium idea, counting on the natural curiosity people had about the ocean and sea life. He opened a shark tank exhibit and a sea lion attraction and quadrupled the size of the aquariums, bringing in exotic fish from all over. A couple of dolphins were added and, before long, the park's attendance doubled, then tripled. James became a partner in the enterprise.

But he wasn't through. In the back of his mind was the idea of expanding the park further and making it into every bit as much of a destination attraction as Disneyland on the other side of the city, which had opened just a little over a decade before. For that, he knew he needed something new. Something special. Something *big*.

"Spotter Boy to Black Death, you read me, over?" The VHF radio crackled and James reached down and grabbed the mike. At the same time, he saw the small seaplane overhead, rocking port, then starboard as it flew low over the marina.

"I got you, Spotter Boy," James said into the mike. "You're looking good up there, Gus. Over."

"Listen, you guys about ready? The pod's about eight miles from here. Couple miles north of Roche Harbor. 48-40 north, 123 west. Copy?"

"Copy that, Gus. We're shoving off now. Over."

Within minutes, the men were all aboard and the small fleet was out of the harbor and into the open water, the sea churning behind it, the wakes of the trawlers cutting large waves into the flat sea.

James Parker was after a killer whale. An orca. Two of them to be precise. The plan was to kill an adult male, from which a perfect replica would be made—something to hang over the newly proposed entryway to the park, a spacious and welcoming open area for which the whale would serve as the ideal focal point. The second whale would be a young juvenile that the fleet would capture. James's trawler was big enough to carry the massive water tank that would hold the juvenile. Then the whale would be shipped alive to Santa Monica where he would become the star attraction of the park. If they kept him healthy, he could reach a size of twenty-five feet or more and weigh in excess of eight tons.

But the expedition was not without risk. Based on all that was known at the time, orcas had earned their nickname "killer" whales and the men on the boats were not without their misgivings and even downright fears. They were man-killers, these whales. No less an authority than the United States Navy had confirmed as much. Actual eyewitness testimony had been hard to come by, and even James, as a boy, seeing the pods of orcas around the San Juan Islands, could never recall an instance of an orca attacking a boat or otherwise presenting itself as a threat to humans—nor could his father who was always regaling his son with harrowing stories of his days at sea. Nevertheless, there was no sense in taking chances. Conventional wisdom and common sense told James that killer whales were killers. It was axiomatic.

The plan was for James's boat and the spotter plane to drive the pod into Reid Harbor on Stuart Island to the north, or, if the pod turned south, drive them into Nelson Bay on Henry Island southwest of Roche Harbor. The rest of the boats would cruise the perimeter and move steadily inward. Explosives would be used to create loud underwater noise sufficient to confuse the whales, or for defense—if it came to that. The men were armed with guns, as well. Once the whales were driven into the harbor or bay, massive nets would be positioned across the entrance to keep them from escaping. It would not be an easy plan to carry out and James knew that the fleet was going to have a fight on its hands.

But how great it was going to be to have that large orca at the entrance to the park. And how special to have a live whale in captivity for all to see and watch grow. He could live for decades—the park's best investment yet. James looked out over the water ahead and smiled at the thought of the young orca out there somewhere, about to become a part of history.

TWO

It was almost showtime. David Parker felt the familiar anxiety coursing through his veins. He controlled it much better these days, but it was still a challenge. He had to mentally pump himself up. Ignoring the anxiety always seemed to make it worse; he fared much better when he took the nervous energy and channeled it into his presentations. Everybody knew him as enthusiastic when he spoke to a crowd. Nobody could have known he was just plain nervous. And nobody would have believed it, anyway. CEOs of multibillion-dollar companies aren't supposed to be nervous, especially whiz kids like David James Parker.

It wasn't stage fright, per se. The anxiety was always there, at least on some level. A presentation such as what he was about to deliver was merely a trigger. There was no identifiable source of the anxiety but over the years he'd learned to live with it and these days his methods—meditation and various relaxation techniques—were better than his old methods. Not that he still didn't find himself engaged from time to time in the obsessive-compulsive rituals that his mind had devised in an effort to instill some control over his life. Open and close the desk drawer six times and everything will be okay. Count to fourteen before putting on your shirt every morning and the day will be a good one. Use only a white coffee cup and trouble can be averted. But at least the rituals were fewer these days.

He picked up his notes from the desk and heard a knock on the door.

"DJ, are you ready?" It was Casey, who opened the door a crack and peered in. DJ's executive assistant was stunning, as usual, in her black, shiny pantsuit and her golden hair. "They're ready to see you, big guy."

DJ and Casey had an easy rapport. She'd worked by his side for eight years—his only assistant. He could have had an entourage of assistants, but that was not his style. Casey did everything he needed and she did it with extraordinary efficiency, one of those people who seem to do everything effortlessly.

DJ was careful, though, to keep their relationship strictly professional. Not that he hadn't had the occasional, random, non-professional thought about her. But honestly he had no idea what he would do without Casey as his assistant and he was always convinced that if he ever tried to pursue anything romantic with her, it would end in disaster, with her leaving him. That wasn't worth the risk. Besides, there was that boyfriend of hers. Or boyfriends. Seemed like every six months or so there was somebody new in her life and each one seemed like "the one," or so Casey would tell him during one of those infrequent conversations they'd have that would stray into the personal sides of their lives. At this moment, "the one" was Jordan, a guitarist in a fledgling band.

But who had time for romance, anyway? DJ's work kept him too busy. His last serious relationship ended in disaster two years before. Julie was the kind of woman he'd consider marrying, something he'd rarely ever considered. But Julie had left him for another man, a betrayal that took him completely by surprise. It should not have. He simply hadn't been paying attention. To Julie or to their relationship. She'd had enough. Since then, it was nose to the grindstone for DJ.

"They're all out there?" he asked Casey.

"Yep. All the major networks. Plus, the entire executive staff, board of directors, upper-level employees, and the usual VIPs. All the software engineers are out there, too. Cripes, those guys have been working so hard on this. Your announcement and presentation today will make them prouder than they've ever been."

DJ felt his palms moisten but forced a smile. "Well then, what are we waiting for? Let's do it!"

He stood up and followed Casey out the door, quickly opening it and closing it twice behind him, hoping Casey wouldn't notice. She did, but like always, she pretended not to. Then they both walked down the short hallway that led onto the back of the stage.

Twenty minutes earlier, DJ had been surrounded by his executive staff for a final strategy meeting. But he had brought the meeting to a close, telling the staff members to all take seats in the audience. He had needed these last few precious moments to himself and now, before going onstage, the only person he wanted near him was Casey.

"How do I look?" said DJ.

"Like a real CEO."

"Very funny."

The suit was not DJ's typical mode of dress, but he felt like the situation warranted a bit more formality. DJ's standard, and therefore the standard for most of the company's employees, was casual. Typically, DJ would be in a white t-shirt, a mala necklace, faded black jeans, and fresh-out-of-the-box Stan Smith kicks, all of which made him look much younger than his forty-eight years, as did the dark brown hair, which curled carelessly over his collar. This became the dress code for pretty much everybody at Yaba except for some of the more conservative employees in accounting who wore ties, almost in defiance of the prevailing style.

Casey walked out on the stage first and the murmuring came to a stop as she began to address the crowd. "Ladies and gentlemen, thank you all for being here today to witness what we here at Yaba believe to truly be a game-changing technology. For those of you in the audience who have worked on this project, we thank you for your tireless efforts. For those of you unfamiliar with the project, we're confident that you'll be more than just a little amazed by today's introduction of it. But enough of me. Let's bring out the man without whom none of this would be possible. Ladies and gentlemen, the chief executive officer of Yaba, Mr. David James Parker!"

At that, the Yaba employees erupted, especially the team of engineers, and DJ walked out, now with a renewed sense of confidence. It was always like this. Once he took the stage, the nerves quieted down and he felt self-possessed and alive. The applause helped. DJ was many things as a CEO—brilliant, visionary, dedicated. But maybe his biggest strength might have been that he was beloved by his employees. Casey said it best to him one day: "These people would walk through walls for you."

"Thank you," DJ said as the applause slowly died away. "Let's end the suspense and let me introduce to you the reason why we're here today." With that, he pulled up his left jacket sleeve to reveal what looked to the audience like a sports watch. It had a dark gray band with a sleek, black face. "Ladies and gentlemen, I would like you to meet Soti. The name Soti is derived from the Greek goddess Soteria who was the goddess of safety and deliverance from harm. The Greek word *soter*, in fact, means savior and the principle of Soteria is found throughout Greek philosophy. The name Socrates is said to be derived from it.

"So, what is Soti? Soti is a personalized artificial intelligence robot that continuously monitors its owner's health and well-being. Observe.

"Soti, say hello to the audience."

"Good afternoon, good humans," came a female voice from the watch. "Or perhaps I will say good afternoon and good evening, as I suspect we are broadcasting to various time zones."

"Your suspicion is correct, Soti. Now, can you please tell the audience your purpose?"

"Certainly, David. My function is to focus on your safety, health, and well-being."

"Thank you, Soti. And what *is* my current health status?"

"Well, your blood sugar levels are off slightly, due no doubt to your decision this afternoon to forego lunch. You're a little more edgy than normal, a probable result of the situation you find yourself in at this moment, addressing hundreds of people." This brought a small wave of chuckles from the crowd. "But it could also be a partial function of the restless night of sleep you had. In fact, you didn't go to bed until one hour and thirty-eight minutes past your usual time. Currently, you're a bit dehydrated, despite my daily reminders that you drink more fluids. Your adrenaline and cortisol levels are much higher than normal, too. On the plus side, you had your daily constitutional this morning at 6:32 a.m. and all appears well, although I must say that with the churning currently going on in your stomach, you might need to pay a visit to the bathroom again not too long from now."

"Okay, okay, that's quite enough for now," laughed DJ, along with the audience. "Ladies and gentlemen, we're talking about 24/7 health and welfare monitoring by your own personalized robotic doctor, of sorts. Soti can anticipate stroke and heart attack. Soti can identify cancer and other diseases *in their very beginning stages*. Moreover, Soti can identify risk factors. So much is known today about the environmental and dietary causes of cancer and other diseases. Soti has access to all of this information and will make recommendations accordingly. This device will not only improve quality of life but will add years to human life expectancy."

The crowd began to buzz.

"How does Soti work?" DJ continued. "From an end-user perspective, it couldn't be simpler. A person's complete medical background is easily downloaded into Soti and then the user merely wears Soti as I am doing now, like an ordinary wristwatch. Soti is small and lightweight. Ah, but Soti is powerful. In short, and to greatly simplify for the time being, Soti relies on audio vibrations—the natural sound waves of the body—to accumulate, on a continual basis, the vital data of the user's physical condition. In a short period of time, Soti becomes intimately familiar with her owner, all the way from the owner's sleep regimen to his daily level of physical activity. From his food intake to, yes, his bowel habits, there is nothing that goes unmonitored. Coupled with a person's health history, and continuous access to the most cutting-edge medical knowledge available, Soti's monitoring allows her to react intuitively to prescribe the proper courses of action to enable a person to live as healthy a life as possible. Ask Soti anything about your body and Soti will have the answer.

"The packets of information you were all handed when you came in go into more detail about the science that's involved. For now, let us just say how excited we are about the technology that we've developed to bring Soti about. Ours is not an ivory-tower, theoretical approach. What we are introducing today is practical usage that we hope very soon to make affordable for everybody."

DJ paused in showmanship fashion and then, waving his right hand towards his extended left wrist, announced triumphantly, "Ladies and gentlemen: *Soti!*" With this, the room rose in unison and DJ basked in the applause. The members of the press remained generally impassive, of course, but even with them, DJ could notice a few wide eyes.

There were some additional comments DJ made, mostly centered on the technical aspects of Soti, the unique way in which Soti was able to derive information from her end user's body. Much of the technology was privileged of course. Everybody from the chief engineer to the cleaning crew had been sworn to secrecy. DJ then opened up the proceedings for questions from the press about testing and governmental approvals and liability issues and other miscellaneous matters, handling most everything deftly, but eventually calling upon various members of the executive staff to take the stage with him to field some of the more technical inquiries, including his top engineers, Paul Taylor and Donny Watkins. In time, he was joined by the director of technology, and Yaba's chief legal counsel. Eventually DJ closed the proceedings by thanking everyone for their attendance, and asking for one final round of applause, this time for the Yaba software geniuses who had risen to the many challenges he had thrown at them in his quest to make Soti a reality. Finally, he invited everybody to stick around for the reception afterward in the company salon adjacent to the auditorium. Almost everybody did so and DJ floated around shaking hands. After a presentation like this was over, his confidence buoyed by success—these were the only times he felt comfortable in social situations of this type. Otherwise he was a wallflower or, more typically, absent.

Casey approached him with a Jack Daniels and soda with a twist. It was his drink of choice, though he typically ordered it more for image than for drinking. He really wasn't much for alcohol and rarely finished any drink he'd be given whether it was a JD and soda, or a glass of wine. Casey found it amusing, correctly sensing that DJ, a tech geek deep down, was not above trying to blend in when he could. The whiz kid, trying to be an ordinary guy.

"Here ya go, boss," she smiled.

"Thanks, Case. How'd I do?"

"Amazing as always. But I have to say that Soti stole the show."

"No shit. Upstaged by a robot. But then that was the idea, you know?"

"You're a wizard, DJ. But what are you going to do to top this? Every innovation you've come up with has been bigger than the one before it. The world's starting to expect the next great technology every time you open your mouth. What's next?"

"I'll let you know as soon as I dream it up. Let's enjoy this one for a little bit first. In the meantime, I better go make nice to the media types. Shake a few hands and make sure we're on track to get some good publicity before they finish all our booze." DJ sauntered into the crowd seeking out the network representatives to personally thank them for coming and to answer any remaining questions they might have.

Casey went off to her office, but returned five minutes later, finding DJ talking with Madeline Velozo of *All World News.* "And that's how we were able to bridge the gap," DJ was saying. "We knew theoretically it was possible. And of course once we could prove it with the computer models, then all we had to do was find a way to replicate it, first in the lab, and then in the real world."

"Excuse me, Mr. Parker," Casey said, calling him by the name she would only ever use in front of the press, "I need a moment of your time."

DJ excused himself and walked a few yards away with Casey.

"What's up, Case?"

"I just took a phone call for you. From a Patrick Callaghan."

"Callaghan? My father's attorney?"

"Yes, that's him. I'm sorry DJ, I don't know how to tell you this. Your father died. His housekeeper found him. He was out by the dock at his place on Orcas Island. A massive heart attack, apparently. Callaghan wants you to call him."

DJ looked down for a moment as Casey calculated what the next best thing to say would be.

"I'm sorry, DJ. Why don't I just get the word spread around here and we can move towards ending the reception a little early. You can call Callaghan and take off. Probably you want some time to yourself. I know what he must have meant to you. Hell, I mean everybody knew your dad. The media people here will probably be getting the story themselves any time now. Why don't we—"

"We have things to accomplish today, Casey. We'll keep the reception going. Besides, afterward, I have that meeting with finance. And then Redfern and I were going to dinner to discuss the product rollout. Call Callaghan and tell him I'll call him when I can. I really just don't have the time right now."

Casey nodded and considered saying something else before settling on, "Sure, boss. Whatever you say." DJ turned and forced a smile and returned to where Ms. Velozo was now engaged with a reporter from *Wired*. That's when it struck Casey that in eight years of working with DJ, she'd never once heard him mention his father, the famous and controversial Dr. James Parker.

THREE

"I'm sorry for your loss, Mr. Parker." Kevin Gloss, the pilot of Yaba's corporate jet was looking over his shoulder back at DJ as he sat alone in the cabin. Gloss, fiftyish, sported a steel gray crewcut and was tall and trim, his clothes always neatly pressed.

"Thanks, Kevin," DJ replied, wondering how often he was going to hear "I'm sorry for your loss" over the course of the next few weeks. "Well, he had a fabulous life."

"He sure did, Mr. Parker. Larger than life, he was."

"Yes. Say, what's the ETA, Kevin?"

"A little under two hours, Mr. Parker. We're wheels up in five. Enjoy the flight."

"Thank you, Kevin."

DJ sunk back into the rich, Ferrari leather upholstered seat. Before him was breakfast: espresso, blueberries, and whole wheat toast with peanut butter. He took a few bites out of the toast and pushed the blueberries around the plate and gazed out of the window as the plane took off, banking over the Pacific Ocean as it left San Francisco behind. He was wearing Soti on his wrist and he noticed a red light flashing, indicating a message. He pushed the speak button and Soti reported:

"Your blood sugar is low, David. Your metabolism has slowed as well. Indications are that you have eaten, but insufficiently."

"I'm not hungry."

"Your body seems to disagree with that assessment, David."

"Who you gonna believe, Soti, me or my body?"

"I'm afraid I don't understand."

"Never mind, Soti," and then he pushed the speak button again to silence her.

Soon he turned his attention to his tablet and scrolled through the morning headlines of various media outlets. Most had a mention of Soti under their business sections. Yaba's stock had risen two points since the announcement the day before. But the big news seemed to be the death of James Parker, founder of the OneWorld Marine Park empire. *Upstaged again,* thought DJ.

One particularly long article detailed the humble beginnings of OneWorld—the park that was more carnival than aquarium. Through James Parker's vision, the park had grown, adding shark and sea lion and dolphin attractions. But the idea that finally put OneWorld on the map was the killer whale exhibit. Parker had brought in a juvenile orca. Several more followed. The original male, noted the article, was still alive: fifty-seven years old. The addition of the killer whales, trained eventually to perform crowd-pleasing tricks, helped vault OneWorld into its place as one of the most successful theme parks in the world. With Parker at the helm, OneWorld expanded. By the year 2000, there were four parks in the United States, one in Canada, and three in Europe. The article mentioned Parker's wife, Katherine, who had passed away in 1987 from breast cancer. James Parker, the article noted in closing, was survived by his two sons David James Parker, CEO of software giant Yaba, and Jonathan Joseph Parker who, the article said, apparently lived at the family compound, Seahaven, on Orcas Island, Washington State.

DJ swiped the article off the screen and closed the tablet. Then he leaned back in his seat to rest his eyes. He hadn't slept well the night before; visions of his press conference interspersed with visions of his father had kept him awake. The family compound. "Seahaven." When he closed his eyes he could see it perfectly. The sprawling house sat on a rocky bluff looking out over the ocean. There was a mammoth dock for the family's boats and even access for a seaplane. A private lane led back to the house from the main road, meandering several hundred yards through old maple trees and tall Douglas firs.

Growing up on the island, DJ had flourished. The house had a million places to play but he'd loved being on the second-story deck at the rear of the house the most. His father had set up a telescope there and DJ would spend hours gazing out at the water, looking at the ships on the horizon and frequently spotting pods of orcas. When he wasn't out on the back deck, you could find him motoring around the islands on the family boat, exploring the shoreline by foot, or riding his bike everywhere it would take him. The island was a magical place for DJ as a young boy. He wondered if he'd feel the same now. He'd been back only on very short trips. As far as Seahaven was concerned, he hadn't stepped foot on the property in seventeen years.

When he'd finally left the reception the night before, finished with the finance meeting, and had eaten dinner with his production manager, he'd gotten around to calling Patrick Callaghan, his father's attorney. He wasn't going to call him even a minute before. Sure, maybe it was a little passive-aggressive, but so what? He didn't have anything against Callaghan, exactly, but it was difficult for DJ to separate his father, or at least his father's business, from his father's lawyer.

Callaghan had presented him with something of a surprise. "You're the executor of the estate," he'd told DJ. "I really need to meet with you here ASAP. As you can imagine, there are a million things we need to go over. Including some final instructions your father had made for you via video."

Executor? Final instructions? DJ was amazed he was even in the will, let alone named as the person to make sure the terms of it would be carried out. He'd just assumed that everything would be going into a trust for Jonathan. Video? For him? "I'll be there the day after tomorrow," he told Callaghan, agreeing to meet in Callaghan's Seattle office. But first, the plane was making a stop at Orcas Island. Jonathan would be waiting for him at Seahaven.

Jonathan. DJ had never lost touch with the brother that was three years his junior, even through all the fights he'd had with their father. Jonathan Joseph—JJ—had become more than a brother; he'd become something of an obsession. DJ had spent an exorbitant amount of time researching JJ's condition. What had started as a diagnosis of autism when JJ was a child became, over time, a diagnosis of savant syndrome. JJ had trouble with rudimentary social interactions but could amaze with his uncanny ability to do complicated mathematical problems in his head. He had an astounding ability to calculate calendar dates. What month and day will it be 738 days from today? you could ask him, and sure enough he'd reply with September 2nd. What day of the week was December 16th, 1906? Sunday, he'd shoot back.

DJ's interest was initially out of brotherly love. He hated to see the way the other kids at school and around the island would make fun of his brother. JJ didn't quite fit in. He was extraordinarily awkward around other people and could never seem to follow a conversation. He had trouble talking, often repeating certain phrases over and over, typically ones he had just heard, or else blurting out something inappropriate. He had no ability to recognize a joke. The nicest thing the other kids called him was weird. Normally they called

him stupid and moron. Either way, JJ couldn't even understand that he was being made fun of. If this happened in
DJ's presence, DJ would go off the rails. "Why don't you try
calling *me* a moron?" he'd shout at the offender and the end
result would often be a bloody nose for somebody, more than
once for DJ himself but he didn't care. He wasn't going to let
anybody make fun of *his* little brother.

Their parents spent good money consulting the best doctors throughout North America and some early therapies
helped JJ's ability to interact socially but it became clear early
on that JJ was never going to be able to live an independent
existence. And so he remained at the Parker estate, being
looked after by Kioko, a full-time nanny that James hired after
Katherine had passed away. "Kioko means 'she who shares
happiness with the world'," the nanny, who was half Japanese,
explained to James during her interview. Not only was she
good with kids, she'd had experience with autistic children
and James hired her on the spot. Quickly, she developed a
strong bond with JJ. She never left, eventually taking on the
housekeeping duties as well, and then becoming James's personal assistant. It was Kioko who'd found James's body.

When the savant syndrome was discovered—DJ was the one
who first noticed JJ's mysterious abilities—JJ started becoming
more popular. Some of the locals got wind of it and would
often approach JJ out of the blue with mathematical or calendar
questions, maybe at a restaurant when JJ was out with James
and DJ. This pissed off DJ just as much as the name-calling. JJ
sometimes seemed to like the attention, so DJ was careful not
to interfere, but sometimes he'd declare to his father under his
breath, "He's not a trained seal, for crying out loud!"

Just the same, DJ was as intrigued as the locals were. After
he'd left Stanford with a post-graduate degree in computer
science, he had found himself with an interest in artificial
intelligence, which naturally led him to start pondering some

fundamental questions about how the process of thinking occurs. How, he wondered, could JJ do the things he could do? For that matter, how was it that he *couldn't* handle the basic socializing skills that others could handle effortlessly? How does learning take place, in other words? This is about the time DJ began throwing himself into his research on savant syndrome. For months, he consulted with the world's foremost experts, read dozens of case studies, and searched through online minutia about the condition until the wee hours of the mornings. Ultimately, he came up empty. Nobody knows how autistic savants do what they do.

"Landing in fifteen, Mr. Parker," came a voice from the darkness. DJ opened his eyes with a start and realized suddenly where he was. He'd fallen into a deep sleep. "Thanks, Kevin," he managed to mumble, rubbing his eyes.

The corporate jet was a fine place to snooze. Up above the world and its problems, DJ never had trouble catching a few winks. He religiously took his tablet with him, promising himself he'd catch up on emails and paperwork but whenever he flew, he always seemed to doze off.

He'd actually fought against the acquisition of the jet at first. Yaba doesn't need one, he'd said when the idea first came up from the executive staff. Regular airlines are good enough. But soon he came to agree with the idea that Yaba needed to portray the proper image. Yaba was the most successful technology company in the world, after all, and what would it look like if he and his corporate honchos were schlepping their way through airport terminals like any other travelers, boarding crowded flights and hoping that for God's sakes there'd be seats available in business class?

Yaba was DJ's dream. Out of Stanford, he bounced around for a few years, working at various technology companies and generally being regarded as something of a genius, but he could never seem to settle in one place or in one role for very long. His father, back when they were talking, said, "You have the same problem I have. You're an entrepreneur. You'll never be happy working for somebody else."

Yaba started humbly enough. Back when DJ's mother had been diagnosed with breast cancer, he'd learned everything he could about it. He'd always wished there was a way for the cancer to have been caught earlier and he never forgot that wish. After Stanford, he found himself obsessed with medical diagnostic techniques. This led to various experiments with diagnostic sonography, the use of sound waves to create internal images of the human body. The technology had been around for a while, but when DJ stumbled across a way to improve on it by the use of vibrations based on varying tonal frequencies, he attracted the attention of a major healthcare company that readily bought his new technology. The legend of the whiz kid had begun. Years later, he would make use of his concept and couple it with AI technology for the development of Soti. In the meantime, with the proceeds from the deal he struck with the healthcare company, he opened Yaba, applying his new idea to the field of music. He started the company in Silicon Valley, hiring the best minds available. Within a year, Yaba had produced the revolutionary and soon to be ubiquitous "Y-Songs" technology. Digital music in its contemporary form was rendered obsolete almost overnight. The deeper, richer, more nuanced sounds from music created with Y-Songs modulation technology—and listened to through the proprietary Y-Songs listening app—thrust Yaba into a class of its own in the tech world and well beyond. "The biggest revolution in music listening since the Edison phonograph," trumpeted the headlines. DJ became a billionaire seemingly overnight.

It wasn't as if James wasn't proud of his son. But it had always been his idea that one day DJ would take over his role as CEO of OneWorld. More than his idea; it was his dream, even from the time that DJ was just a kid. And why wouldn't he? DJ's interest in sea life matched his own. When he was little, he couldn't get enough of OneWorld. James would fly the whole family to L.A. on the weekends and the boys would spend all of it at the park, DJ soaking in every exhibit and JJ typically with his face pressed up against the thick glass of the orca tank seemingly mesmerized by the whales.

When their mother, Katherine, became ill, the weekend trips ended. When her condition became worse, James moved the corporate headquarters closer to home, taking over an office tower in downtown Seattle. Besides, by then, OneWorld was going international and the executive offices had outgrown the cramped administration building at the Santa Monica park. It was now a quick commute for James and he could spend a lot more time with his wife.

DJ's interest in sea life continued unabated, but somewhere along the line it shifted. As a teenager he found himself with conflicted feelings about his father's line of work. Maybe it was all the time he'd spent watching orcas in their natural habitat, but suddenly it bothered him to think of the ones confined to the tanks of OneWorld. The more he thought of it, the more distasteful the idea became. Eventually he got into long arguments with his father about the whole concept of putting animals on display for human amusement.

"It's not amusement," James would say. "It's education."

"Right," DJ would counter. "All those people coming to your parks are there to be educated."

The arguments always took the same course, typically getting louder as they progressed.

"Look, it doesn't have to be either-or. You can be amused and still learn something."

"Learn what?! How animals behave in zoos? What's that got to do with anything in the real world? Look around! Somebody can come here to the San Juan Islands and learn more here than they ever could at a OneWorld park!"

"Ah, but not everybody can afford to come here, can they? We're showing things to people that they otherwise would never, ever see! They get to learn something about nature they'd otherwise *never* learn."

"But what's the cost to the whales and the dolphins and the sea lions? Think they want to be caged up so that some fat slob tourists can 'learn' something?!"

"Those whales and dolphins and sea lions live the kinds of lives in our parks that other animals would kill for! They're safe, secure, healthy, and well-fed."

"You forgot to mention imprisoned! Orcas in the wild can cover up to a hundred miles or more in a day, did you know that? The Southern Residents' territory is the entire Salish Sea and the Juan De Fuca Strait, north all the way to Tofino! How far do your whales go in their tiny concrete pools each day?"

Ultimately, one or the other would storm out of the room. Katherine would eventually bring them back together. She was the glue that held the family together and when she died on DJ's fifteenth birthday, the eventual split between father and son became a foregone conclusion.

FOUR

Callaghan had arranged for a car and a driver for DJ at Orcas Island Airport. The car was a well-worn 1995 Lincoln Town Car and the driver was its owner—Bill Covington, a local and a long-time friend of the Parker family.

"Good to see you, David!" Covington smiled, taking DJ's suitcase and tossing it into the trunk. Covington was sixty-eight, a heavyset man with a high forehead and a friendly face that seemed to be in a perpetual state of amusement. A real estate man, he'd known the Parkers since they first arrived on the island, renting them a temporary house until their waterfront estate was completed. James had wanted to be close to the construction, overseeing the progress of his lifelong dream home.

"Wish it were under better circumstances," Covington continued. "Hop in." DJ slid into the passenger side while Covington more or less fell into the driver seat, the Town Car's suspension bouncing and creaking under his weight. "Yeah, we all loved your father. The whole island is in mourning. Boy, it's been a while, huh? I think you'll find the place hasn't changed much since you were here last. When was the last time you visited your dad's place?"

Covington drove the car out of the airport and before long they were heading south on Orcas Road. That would eventually become Deer Harbor Road, a long, winding corridor through the trees, which would take them along the upper waters of West Sound to Channel Road towards Spring Point Road and Steep Point.

"Gee, I don't really know, Bill. A while, I guess." Suddenly, seventeen years seemed like a very long time to be away from his father and the home in which he'd grown up, and DJ couldn't bring himself to say it out loud.

"Well, you're looking good! Gosh, seems like just yesterday you were running all around here, out on your boat or riding your bike. You know, we've all followed your career. You've done pretty well for yourself, haven't you? I won't pretend to understand all this new technology stuff, but the kids sure seem to like that music thing of yours. And I'll have you know that the missus has put some of our retirement into Yada stock."

"Yaba."

"But of course not as much as we've got in OneWorld. Ha-ha! Gee, your father sure had a Midas touch, didn't he?"

"Yes, he sure did."

"A Midas touch. Funny thing is, he used to talk about your success all the time."

"He did?"

"Oh, sure. 'DJ's doing this' and 'DJ's doing that.' You know, when he'd fly in for the weekends, we'd see him every Saturday night at Spanky's. He'd come in for a beer and he'd always buy the house a round. I tell ya, no matter how big that guy got, he stayed the same old Jimmy that everybody got to know when your family first moved here. Orcas Island won't be the same without him. But anyway, he would always mention you."

Covington went on about James some more, turning onto Spring Point Road, which eventually led along the shore above North Pass. Then he turned down the long, private lane towards the Parker compound. "Hope it looks familiar," Covington smiled. "You know, I'm kind of surprised you haven't come around more often. But I guess the corporate tech world can keep you busy, huh?"

"Yep. It's tough to get away. You know how it is."

"Sure, sure. Well, here ya go. Let me open the trunk for you. There ya go. Now, just call me in the morning when you're ready to go back to the airport!"

Kioko opened the door to let DJ in.

"Hello, Mr. Parker. Welcome home. It's very nice to see you. It's been...quite a long time." Kioko was in her mid-sixties now, but she looked younger. Small and slender, with nut-brown hair that hung loose down to her shoulders, it seemed to DJ as if she'd hardly aged at all.

"Hi, Kioko. Thanks. Yes, it has."

The two looked at each other for an awkward couple of seconds and DJ noticed the redness in Kioko's eyes. She'd been crying, although at the moment she stood stoically, a half smile planted on her face. The two quickly embraced. To both it felt obligatory. Kioko was careful not to take sides in family business, but of course James, not DJ, had been her employer and it was hard not to gravitate towards the master of the house, especially in light of the fact that DJ had made himself so scarce. To his credit, he hadn't lost touch with JJ, however, calling him every other day or so. Kioko would answer the house phone and so it wasn't as if DJ and Kioko hadn't talked at all in the past seventeen years. And of course there were those visits to Orcas Island, timed to coincide with trips James might be taking overseas. DJ would stay in a hotel in town and Kioko would drive JJ to see him.

Once, Kioko even flew with JJ to San Francisco to see DJ. That had been ten years ago. They'd driven over the Golden Gate Bridge and JJ, who had done some reading about it, had reported that "the Golden Gate Bridge is 8,981 feet long." Then he did some quick calculations in his head. "That's 2,993.666 yards. It's also...107,772 inches or...273,740.88 centimeters." Then they'd gone to Fisherman's Wharf and walked out to the end of Pier 39 to see the sea lions that have made the docks their own. Kioko and DJ practically had to drag JJ away.

"I wish you and your father got along," Kioko had mentioned later that afternoon in San Francisco. "I know it's not my place to say. But family is important."

DJ had known this to be true about Kioko. Hell, she'd become a vital part of the family. Of course, it was important to her. And if it wasn't her place to say, whose was it? Never married and unable to have children of her own, Kioko was nothing less than a second mother to JJ and seemed to have an intuitive gift for communicating with him. Nobody understood JJ better. And over the years, she'd become close to James, too. In fact, DJ found himself wondering every so often just how close.

"My father and I just disagree on some things," DJ had offered, hoping his explanation would be enough to change the subject.

"You're both stubborn," Kioko had said. "Your father loves you. And I know you love him."

DJ hadn't said any more and Kioko never brought the matter up again.

Now, standing in the foyer of the family home, the two knew that the only reason DJ was there was because of his father's death. If there was ever going to be a reconciliation, the time had passed.

"So where's JJ?" DJ asked.

"He's out back, on the dock, of course."

"Of course."

DJ walked through the large living room to the back deck and down the steps to the dock. JJ was staring out at the sea. "JJ!" he called. "How you doin' buddy?"

JJ turned and saw DJ and then pointed out to the water. "There's five whales out there," he said. "Five of them. Five whales."

"Is that right? Gee, I don't see any."

"They're out there. Out by Reef Island. Reef Island. Five of them. Three females, a bull, and a juvenile." Then he added, "They're from J pod," referencing the identification system used by researchers to track the movements of killer whales. Local to the Salish Sea was the whale community referred to as the Southern Resident Killer Whales. The SRKW group was a single clan consisting of three pods known as J, K, and L. JJ followed the community religiously.

"No kidding? Well, listen, can you come here a second and sit down with me? We need to discuss some things."

"Okay." JJ dutifully walked over to his older brother and they sat down in a couple of Adirondack chairs turned slightly towards each other. DJ could hear the gentle lapping of the waves against the dock pilings as he took in his brother. Though JJ was younger by three years, he looked younger still, gangling and wiry with long, tousled hair that fell down over his shoulders. Sometimes he'd be smiling for no apparent reason, and other times he'd be impassive and expressionless. At this moment, DJ observed the latter.

"Well, first of all, how are you, little brother? It's good to see you. I guess it's been a while since I've been home, hasn't it?"

JJ glanced around as usual. It was hard maintaining eye contact with him and DJ always had the impression that no matter how much it might appear that JJ was following the conversation, his mind was elsewhere.

"Yes, it's been awhile," JJ nodded. "Been awhile. Been awhile."

"Let's see, it was probably May of 2003."

"What date?"

"I don't know. Let's say the fifteenth."

"Um...6,245 days."

"Yeah, that sounds about right," DJ smiled. "Hey, guess what? I'm still wearing the mala necklace you made me. See? I wear it all the time."

JJ nodded. He had a flair for art. Making necklaces was a small talent of his, but his real strength was painting. James, in fact, had provided him with a studio, a casita next to the main house where he'd spend hours at a time drawing and painting stunning pictures of seascapes and marine life. Several of his pieces were showcased throughout the house and DJ had a few hanging up in his own place. Guests of both homes would ask about the paintings, wondering if there were more that could be purchased, but JJ could never part with any of his creations to a non-family member.

"Listen, JJ," DJ said, leaning in towards his brother, "we need to talk about what happens now."

"What do you mean? What happens now?" JJ's eyes were darting about.

"Well, now that Dad is...gone."

"I don't want to talk about that." JJ looked away, over towards the water. "Don't want to talk about that!"

"I know, JJ. But we have to."

"Don't want to talk about that!"

"Well, we need to talk about where you're going to go."

"Go? Go?"

"Yeah. I mean, you can't stay here. I imagine we'll be selling—"

"No! No! No! No! No!" JJ screamed, and then he stood up and with quick and jerky movements began pacing back and forth, still saying "no" but now muttering it under his breath.

"Okay, okay, listen, JJ, it's all right." DJ rose and stood beside his brother, putting his arm around his shoulder. "I'm going to take care of you, JJ. Remember San Francisco? How would you like to come back to San Francisco with me? I have a place on the ocean just like this. Remember? It'll be just like here."

"I don't want to leave! I don't want to leave...I don't want to leave..."

"Okay, okay, calm down, JJ. Take a deep breath. We'll talk more about it later. It's going to be alright. I'll make sure. You trust me, don't you? Of course. Now, listen, I have to meet with Mr. Callaghan tomorrow in Seattle. Afterward we'll figure out our next steps. Okay? We don't have to worry about it now. Tonight we'll go into town. Just you and me. We'll eat burgers. How does that sound?" Only two people in the world could calm JJ down when he was agitated—Kioko and DJ. But DJ knew that keeping him calm about the move was going to be an ongoing battle. Taking him out of his routine was not going to be easy. He'd warm up to it eventually, but DJ was going to have to take it slow.

"So what do you say, buddy? Burgers tonight?

"Okay," JJ said. "Burgers."

"In the meantime, I have to go through Dad's desk for some papers to give to Callaghan. Insurance stuff and bank account information and that kind of thing. I'll see you a bit later, little brother."

DJ went into the house and walked towards his father's study. Kioko meanwhile was on her way out to the dock with a couple of glasses of lemonade.

"Mr. Parker, I was just bringing you and JJ something to drink."

"Oh, sorry, Kioko. I have to grab some things of Dad's. But JJ's still out there. Hey, listen, Kioko...I don't know exactly what happens now with JJ, you know? I think I'm going to bring him to San Francisco. I think I should have him close to me. So...we'll be selling the estate. I know how valuable you were to my father, Kioko. And to me, of course. It's a lot to ask, I know, but I'd like you to consider staying on. I'll pay you what Dad paid you. And of course all moving expenses to San Francisco. You'll have your own quarters and everything."

"Thank you, Mr. Parker. I will consider it. I'd be lying to you if I said I hadn't been thinking about what becomes of me now. But I've been here so long. I have friends here. My life is here. As you know, I grew up on Orcas Island. I have a sister here and we are very close. And I'm not getting any younger, Mr. Parker. Your brother means the world to me, but I'm just not sure I can leave."

"I understand, Kioko. Please think about it. We need you."

"Of course, Mr. Parker, thank you," Kioko nodded, and then she walked towards the back door to the dock.

DJ stepped into his father's study and looked around. It hadn't changed since he was a kid. The large oak desk sat imposingly in the center of the room, the dark leather swivel chair behind it—the chair he'd often sit in as a boy, pretending to be his father. One whole wall was a bookcase, filled with books on marine life, interrupted every ten books or so by books on ships and shipwrecks. On a large table near the bookcase sat a four-foot replica of the *Essex*, a whaler that had been attacked by a sperm whale in 1820 and sunk, the only known case of a whale ever attacking a ship. The twenty-man crew spent ninety-five days stranded in the South Pacific with no food or water. Ultimately they resorted to cannibalism. Eight crew members survived and their accounts later inspired Herman Melville to pen *Moby Dick*.

The other walls of the study were adorned with plaques and photographs and memorabilia collected over the years. There were pictures of business associates and company functions. DJ recognized a shot taken at one of his parents' annual clam bakes. It was always the event of the year. Eighty or so friends and colleagues would be invited to Orcas Island and James would put most of them up at the Rosario Resort on Rosario Point, looking out over East Sound. DJ remembered one party in particular very well. He was nine and the house was full of guests. His mother was wearing a silk, watercolor dress that James had bought her in India and she looked magnificent. His father was in charge of the music, as usual, and DJ could recall the sounds of the Beatles, the Rolling Stones, Cat Stevens, and Queen blaring throughout the home. He'd gone to bed but had awakened in the wee hours of the morning to the sound of "Peace Train" skipping on the turntable, replaying the same phrase at the end of the record. He'd gone downstairs to the main living area to turn off the music and had been hit by the smells of cigarette smoke, spilled alcohol, and a pungent odor he would later in his life identify as marijuana. To get to the stereo, he had to step over more than a couple of passed-out party guests and he thought at that moment how cool his parents were to be hosts of such a bacchanalia.

Centered on the near wall of the study, under a bronze picture light, hung a large painting JJ had made. It was of an orca, the first orca that had been captured by James, the one still alive in the Santa Monica park. He'd painted it from memory after a visit to the park, but he'd put it in its natural habitat, swimming alongside its mother as a young juvenile. At the bottom right corner of the picture, DJ noticed for the first time an apparent title: "Boo and Chumley," it read in small, scripted letters. Just like JJ to imagine the whales with names.

The rest of the wall was family photos, several of them with Katherine and her two boys. DJ noticed how young she looked, how alive. One picture was taken on the beach and it must have been taken by James. DJ was probably about six, JJ around three. They were at the edge of the water, one on each side of Katherine as she walked with them, holding their hands and heading towards the breaking waves. They were all in stride but were all looking back over their shoulders at the camera. Everybody was smiling but as DJ gazed at the picture, it struck him that it was his mother's gentle smile that lit up the scene. He would see that same smile on her face up until the day she died. Even then, even close to death, she exuded a kind of warm contentment, an ongoing equanimity that had been her life's trademark. Her easygoing disposition had always contrasted with her husband's ambition and determined striving. He'd always wanted more; she'd always been happy with whatever she had. Her death had hit DJ hard, unmooring him. His normal anxieties had intensified and later on he would realize that his obsessive-compulsive behaviors started about this time.

DJ's eyes moved to another picture just of JJ on the dock. He must have been around eight or nine and he was staring out to sea with a look that seemed equal parts pensiveness and innocence. Another photo was of DJ, age twelve, standing at the wheel of the family yacht with James's arm around him. James was gazing down at his son. He looked proud. DJ glanced around the walls at all the photos he had not seen in years and was struck by how long ago his childhood suddenly seemed.

Finally, he sat down in his father's chair and leaned back. It was impossible not to feel his father's presence. Later, Kioko would pass the room on her way to the kitchen and glance in to see DJ sitting in the desk chair, facing the wall. His shoulders were shaking and he was holding his head in his hands, silently sobbing.

FIVE

Patrick Callaghan, sixty-four, was a tall, trim man with an elongated face and ginger-gray hair that had been a shade more crimson in his younger years. When DJ had arrived at his office, he'd ushered him right in. "As you might guess, we have a lot of ground to cover," he had said, guiding DJ into the conference room where various files had been neatly stacked on the long table. Collectively, they described the estate of James Parker—everything he'd acquired and owned, all of it reduced to paper representations, the digitized versions all sitting on Callaghan's laptop.

"Listen, David, I know you and your father didn't get along," Callaghan said. "In fact, I know you two hadn't talked for quite a while. I was his attorney for thirty years. More than his attorney. His friend. He was very proud of you, you know. And I think he would have wanted you to know that."

"Uh-huh," DJ said, with a slight roll of the eyes that was not lost on Callaghan.

"It's true. And I'm sure he would have wanted to tell you that himself, but your father—well, he was a proud and stubborn man. Don't get me wrong. You couldn't ask for a better friend. And I'm not going to pretend I know what was said between you two to cause your estrangement, but whatever it was, well, it hurt him."

DJ knew what it was. DJ knew exactly what it was. He could picture it like it was yesterday. He'd been visiting Orcas Island over a long weekend, staying at the compound, mostly to see JJ. In their conversations, he and James had done a fair job of skirting around their respective careers. James would forever harbor feelings of disappointment that DJ hadn't followed him to OneWorld and consequently rarely asked about Yaba's success. And DJ had made his opinions about James's work all too clear. And so the two mostly discussed family, fishing, and sports. It had been cordial, if a bit tense. But then OneWorld came up again, and it was DJ's fault.

On that Sunday morning, a pod of orcas had come into view of the house. James, DJ, and JJ had been sitting on the dock, with James and DJ paging through different sections of the Sunday paper and drinking coffee. JJ had pointed the whales out to them. "From K pod," he said. "They're going three knots, looking for salmon. K pod's not as big as L pod, which is the biggest. The Southern Resident community has eighty-two members."

"That's great, JJ," James had remarked.

DJ snickered lightly, ostensibly to himself.

"Something you want to say?" his father sighed, raising an eyebrow.

"Nope. Not really." Then, "Well, since you asked, I was just thinking how great L pod would look in one of your tanks." DJ would never know why he said that. Why he couldn't just leave it alone. Maybe it was the hangover he'd been nursing from the night before. He'd hooked up with some old buddies from his youth and, despite his typical aversion to drinking heavily, he'd managed to tie a good one on. He and his friends had closed down Spanky's.

"Okay, there it is," James said. "I wondered when I'd finally get to hear one of your snarky remarks. Just like you to criticize and insult my life's work. Let me ask you something. What do you think paid for this house where you grew up? What do you think paid for Stanford? Where do you think the money came from?"

"So what are you saying? You want me to pay you back? Because I can, you know."

"What, ask you to pull money out of your precious computer game company? I wouldn't dream of it."

"We don't make computer games! You know what? Screw you, Dad. I don't need this shit. As a matter of fact, I *will* pay you back."

"You sure? You know me—I'm liable to take the money and imprison and torture more animals! Right?"

JJ had become agitated and had started pacing with his hands over his ears and humming loudly so as to drown out the sounds of the argument, which only escalated from there. This was a good thing, DJ would think in retrospect, because hopefully he never heard DJ's final statement: "Fuck you, you're nothing but a goddamned prison warden!" Then he'd gone into the house, packed his bag, and left early for the airport. That had been seventeen years ago.

"Well, in any event," Callaghan continued, "It was always my belief that he wanted to make things right with you. The fact is, he was ready to take OneWorld in a different direction, a direction I think you would have approved of. Just between you and me and the lamppost, I don't think he ever stopped thinking that maybe someday he could get you involved in the business."

"Me? Involved in OneWorld?"

"Indeed. Listen, we need to go over his will, but before we do that, I think you're going to want to watch the video he made for you. It's about six months old. Now, I don't know how much you knew about your father's health. He'd had some heart trouble over the past couple of years. He'd had a stent put in but the doctors told him that he'd need bypass surgery. Preferably sooner rather than later. Well, he kept putting it off. Said he was too busy. I never thought he was taking it seriously enough. Then again, he made this video, so I guess it must have at least crossed his mind that his problems weren't exactly trivial. He never did get the surgery and, well, six months later, here we are."

"Okay," DJ said, "let's get on with it."

Callaghan turned on the flat screen TV that hung on the front wall of the room and, in a moment, the face of James Parker materialized.

"Hello, DJ. If you're watching this, then you know that my time has come." James was seated in the leather chair behind the desk in his study, the same chair DJ had occupied the day before. He was composed, relaxed. He looked directly into the camera and he spoke without notes. "Maybe you're mourning me in some way, I don't know. Or maybe not. Either way, whatever's come between us in the past doesn't really matter now, does it? I'm sorry we ended up like we did. Profoundly sorry. You're my son and you never stopped being my son. And I have never stopped loving you. No matter what, please know that."

Callaghan glanced over at DJ out of the corner of his eye for a reaction but DJ was sitting impassively. Inside, he was anything but impassive. The talk of fatherly love tugged at him and the sight of his father after seventeen years threw him for a loop. Aside from the occasional news clip or photo, the last time DJ had seen his father, he was sixty-two. Now, DJ was looking at a seventy-nine-year-old man. Still, he could see the familiar glow of energy in his father's blue eyes. He hadn't lost that. And the handsome, powerful presence was still there, maybe not as pronounced, but it didn't take much for DJ to imagine his father as he'd known him years before. And there he was, his father, speaking to him directly as if they were in the same room. The whole thing was disquieting and if Callaghan would have looked under the conference table, he would have seen DJ silently tapping his foot against the carpet, ritualistically counting the taps.

"Onto the business at hand," James was now saying. "I have something to share with you, DJ. Something important. Something I think you may appreciate. It begins with a story. You know, of course, about our capture in 1964 of the very first orca for the Santa Monica park. I had told both of you kids about it long ago, back when you were interested in my work. But I didn't tell you everything.

"You see, on that day, we had plans for more than just a capture. In addition to the young whale, we had wanted to take a large, grown male orca. Kill him, that is to say, and take him back to Santa Monica using his body to manufacture a perfect replica to hang at the entrance of the park. Then we'd hang the skeleton inside the park in a separate exhibit.

"Now, you have to understand, we didn't really know anything about orcas back then. Killing a whale was like killing a fish. To us, an orca might as well have been a big...salmon. Worse, even. These were *killer* whales, after all. They were dangerous and predatory. Lethal. Who would have thought back then that they were intelligent and peaceful enough to be trained? You can criticize the parks all you want, but even you have to admit that without the work of OneWorld, we'd still be largely in the dark about these magnificent creatures.

"Well, anyway, it was a beautiful day on that September morning as our little fleet set out from Friday Harbor to intercept a pod of orcas. We used the boats and a seaplane to drive them into Reid Harbor. Well, and some explosives. Then we set up nets across the entrance to the harbor. There must have been twenty or thirty orcas trapped right where we wanted them. One of our boats motored alongside a large male and they radioed over to me. 'Okay to make the strike?' they asked. I gave them the go-ahead and one of the guys heaved a harpoon towards it, hitting it right on the head. The harpoon glanced off the whale but it obviously stunned him. He began to sink. My boat had moved over to the scene by then and I was pretty much right on top of the action, watching what happened.

"Well, I don't have to tell you that orcas don't breath involuntarily like you and I. If they fall unconscious, they simply stop breathing. So this particular orca started sinking into the depths, nearly out of sight. I figured he was a goner and it was a shame because he would have fit the bill perfectly for what we were looking for. Then, just when I was about to shout a command to turn the boat around, I saw something amazing. Through the murky water, I suddenly saw the whale rising. But he wasn't rising by himself. There were two other orcas with him, using their pectoral fins to raise him up. Pushing him upwards to save his life! They had seen what had happened and they had come to his rescue. I was astounded, needless to say.

"As all three whales came close to the surface, I heard the man from the other boat again, but this time we were close enough that he was just yelling over to me. *'Should I strike again?!'* He had a hold of the harpoon again and he was poised to throw it. Both boats were right on top of the whales. We could have had our pick of the three. I looked around to see two men on my boat with harpoons, too. It would have been so easy.

"'No!' I yelled back. *'No!'*

"I got some quizzical looks that day, let me tell you. But once I saw how hard these two whales were working to save the other, I just couldn't bring myself to order its death. In the end, the whale seemed to regain its senses and the three went off together. We never did kill a whale that day.

"Well, in the meantime, another boat had identified a juvenile and I ordered my boat to close in. We waited until it surfaced and launched a net over it. Took us a couple of tries, but we got him. We reeled him in using one of our biggest winches. He might have been a youngster, but he weighed about twelve-hundred pounds. Anyway, as you know, that was Eilio, the whale that put OneWorld on the map.

"I've told you about his capture before. But here's what I never told you: as we reeled him in, a solitary whale followed him to the boat. A female. And as we lifted Eilio onto the deck, this female spyhopped literally next to the boat. One of my men even raised a harpoon, almost instinctively, like in self-defense. But the whale wasn't threatening or anything. She was just watching. Now, here's the kicker. She kept looking at *me*. It was disconcerting, to say the least. Then I noticed the other whales gathering around. They showed no fear. Nor did they show any hostility. The just seemed...concerned. Anyway, we secured the juvenile, kicked the boat into gear, and left. The other boats rolled up the nets going into the harbor and we all went back to port. The pod followed most of the way.

"Now, I've never forgotten about the behavior of those whales. And I've especially never forgotten that female that came up to the boat. It occurs to me that she was Eilio's mother. I probably sensed that at the time, but, truthfully, I'd put it out of my mind for all these years, just like I put it out of my mind that she was looking at me. Had to be my imagination. That's what I told myself. The same with the two whales rescuing the other. I don't know...I guess I convinced myself it was all just coincidence. Whales might be smart enough to train, but they don't have emotional intelligence like we do, you know? That's what I made myself believe. Hell, that's what I'd *come* to believe.

"And so I never really thought about it anymore until about three years ago. As you know, that's about the time we were starting to get some flak from the animal rights people.

There was that investigative piece on 'Newsline,' and then there was that damn book that came out where some of our ex-trainers were quoted telling stories about the orcas, anecdotes that presumably demonstrated the fact that the whales had a sophisticated language and even feelings. Suddenly, these killer whales were smart, sensitive beings.

"We decided to go on the offensive. My plan was to show the world that orcas were not as smart as people were suddenly thinking they were. We opened a research lab to determine once and for all the actual level of intelligence of orcas—both cognitive and emotional intelligence. We spent millions. Then we ran the research through a third-party company to give the impression of neutrality. We paid for it and we directed it, but we needed them to monitor it, to sort of audit our work. It was all on the up and up, but of course we were hoping our research would reveal that there really wasn't anything extraordinary about orcas.

"Well, we were wrong. Through various experiments with different whales, we learned these animals are incredibly smart. It wasn't just tricks they could do, which of course had always been our main interest. It was problem-solving skills. We set up challenges for them. At the Santa Monica park, outside of the public viewing areas, we built enormous obstacle courses that the whales would have to navigate to find food. Mazes, of sorts. We made them so they could easily be reconfigured into different courses. Well, the upshot was that we couldn't create anything that was too difficult for them, no matter how complex.

"But there was more. We learned something about how they communicate with each other. On any given obstacle course, a single whale might take several minutes to find his way. But then the next time, he'd conquer the course in seconds. He had memorized it, you see. And this would hold true even if we waited days or even a week or more to run him through the course in question. We'd mark the course in particular ways, letting him know which one of several it was by clues, like certain shaped buoys for instance. Any given whale could hold as many as twelve different courses in his head at any given time. A single clue would tell him whether it was, say, course number four or course number nine. Good God, most humans can't even do that!

"Okay, so that's amazing enough. But here's the communication part I mentioned. If we brought another whale into the tank with the same course, and left the first whale there, but prevented him from actually swimming the course and showing the way, the second whale would conquer the course just as quickly as the first. His first time on it, mind you. How was he able to do it? We determined he was able to do it because the first whale, within earshot, so to speak, *would tell him how to do it.*

"Now, we had every underwater listening apparatus known to man and we heard some basic echolocation sounds, but we heard nothing that would warrant the second whale being able to 'hear' from the first whale the kind of detailed instructions necessary to successfully navigate the course. But there was no other explanation. Leave that first whale out of the equation, and the second whale would have just as much difficulty with the course on his first attempt as any other whale. He'd do it, but it would take a while. Put the first whale into the equation by keeping him close by, and the second whale would run the course as if he'd done it a hundred times.

"We still don't know for certain how they did it. We suspected they must have been on some strange frequency. A frequency that's unknown, at least to us. So we adjusted our equipment every which way possible, but we could never pick up on how they were talking to each other. It's still a mystery. But there's a frequency of some description that's out there somewhere. One that we missed. How else can you explain it?

"Now, the other component in these experiments was the first whale's motivation. He had nothing to personally gain by communicating the course direction to the second whale. It was the second whale that was trapped in the maze, looking for the way out and the way to the food source. Was it empathy? When I think of those two whales saving the other whale's life on that September day back in 1964, I have to believe it was. Empathy and understanding. Human attributes, you might say. Exclusively human—or so it's been believed.

"Well, of course, these weren't the results we expected, nor what we were hoping for. If word got out about the true nature of our whales, the public would be fit to string us up. The board of directors, on seeing our preliminary report, shut the project down immediately. So ended the research. At least as far as anybody with the board knows. But I've kept it going. Secretly. The board would have my head if they knew. But, DJ, all of our findings about the intelligence of these orcas has thrown me back into time, to that day when we captured Eilio. And now I'm haunted by it, haunted by the sight of that mother looking at me as I snatched her son away from her forever. It was me, DJ. There were nine men on my boat. *Why was she looking at me?*

"I have to make it right. I have to keep this research going and I have to find a way to make it public without simultaneously destroying OneWorld. You can disagree, but I really believe the park has done amazing things in marine education. I dedicated my life to it. I don't want to see the parks shut down. On the other hand, I can't in good conscience remain silent while these amazingly intelligent animals remain captive. Christ, DJ, you were right. I was a prison warden.

"But now I have a plan. Somebody has to carry it out and there's nobody in the world I trust to do so besides you. Patrick will go over the details with you and make you privy to all the research. DJ, I don't want my legacy to be that I was a zookeeper of beings that I have come to believe are every bit as intelligent—maybe even more so—as we are. My life's work has to mean more than that. And it can, with your help. Can you do it, DJ? Can you help me? And if you don't want to help me, can you help the captive whales of OneWorld? There's nobody else. Just you, my son. Just you."

James Parker's face faded out as the video ended. Callaghan sat quietly allowing DJ time to process what he'd just seen and heard. DJ continued staring at the blank screen for several moments, saying nothing, and hardly breathing.

SIX

The funeral was well-attended. Most of the people from OneWorld's corporate headquarters in Seattle were there, as well as colleagues from all over the world. A few members of the media were there, too. They had set up shop on Orcas Island two days before and apparently had been interviewing locals about James Parker. Soon, they were interviewing them about DJ. Word was getting around about the estrangement of the famous sea park operator from his also-famous, tech-company CEO son.

One woman from the *National Globe* had actually approached DJ at the public viewing the night before the funeral, asking him for a comment about the relationship. "I'm just here to honor my father," DJ had managed before turning and walking away. A security guard was then called over and from that point on, the funeral home was more careful about whom they let in. At the funeral itself, family and close friends were sequestered in the front row with a couple of beefy guys in suits sitting right behind them, keeping a close eye on anybody who approached.

Darren Wheeler, longtime friend and associate of James, delivered the eulogy. He'd been retired for years but was with

OneWorld almost from the beginning, working first as an independent consultant at the Santa Monica park, and then as a full-time officer of the company. He and James had become best friends over the years. His tribute was a long, rambling thing and DJ's mind wandered throughout.

Mostly, he was thinking about Patrick Callaghan's words to him in his office two days before. The fact is, he'd barely been able to focus on anything else. After the video, Callaghan had given DJ a broad outline of James's plan. OneWorld would concentrate its resources on one giant project: a two- or three-hundred-acre "sea sanctuary" where the thirty whales currently scattered throughout the parks would be relocated. Whales held their whole lives in captivity, having never learned to hunt, cannot safely be returned to the open ocean. But the sanctuary would mimic real life, giving the whales their freedom. James could only speculate as to what would become of the parks once the orcas were removed, but he imagined that, absent the main attractions, they would probably have to close.

"Just as well," Callaghan had said. "Your father believed that funding the sanctuary would actually require the closing of the parks. He'd written several pro-formas, which I have here for you, based on various scenarios. None of them seem to work without the closing of the parks and the selling of the land, buildings, and everything else. Naturally, the fly in the ointment is trying to get *that* past the board of directors. Frankly, your father could only see one way his plan—his *dream*, I should tell you—could happen."

"And what's that?" DJ had asked.

"By taking it to the public. By making the case so strong that the publicity would steamroll the board into compliance."

"But...what case?"

"The case for the intelligence of the whales, of course. Your father wanted to release his research. By so doing, he imagined a clamor from the general public. This would be answered by an organized marketing campaign touting the new sanctuary. If done properly, OneWorld would look down-right responsible. Hell, maybe even heroic."

"I guess that sounds reasonable."

"Yeah, but there's only one problem. Your father never finished the research. Now, I don't know any more about the research than you now know. I'm a lawyer, not a scientist, and it might as well all be Greek to me. But you're a com-puter guy. You have a scientific mind. And you know as well as anybody that just saying something is so without telling why or how isn't anything more than conjecture. This com-munication thing that James talked about—his evidence of intelligence—will be derided without some type of proof of how the communication takes place. Even the problem-solv-ing trials, the courses that the whales had to navigate and the apparent sharing of information—as impressive as that all is, it only provides anecdotal evidence. How is one whale able to talk in such detail to another? That's the thing that your father felt had to be answered before taking the research public. It's that unknown frequency that he mentioned. That's what we need to discover."

DJ had said nothing as Callaghan continued, though his mind was racing.

"Now, DJ, your father wanted to present all of this to you specifically, and I'm sure you can guess that a big part of that is because of your work at Yaba with sound. But there's much more. It's because of your love for the whales. Your philoso-phy, which all these years had been diametrically opposed to his. But, you know, your father was just being a good busi-nessman, DJ. In that, you and he are probably more alike than you know. But there's something else, something stronger. He never said it in so many words, but I know that him wanting you to take over his plan was his way of apologizing and, well, winning you back as his son. Of course it's a posthumous thing, but, nevertheless..." and then Callaghan's voice had trailed off. The meeting had ended with Callaghan telling DJ the research was ready to be delivered to him whenever he was ready to receive it. All the details of the experiments. DJ had no legal obligation to take over, of course. "It's completely up to you," Callaghan had assured him, though the assurance seemed half-hearted at best. Callaghan wouldn't say so, but DJ was sure that he felt DJ had a moral obligation if not a legal one.

Now, sitting in the front row at his father's funeral and listening to Wheeler drone on, DJ felt more conflicted than he ever had about anything in his life. He pulled at his shirt collar, feeling as if he couldn't breathe and wishing like hell that he could yank his tie off. Soti was flashing red under his sleeve, alerted by the change in heart rate. It didn't help DJ to know that Callaghan was sitting exactly one row behind him. He could practically feel his breath. Thoughts kept hitting him from every direction. It was crazy to take over his father's plan. For one thing, strictly from a practical standpoint, he didn't have the time. Yaba was just beginning the biggest product rollout of its history. He didn't have the resources either. Or, more accurately, he was reluctant to spend them on research that might come to nothing. Sure, the experiments were impressive, but there was an intimidating distance resting between what had been observed and uncovering the science behind it. It could take years. Maybe decades. And in the meantime, who would he hire to do the research? He couldn't take his own engineers away from their duties at Yaba. Then he'd be in trouble with his own board of directors. And even if he did somehow uncover this mysterious frequency his father was so sure existed, even if he could reveal how it was that the whales presumably communicated, and then released his findings to the public, how could he be sure that would provide enough of an impetus to ultimately force the board of directors of one of the most popular theme parks in the world to close eight locations and invest in a brand new project that, according to DJ's quick calculations, couldn't possibly cost less than a cool *billion* dollars?

No, there just wasn't any way he could do it. It made no sense. Moral obligation? What did he really owe his father anyway? He certainly didn't ask for this to be thrust upon him. Frankly, it wasn't fair. Screw it, he decided. By the time Wheeler wrapped up his eulogy, DJ had made up his mind.

It was getting near dusk by the time the last of the guests had left the compound. The funeral was late in the morning and Kioko had arranged for a catered lunch afterward on the waterfront at Seahaven. The lunch stretched out for what seemed to DJ to be forever. After a couple of hours of condolences uttered to him in a myriad of ways, he finally excused himself and retreated to his room, locking the door, taking some aspirin for his pounding headache, and removing the damnable tie. Then he lay down for a nap, the words of his father echoing in his head, and then the tender feeling of loss. Maybe it was this that soon had his mind drifting back to his mother. Her words echoed, too—the last coherent thing she'd said to him on the day she'd died. *Be happy.* Soon, he fell into a deep sleep. When he awoke, he was just in time to hear the last mourner's car driving off.

DJ rose and walked downstairs, through the kitchen where the caterers were busy cleaning up, and then outside to the deck and down the steps to the dock. Kioko was sitting by herself, looking out at the glowing red sky of the horizon as it reflected off the flat water. The sun was setting and above the horizon there was only a scattering of wispy clouds over-head, leading upwards to the gradually darkening sky. A lone bald eagle sailed past low in the sky and the setting seemed so serene to DJ that he could practically feel the air meeting the wings of the eagle with each graceful stroke. He real-ized just then that his headache was gone and he stood for a moment taking in the sunset, breathing in the clean, cool air, and surveying the panorama before him—the watercolor sky, rising up behind the water, which was blending now into the adjoining skyline of towering trees, the orange sun slipping downwards, mirroring flashes of scarlet off the sea. This might be the most beautiful place on earth, he thought.

"It's really something, isn't it?" he said at last to Kioko.

"Yes it is," Kioko said, her gaze remaining fixed. DJ took the chair beside her, and as he sat down, he glanced over at Kioko's face and could see that she'd been crying.

"I know my father meant a lot to you, Kioko."

"I...loved him, DJ."

"Yes, well, we all did. I mean, of course, we had our prob-lems, he and I, but—"

"No, I mean I loved him."

"You mean...*loved* him?"

"Your father was a great man. For years, I'd been in love with him. I never said anything. I loved it here, loved working with JJ, loved being in charge of Seahaven, and loved being your dad's assistant. I didn't want to risk any of that. And I sensed your father wouldn't have wanted to get involved anyway. He was so into his work, you know?" The thought of Casey suddenly flashed into DJ's head. "Well, anyway, I don't know why I mention all this. I guess I just needed to tell somebody. I hope you don't mind."

"No, of course not. And I'm sorry, Kioko. This must be harder for you than I imagined. Well, your secret is safe with me."

"Thank you."

Neither said anything for a few minutes until Kioko finally broke the silence. "You will help finish his work now, won't you, DJ?" she asked. "Towards the end, that was all he ever thought about."

"Yes, well, about that...we'll see, I guess. I mean, I have a lot going on with Yaba, you know."

DJ didn't know how to tell Kioko he'd decided to pass on his father's plan. Maybe he would pass on it gradually. Tell her he'd look into it, then keep putting it off until, finally, it would just sort of become forgotten. For the moment, he decided to switch the conversation, putting her on the spot instead.

"Have you thought any more about coming to San Francisco with JJ and me?"

"No, I really haven't been able to focus on the future very much, I'm afraid." Truthfully, she had given the matter a great deal of thought. Inside, she was torn and confused. Her inherent sense of duty was conflicting with her deep personal desire to stay on her beloved Orcas Island. She had no way to convey to DJ her level of turmoil but knew that it was her burden and hers alone. It was perfectly reasonable for DJ to sell Seahaven, return to San Francisco, and take JJ with him. She'd always known this time would come, but she'd always imagined that when it did, she would know what to do. It surprised her that she didn't.

"I understand, Kioko," DJ said gently. "Take all the time you need. Well, there's JJ down at the end of the dock. Think I'll see what he's up to." Then he rose and strolled down to where JJ was sitting on the edge of the dock, his legs dangling over the side.

"Whatcha up to, buddy?" DJ said, sitting down beside him, dropping his own legs over the side. "See any orca today?"

"Yesterday, the T18 transients came by looking for a harbor seal. T19B is in that pod with his mother and brother.

His name is Galiano. Galiano. His name is Galiano. He's the largest known orca in the Pacific Northwest. He weighs over eight tons. Eight tons."

"No kidding?"

"T18 is his grandmother. Scientists aren't sure if she's his aunt or grandma. But she's his grandma. She's his grandma. Grandma. Orcas are apex predators. They have no fear and are the largest member of the dolphin family. Transients eat mammals; residents eat fish. Usually only Chinook salmon. Residents usually eat only Chinook salmon."

"How about that." DJ had heard it all before, maybe a hundred times, and although it was awkward at times to stay in the moment, he always made sure to seem interested. Sometimes he wondered who JJ was speaking to. Surely he knew he was repeating himself. Truthfully, however, DJ marveled at his brother's ability to spit out data and information so matter-of-factly.

"The residents are having a harder time finding food locally this year so they're staying out in the Juan de Fuca Strait where there's more salmon. They don't come by as often now. I miss them. I miss my friends. They don't come by as often now. Dr. Lilly says orca are as intelligent as humans and perhaps more social. I've read all his reports and manuscripts. Dr. Lilly. Dr. Lilly. He did experimental tests on dolphin brains. He killed some. He felt bad and stopped. Dr. Lilly stopped."

DJ remembered the name John Lilly. He was the neuroscientist who studied dolphin communication in the 1960s, '70s, and into the early '80s. Although Lilly's methods were considered radical, he uncovered many interesting truths about the dolphin family. He also attempted communication between humans and dolphins and envisioned a time when the killing of whales and dolphins would cease, not from laws being passed, but from humans' eventual awareness of their innate understanding that these are ancient, sentient earth residents with extraordinary intelligence and incredible life force. Not to be killed—indeed to learn from. His work helped the creation of the United States *Marine Mammal Protection Act of 1972.*

JJ sat silently then for a minute or two, pensively. From the distance, a ship's horn could be heard.

"The speed of sound is 1,125 feet per second," he said suddenly, perking up. "1,125 feet per second."

"Yep, that's right," smiled DJ.

"Of course it's faster underwater. Sound in the ocean travels at 4,838 feet per second. Faster underwater."

"Is that so?"

"That's 4.3 times faster. Dr. Lilly's research determined that dolphins process information faster than humans. Much faster. Much faster than humans. Faster."

"Hmm...I didn't know that, JJ. Interesting." And indeed it was. DJ couldn't help but be intrigued by theories of sound. It was an occupational hazard.

JJ's eyes darted around. "James Parker is dead," he said. "He died right over there last week. I miss him. He was my dad. He was working on a plan to help the captive orcas of the OneWorld parks. He had a plan. James Parker."

DJ studied his brother's expression and could feel the hurt. JJ had lost his mentor, protector, father, and provider. No more Mom; no more Dad. James may have spent a lot of time away from home traveling over the years, but he unfailingly returned. Not anymore.

Later, long after the caterers were through and long after Kioko and JJ had retired to bed, DJ sat in his father's leather chair in the dark. He thought about sound. He thought about frequencies and communication. He thought about Kioko and her feelings about James Parker and his research. And clearly JJ was aware of their father's intentions. He thought of his own childhood and his love of the sea and sea animals. What had happened? He'd gotten away from it. Gotten away from his roots. Christ, when was the last time he'd taken the time to gaze at a sunset like tonight's?

Finally, he thought about his father. Their estrangement. Maybe it didn't have to continue. Maybe, even after death, there are ways to mend fences. He took out his phone and called Casey, because, well, there was nobody else to call. She listened to him and heard the anguish in his voice but stopped short of offering any tangible advice. Follow your heart, she'd said. Typical Casey, DJ thought. Then she'd said get some sleep and DJ decided maybe that was the best advice of all.

He awoke the next morning to the sun streaming through his bedroom window. He went downstairs and poured himself a cup of coffee and then placed a phone call to Callaghan. "Okay, Patrick," he said, "I'm ready to see what you've got."

SEVEN

"And what of OneWorld?" Boris Kucherov looked around the conference table, his dark steely eyes glaring from under his bushy black eyebrows. Kucherov was a solid, barrel-chested man of fifty and he dominated the room with his presence at the head of the table.

Five other men were sitting at the table with him, all of them senior VPs. The conference room was situated at the top floor of a renovated office building from the Soviet era that sat on Bolshaya Gruzinskaya Street in the Tverskoy District of Moscow, a twenty-minute drive to the Kremlin. Close, but not too close. Neftkomp was ostensibly a private concern, but the majority interest happened to be owned by the Russian government. CEO Kucherov liked to think he operated the company with a certain amount of autonomy, but he knew without a doubt which side his *khleb* was buttered on.

"Things will be easier now that James Parker is dead," spoke Alexander Kovalchuk, the man sitting to the left of Kucherov. "There was no hope of a takeover with Parker still influencing the board. Now that influence is gone."

"But his son," Pavel Fetisov chimed in. "He could be a problem."

"He has no interest," said Kovalchuk. "Oh, of course, he'll have a financial interest once the estate is settled, but the man is head of Yaba. What does he want with marine parks?"

What do *we* want with marine parks? thought Kucherov to himself. How did the largest conglomerate in Russia, owner of oil, utility, transportation, and manufacturing companies, get saddled with the task of bringing on board a chain of entertainment facilities that boasted, so far as he could tell, nothing more than glorified fish tanks? The order had officially come from the minister of industry and trade, but it had been made clear to Kucherov that it had originated at the Kremlin. The president himself wanted OneWorld. It was part of the new Russian policy of *Zakhvat*, the economic strategy of investing in iconic foreign businesses, a means by which to better align the country with the peoples and cultures of the world. A healthy, more connected relationship with the world, so went the thinking, meant healthy economic returns. It was win-win, with a more globally engaged Russia. Kucherov liked things just the way they were, but he was nothing if not loyal. The president was an old friend, after all. More than a friend. Kucherov knew that he held the CEO position of Neftkomp only because of the president's influence.

"Still, we need to move fast," said Fetisov.

"Then we need to...encourage...the board of OneWorld to sell," said Kucherov.

"We already have one of the board members in our pocket," offered Evgeni Sergachev with a sly smile. "A well-respected member of the board." Sergachev was a tall, thin man with narrow, beady eyes and a receding hairline. He rarely smiled and when he did, one knew immediately that it was for good reason.

"A board member, you say?" said Kucherov, arching his bushy eyebrows.

"Indeed. We've made great inroads over the past month. We think this member will be able to adequately persuade the rest of the board to sell. It's a good time for it, anyway, what with the death of Parker. Plus, the animal rights crybabies are still making noise."

"This is good news, Evgeni," said Kucherov. The kind of good news Kucherov could use. Acquiring good news was actually his purpose for the meeting. He was having coffee with the president at the end of the week and was expected to make a full report on Neftkomp's operations. Being an old friend of the president's notwithstanding, these meetings went much smoother if Kucherov could show company progress. Sometimes the coffee would be followed by vodka.

Vodka would be nice, thought Kucherov. It wouldn't be like that meeting three years ago. How could he forget that? Neftkomp's oil concerns were in dire straits. The president was not pleased. There was no vodka that day. "I cannot control the world's supply," Kucherov had said in the face of an uncomfortable berating. "If there is a glut, there is a glut." The president knew he was right but it still wasn't pleasant being the messenger of bad news. Meanwhile, the president had his own people to report to. Nobody was supposed to speak about them, but everybody knew who they were. On the surface, they were successful, wealthy businessmen. But they were also men of great influence, with their hands all over the inner workings of the Russian Federation. The *oligarkhi*, they were called. The president would have to face his own berating. A month after his meeting with Kucherov about the oil, Russian military presence in the Middle East was expanded. The president himself made a whirlwind tour of the oil exporting countries. Shortly after that, the global price of oil increased and Neftkomp's financial numbers were a lot more palatable.

"Yes, I think we'll be able to proceed nicely," said Sergachev.

"And then of course will come the expansion," said Ilya Larionov.

"You get ahead of yourself, Ilya," said Kucherov.

"Perhaps. But it's exciting, no? We have all seen the plans from our engineers for the bigger parks. And a total of twenty of them in ten years! Here in Russia, in China, all throughout Europe. Sea life from all over. Six killer whales in each park. I can't wait to take my kids."

"Yes, yes, there are grand plans," said Kucherov impatiently. "Fish, fish, and more fish."

"Well," said Larionov, "it will be an improvement at least over the Moscow People's Aquarium, no?" This brought laughter from the room. The People's Aquarium had been built in the 1970s under Leonid Brezhnev by a committee of Soviet officials highly experienced in construction and engineering and poorly trained in ichthyology. The place looked like a palace but the fish kept dying. Experts were brought in to run the facility, but their budget was severely limited, the cost of the construction having ballooned twenty times over initial estimates. The crowning moment of the aquarium had come during a state visit by the secretary of the Socialist Unity Party of East Germany. The curtain came back on the massive dolphin tank and floating on top, in plain view of the secretary, was a dead dolphin. Nobody knew how long it had been deceased. The trainers were found drunk in the basement. Since then, the aquarium had fallen into complete disrepair and had become the butt of many jokes about Soviet inefficiency.

"Let us focus," said Kucherov, stifling the laughter. "Tell me more about this board member, Evgeni."

"Robert Mackinnon. He seems more involved in the day-to-day activities of the company than the others. He has spoken to my man in Seattle in depth about the assets of the company, shared with him some inside information. Apparently, there is some research, too, which he is trying to interest us in."

"What kind of research?"

"I don't know. Something about the intelligence of the whales."

"So what? Tell him he can keep his research. That needn't be part of the deal."

"Apparently, he'd sell the research himself. A side deal. The board wouldn't want it released, from what I am told."

"A side deal? Hmm…interesting. There must be some value to this research, though I can't for the life of me imagine what it could be. Research on whales? They're big fish. And they entertain crowds who pay good money to see them. What more is there to know?"

"Mammals, actually," corrected Larionov.

Kucherov ignored him and looked thoughtfully at the ceiling for a moment before turning back to Sergachev. "Have your man in Seattle look more deeply into this research. We're not going to pay for information we could find ourselves online at *Vikipediya*. But if there is something of realistic value, I suppose we should know about it."

"Yes, I will do it."

Sergachev was a good man. If he said he would do something, it would get done. Kucherov had known Sergachev from his university days in Saint Petersburg. Both had graduated with honors from the State University of Economics and Finance. Kucherov had had the contacts, though, and rose higher in the Russian corporate world. Evgeni Sergachev, on the other hand, had his own talents. Mainly, he wasn't afraid to get his hands dirty. He always seemed to be able to find ways to get the hard things done, or else he knew the right people to get those things done for him. His man in Seattle, for instance. Who was he? How did Sergachev even know him? Sergachev seemed to have a network of mysterious men who reported to him and made things happen. How they made things happen, Kucherov never asked. Part of it was that he trusted Sergachev implicitly. Another part was the desire to maintain deniability if something went wrong.

"Well, let us waste no time then," said Kucherov. "The sooner OneWorld is a part of Neftkomp the better. But enough of that. Pavel, tell us how things are going with our rail service."

Kucherov was happy to change the subject to an industry he understood, one of real significance. Entertainment held no interest for him. Rail, oil, coal, electric—these were industries you could hang your hat on. He was proud of his leadership in these areas. Most days he went home satisfied with the work that he was doing—home to Natalya, his wife of thirty years. Tonight, their grown children were coming over for dinner: their son Andrei and their daughter Anna. Anna would be with her husband. The couple was expecting their first child, Kucherov's first grandchild.

As for OneWorld, it would surely take care of itself. Sergachev was on the job. Soon enough, Neftkomp would own OneWorld and then would come the expansion. More fish for people to see, thought Kucherov. *Bol'shaya sdelka.* Big deal.

EIGHT

OneWorld had buried the research. In fact, it had been destroyed, so far as anybody at OneWorld knew. Nobody had a copy of it. Nobody but Robert MacKinnon. And Robert MacKinnon knew that he alone possessed it. His fellow board members had tasked him with making sure every piece of research had either been shredded, or wiped clean off of any computer that had come in contact with it. He had promised the board he would take care of it and then happily reported that the job had been done. Good old, trusted MacKinnon. He was the guy you gave the difficult work to. That's why he was on the board and he knew it. Every successful business enterprise needs a son of a bitch. MacKinnon was proud to be OneWorld's son of a bitch.

MacKinnon had been around long enough to know the score. The way you get anywhere in this world is to find weaknesses and exploit them. The lion doesn't go after the strongest, fastest gazelle. He goes after the feeble one. Weaknesses were everywhere. OneWorld's implicit trust in him was a weakness. So was loyalty. When he had decided to hang on to the research, MacKinnon wasn't sure exactly what he'd use it for, but he knew that it gave him a leg up. It left OneWorld in a vulnerable position. OneWorld had gotten just a little weaker while he had gotten just a little stronger. That, he calculated, would someday come in handy. All he needed was to bide his time until the right opportunity presented itself.

He was concerned at one point, after it was decided to kill the research, that James Parker would object. But Parker seemed to understand that the board was not going to be talked out of squelching this sudden threat to the profitability of the company and he'd willingly gone along with it. Almost too willingly. But of course he'd probably not been feeling himself, what with the heart condition. One thing was for sure. Once he died, any threat from Parker died with him. It's possible, of course, that he might have kept some of the research himself, but who would even know to look for it? Nope, MacKinnon was the only one who had it.

And then the opportunity had come, one that wouldn't even require any betrayal of OneWorld: the man who had approached MacKinnon at the diner on Pike Street in downtown Seattle where he always had his morning coffee. Every day at 8:00 a.m. before going to his plush office suite. You could set your watch by it. The man, tall and sturdy and wearing an expensive, well-tailored suit, had approached him at the breakfast counter and said, "Mr. MacKinnon? My name is Gardner. I don't mean to disturb your breakfast. I just wanted to give you my card. I represent a client who would love the opportunity to chat with you about a company you have an interest in." MacKinnon noticed a subtle scar running down the man's cheek, which seemed somehow incongruous with his manner of dress and demeanor. It appeared as if the man had tried to conceal the scar with makeup, but it was still partially visible.

Robert MacKinnon had an interest in several companies. In addition to his seat on the board of OneWorld, he was still active in the financial consulting firm he founded, was president of a real estate brokerage, and sat on the board of trustees of a mutual fund. "I'm listening," he had replied. "What company? What client?"

"Oh, please," Gardner had said with a disarming smile. "I have already taken too much of your time. Please, hold onto my card and call me when it's convenient for you. We can meet at a time and place more suitable." And then he'd turned and left.

The bone-white card said simply:

Nelson Gardner Investments
Seattle, Washington

At the bottom was a phone number. Curiosity had gotten the better of MacKinnon and the next day he had called the number and two days after that they'd met at Elliott's Oyster House for lunch. Gardner's client was a foreign entity. A *big* foreign entity. Their interest was in OneWorld and they were willing to pay whatever the cost. Gardner had mentioned this and then had said, "In fact, Mr. MacKinnon, their interest is such that they'd be willing to pay a substantial...commission...to the person who could help procure the sale."

"A commission?" MacKinnon had said. "Well, I can't help you there, Mr. Gardner. I'm on the board. Conflict of interest, you know."

"Of course. Well, naturally the commission needn't be publicized. It could remain just between my client and...and the procuring cause of sale. A consulting fee, let us say, Mr. MacKinnon."

"A consulting fee, eh?" MacKinnon had rolled the idea around in his head and decided he kind of liked it. "How much of a consulting fee, Mr. Gardner?" The two had then discussed some numbers, all of it very hypothetical, of course, as both were equally quick to point out.

Interesting that out of all the board members, it was MacKinnon that Gardner had approached. Smart guy, MacKinnon thought. Must have done his homework. MacKinnon was the one man on the board who could get things done. That explained the house on Mercer Island, the Ferrari, the speedboat. MacKinnon loved the good life. Almost as much as showing it all off. But, really, what's better than feeling the envy of others? Isn't that what it's all about? What's the use in winning if you don't display the trophies?

The lunch had been two months ago. MacKinnon had since approached each board member privately and discussed the contact he'd made who had evinced an interest, on behalf of a large foreign entity, to buy out OneWorld. "A once-in-a-lifetime windfall," is the way MacKinnon had put it. Nobody seemed to dismiss the idea out of hand, although a couple of the members had cringed a bit at the idea of relinquishing American ownership of such a longstanding American institution. "A genuine piece of Americana," one of the board members had said. "The way of the world," MacKinnon had replied, shrugging. "Budweiser is owned by a Belgium company now. What are you gonna do?"

Since then, Parker had died and Parker had represented the biggest threat to selling off the company. It was his baby, after all. But now that threat was gone and with just a little arm-twisting, MacKinnon was sure he could convince the board to vote in favor of the sale. That's what he did, after all. That was one of his two major talents—the ability to put complex deals together between people. That's what his real estate brokerage was all about and this was really just another real estate deal, albeit it a billion-dollar one.

His other major talent was his willingness to skirt around legalities. Insider information was his stock-in-trade. That's what made his financial consulting firm so successful. And not just the skirting around of legalities, but the ability to do so without leaving fingerprints. Three times the SEC had investigated his firm and three times they had come away with nothing. This, MacKinnon knew, was what separated him from the pack. You have to bend the rules to be successful, he always said. *Really* successful. And who wants to be anything less? Hell, sometimes you just have to flat *break* the rules. Just never leave tracks.

In the end, MacKinnon knew that the business world was a game of negotiation. A game that's not for the faint of heart. And he never lost. Well, almost never. He could think of three negotiations he'd lost convincingly: his three divorces. The third sealed it for him: he would never marry again. Hell, if women were going to be that expensive, he figured he'd just buy them one night at a time. At least a hooker lets you know going in how much it's going to cost you. "I don't pay women for sex," he once bragged to a stranger in a bar. "I pay them to leave."

But in the business world, MacKinnon was a negotiator par excellence. What made him so was that he was not above using powers of persuasion that others might never in a million years use. Blackmail, bribery, extortion—well, these were just harsh words to describe intelligent negotiating tactics. You could be smart and use such tactics and reap the rewards, or you could be a sap and kowtow to misguided, outdated notions of ethics and morality that are designed to keep the suckers of the world in check. And in the poorhouse.

This research, for instance. The research that he just sprung on Gardner as the two were sitting at Elliott's again. It was a beautiful little nugget of information and MacKinnon knew that in the hands of a master like himself, the nugget would mean a huge payday.

"And the research is all yours for a simple ancillary fee," MacKinnon said over his clam chowder.

"Ancillary? How 'ancillary'?" replied Gardner.

"Let's say the same amount as the commission. That seems fair, wouldn't you agree?"

"So you want my client to essentially double their commission to you? Explain to me again the value of this research."

"Well, it's not exactly that the research in and of itself is valuable," MacKinnon explained. "It's a matter of what one does with it."

"And what should one do with it?"

"Nothing," MacKinnon smiled.

"I'm afraid I don't understand."

"The research is a ticking time bomb designed to implode OneWorld. It needs to be dismantled like any other bomb. Should this research get out, there'd be a public clamoring for OneWorld to be shut down. Clamoring? Hell, there'd be a lynching. Don't you see? If it got out that orcas are every bit as intelligent as humans, maybe even more so, the outcry over their captivity would be overwhelming."

"If they're so intelligent," Gardner joked, "Why aren't *they* bidding to buy OneWorld?" This caused both of the men to laugh heartily but there was a grain of cynicism in the joke that MacKinnon picked up on. He knew he had to sell his prospect on the validity of the research. And so for the next twenty minutes he related the findings—the problem-solving skills of the whales, the obstacle courses they had navigated, their empathy, and their unknown means of communication. Gardner listened attentively and MacKinnon could sense that he had him hooked. Gardner wasn't joking anymore.

"So how do we dismantle this ticking time bomb?" Gardner asked flatly.

Time to reel him in, thought MacKinnon. "That, you can leave up to me," he said. "I have the research safely hidden away and I can guarantee without reservation that it exists nowhere else but where I have it. For the fee, it's yours."

"And what if my client won't pay this fee?"

Now MacKinnon had to be especially careful in choosing his words. But this is why he made the big bucks. "Well, of course, I can't be responsible for what might become of the research. Leaks happen, you know. Just when you have something safely hidden away, somehow it gets out. Nothing is foolproof. Naturally, I'd hold onto the research as best I could, just in good faith. But you never know when it might, somehow, get in the hands of, well, the media, for instance. What a shame that would be for your client."

Gardner seemed a tad irritated, but that was to be expected. His client will initially chafe at the extra fee, but they'll go along with it in the end, MacKinnon thought. They'll have to. What possible choice will they have? And just as a token of civility and good faith, MacKinnon picked up the lunch check.

"I'll be in touch," Gardner said brusquely on the way out, to which MacKinnon smiled and offered his hand. The two shook and Gardner walked off. MacKinnon was pleased. The meeting had gone well. It would have been possible to have overplayed this hand of his, but MacKinnon had known just what to ask for and how to present it. This wasn't his first rodeo. This foreign entity, whoever they were, would learn how shrewd he could be. If you're going to deal with Robert MacKinnon, you'd better be prepared to play hardball. Yes, sir. That much MacKinnon was certain of.

NINE

DJ sat in the living room back at Seahaven with files of material spread out all over the coffee table, the sofa, and the floor. There were photographs and videos and index cards, thumb drives and handwritten notes, digital copies and hard copies. It was everything Patrick Callaghan had— all the research that had been done on the orcas. Now DJ was sifting through it all, trying to make sense of it. His father's conclusion seemed reasonable enough. It was hard to deny the fact that, somehow, the whales had a hidden means of intelligent communication. But for all the research that had been done, this is where all hypotheses seemed to dead-end. There was absolutely nothing that would indicate how that communication took place.

DJ thumbed through a book of handwritten notes, all of them signed "B.L." The book detailed one of the experiments and judging by the reactions of "B.L." it must have been one of the very first. Astonishment practically dripped from the pages. "They shouldn't be able to do this," read one of the entries. "Would not believe had I not seen with my own eyes!" read another. The note on the final page said simply: *WTF??*

DJ thought for a second and then reached for his phone and called Callaghan. "Patrick," he said. "I need some more information."

"I don't have anything more than what I've given you, DJ."

"Who's B.L.?"

"Huh?"

"There are notes here signed by a 'B.L.' I sure would like to talk to him."

"B.L.? Okay, let me call OneWorld. Maybe I can wrangle something from Human Resources. As your dad's legal representation, I ought to be able to get them to share something with me about him. I'll be in touch."

DJ glanced down at his wrist to see Soti flashing red.

"I'm concerned, David," Soti said when he pushed the button. "Your physiological signals indicate stress consistent with the denial or repression of feelings."

"What are you talking about, Soti?"

"Occasional, temporary stress of this kind is not in and of itself unhealthy. But the stress I have sensed has now been fairly steady for the past forty-eight hours, David. Consequently I am bringing it to your attention."

"Okay, so what kind of feelings am I repressing, Soti?" DJ asked, more amused than curious.

"There are many feelings, the denial of which could trigger these physiological indications. Fear or anger, for instance."

"Well, I can't think of anything I'm afraid of right now, or angry about."

"Or grief," Soti continued. "The feelings, not recognized consciously, can create unhealthy stress."

Forty-eight hours? Two days before was his father's funeral.

"Okay, Dr. Freud. Thanks, but I have work to do." Then he pushed the button and Soti went mute once again.

JJ ambled into the living room and sat down on a chair next to the sofa.

"How you doin', buddy?" DJ said.

"Good. Good. Good. What are you doing? Doing?"

"Trying to solve a mystery, brother," DJ sighed. "Trying to solve a mystery."

JJ picked up a stack of photos and began flipping through them, stopping at a picture of one of the orcas swimming through the maze. "Kuniki," he muttered under his breath. "Kuniki. Kuniki. Kuniki."

"Hmm?" DJ said, absently scrolling through a digital report he had loaded onto his tablet. "What's that, buddy?"

"Kuniki. This is Kuniki," JJ said, holding up the picture. "Kuniki."

DJ picked up a report that was lying on the coffee table listing the whales in the experiments. He looked at the photo of the whale JJ was holding and the date on the picture. The report mentioned the whale's name in that experiment: Kuniki. The name wasn't on the photo.

"JJ, how do you know the name of that orca?" asked DJ.

"I don't know. I don't know. It's Kuniki."

"How do you—" DJ's phone rang. It was Callaghan.

"Sorry, DJ. OneWorld is a big corporation with hundreds of employees. There have been a few 'B.L.'s' but nobody that could possibly have been involved in the research. Nobody, in fact, that was even employed during the time the research took place."

"My dad mentioned a third-party research company."

"They were only monitors. They examined the research but they never actively participated in it. They would not have made contemporaneous notes."

"Well, there had to have been somebody with OneWorld with those initials."

"I don't know what to tell you, DJ."

"Thanks, anyway, Patrick." DJ hung up the phone and picked back up the book with B.L.'s notes. "B.L., B.L., B.L...." he mumbled to himself.

"Brooke Lewis," said JJ.

"What?"

"Brooke Lewis, Brooke Lewis, Brooke Lewis." His eyes were darting about the room.

"JJ, do you know this B.L. person?"

"It's Brooke Lewis."

"How do you know that?"

"The whales knew. The whales knew."

"The whales knew?"

"They knew Brooke."

"Well, how do *you* know?"

"It's just in my head. My head. Her name is Brooke Lewis. She was a trainer. Brooke Lewis."

DJ reached for his phone and called Callaghan back. "What can you get me on a Brooke Lewis?" he said. "She might have been a trainer."

"Where did you come up with that?" asked Callaghan.

"From...I'll tell you later. Find me what you can and get back to me, would you?" DJ hung up and turned to JJ.

"JJ, what do you know about these experiments? Did Dad talk to you about them?"

"He mentioned the experiments. My dad was doing experiments on the intelligence of orcas. James Parker was researching the intelligence of orcas."

"Yes, yes, and did you attend any of the experiments?"

"No."

"Did Dad share with you any details? Did you read some of Dad's notes?"

"No." JJ was slightly rocking back and forth, his eyes fixed once again on the photographs. "Orange juice," he blurted out and then rose and walked off in the direction of the kitchen. DJ realized his father must have talked to JJ about the research. He couldn't have imagined that he would have gone into any great detail with him, but at some point he must have dropped the name Brooke Lewis into the conversation. How else would JJ have known it?

A half hour later, Callaghan called back. "DJ, my contact in Human Resources was familiar with the name Brooke Lewis. She's pretty sure she was a trainer in Santa Monica. But here's the strange thing: there is no record of her anywhere in the company's computers. No personnel file. Nothing. It's as though every trace of information on her was wiped clean."

Kioko made dinner for the boys on DJ's last night at Seahaven. The three sat in candlelight at one end of the long dining room table as a steady rain pelted against the huge bay window. Andrea Bocelli, Kioko's favorite, was playing on the room's sound system, a Yaba system, DJ had noticed.

DJ had boxed up all the research and was heading to the airport first thing in the morning. Kevin Gloss had flown the corporate jet in and was coming over in a cab that evening to take the boxes and load them on the plane. DJ had already decided to use the resources of Yaba to continue the experiments. His plan...well, he didn't exactly have one. His idea was to show the research to a couple of the top Yaba engineers and together, maybe they could all come up with a plan for how to continue the work DJ's father had started. Somehow, some way, the means of cetacean communication had to be uncovered. The true level of intelligence of the whales had to be revealed. Simultaneously, DJ hoped to start working, in broad brush strokes if nothing else, on the idea of the sea sanctuary.

In the meantime, he sure would like to talk to this ex-trainer, this Brooke Lewis person. It would be helpful to talk to an eyewitness, somebody who was actually there at the experiments. There were other names and initials attached to various notes, but there was just something about Brooke Lewis's scribblings. They were candid and authentic. Refreshingly unscientific. Why would her records have been expunged? Computer glitch? Maybe.

"I'll be flying back quite regularly," DJ explained to Kioko over dessert and coffee. "Callaghan and I have a lot to do with respect to the estate. But I want you to know that there have been no plans for Seahaven yet. We're in no hurry. No hurry at all. Naturally you're welcome to stay for as long as you'd like, Kioko."

"Thank you, DJ."

"You hear that, buddy?" DJ said to JJ. "I'll be coming back a lot. We'll be seeing a lot of each other."

"There's the buzzer for the front gate," said Kioko. "It must be your man. I'll let him in. It's a mean night out there."

DJ finished his coffee and walked out to the foyer where the research was all neatly stacked. Through the front window he could see the headlights of the cab shining through the rain as the cab pulled around the circular drive. Somebody in a white rain slicker with a hood stepped out of the backseat, and it didn't look like Kevin Gloss. Whoever it was, they tossed a few bills to the driver and then stepped lively up the porch steps, then right on through the front door, which Kioko had been holding open in anticipation of Gloss.

No, this wasn't Kevin Gloss at all. This was a woman, tall and athletic, and, when she pulled down her hood, a brunette with tanned skin and crystal blue eyes.

"David Parker, I presume?" she said, looking at DJ. "I need to talk to you. I worked with your father. My coming here this evening is a risk to me, but a risk I'm willing to take. I need to talk to you about some research your father was involved in at OneWorld. I was helping him. By now, I assume you must know something about the research. I wonder if you know how important it is. It must be continued, no matter what they do to try to stop it. I want to help." Then, taking a breath and extending her hand out to DJ, the tall, athletic brunette said, "Hello, Mr. Parker. My name is Brooke Lewis."

TEN

"B.L.?!" said DJ, shaking Brooke's hand. "You're B.L.?"

"Excuse me?"

"Oh, sorry. It's just that I've been reading your notes. Yes, I am aware of the research. My plan is to continue it. I was wondering how I was going to get in touch with you. Come in, come in. Please. Kioko will take your raincoat. Please, come into the living room and sit by the fire. Do you want a cup of coffee?"

"Do you have anything stronger?"

"Um...sure. Bourbon?"

"There ya go. Neat."

"Kioko, would you mind?"

"Two bourbons?" Kioko said.

"Two glasses, Kioko. And leave the bottle. Ms. Lewis and I have a lot to discuss."

Brooke and DJ walked into the living room and sat down by the fireplace in matching chairs that slightly faced each other.

"Wow, I don't know where to start," DJ said. "I have so much I'd like to ask you. But, listen, why did you say that coming here is a risk for you?"

"You're not the only one with an interest in the research, Mr. Parker."

"What do you mean? And please...call me DJ."

"DJ. Thanks. Well, there are certain people who would like to keep the research from ever being released to the public."

"Well, sure, I would assume the board of OneWorld wouldn't care for it to get out."

"And these people," Brooke continued, "would stop at nothing to prevent that possibility."

"What do you mean 'stop at nothing'?"

"I mean stop at nothing. How familiar are you with the board members?"

"Truthfully, not at all. I have to confess I haven't spent a lot of time following my father's business. Until just recently, as a matter of fact, I've more or less been ignoring it."

"Have you heard of the name Robert MacKinnon?"

"No, not really."

"Robert MacKinnon is a board member. Perhaps the most influential. He's also a twisted, evil, son of a bitch."

"He is? MacKinnon? Robert, did you say?"

"Look, Mr. Parker—DJ—let me start at the beginning."

"Please."

Brooke took a deep breath and downed her drink. "I was a senior trainer at OneWorld in Santa Monica. I grew up in Florida. Saint Petersburg. When I was eight years old, we took a trip to Naples, Florida and my parents took my brother and me to the OneWorld park there. I fell in love with the orcas. From that time on, I told anybody who would listen to me that someday I'd be a OneWorld trainer, that someday I would swim with the orcas. I never swerved from that path. I went to Florida State and got a degree in marine biology. I was on the university swim and volleyball teams. I was a pretty good athlete. Even made it onto the Olympic volleyball team in '08."

"Wow," said DJ, pouring Brooke another bourbon.

"Silver medal. Lost to Brazil in the finals. Anyway, no matter what I did, I never lost interest in the whales and when I graduated from FSU, I moved to Naples and became a trainer. I loved it. Loved every damn minute of it. I was there for five years and then an opening came up in the Santa Monica park for a senior trainer and I applied and got the job and moved. I don't mind telling you that I was good at it. Maybe the best trainer in the system.

"DJ, my experience with the whales was magical. I witnessed behaviors that were amazing. One time, for instance, with a full audience, I was set to do a rocket hop with a fifteen-year-old orca named Keira. Now, a rocket hop is when the trainer joins up with the orca at the bottom of the pool and then the orca drives the trainer upwards, thrusting her into the air once they break the surface. I'd been doing the rocket hop for several years with Keira. We must have done it over two hundred times. Anyway, on that day, I dove into the water and somehow—I don't know how—I took in a mouthful of seawater. So I'm on the bottom and Keira is getting under where I have my feet positioned but I'm beginning to cough and choke. Keira's about to launch me upwards, but she senses that something's not right and instead of launching me, she gently nudges me to the surface where I cough up some water and manage to catch my breath. And then she stays right beside me, as if she's making sure I'm okay. No, not 'as if.' She was making sure. I stroked her for a few moments in gratitude and then we tried the maneuver again, pulling it off flawlessly.

"I saw a lot of emotions from the whales. If they were given the wrong food or asked to do something they didn't want to do, they'd spit water at the trainers. One time, one of our trainers, a guy named Gary, was being too aggressive with a female orca. Well, I guess one of the male orcas didn't like what he saw. He came over and grabbed the trainer by his foot and dragged him under, thirty-four feet to the bottom of the pool. Then he held him there for thirty seconds before releasing him. Gary came to the surface just in time. He might have drowned, but, you see, Eilio didn't want to kill Gary."

"Eilio?"

"Yes, the male. OneWorld's first whale."

"Yes, I know."

"Well, anyway, Eilio didn't want to kill Gary. He just wanted to teach him a lesson. But how did he know just how long he could keep him under water? I started wondering just how smart these creatures were. After working hours, I began doing a few experiments. I played music to test the whales' reactions. I played the Bee Gees once to a female orca who vigorously shook her head. Then I played some Led Zeppelin and she breached and swam enthusiastically around the pool. I tried all different kinds of music. She was non-responsive to Beyoncé but she loved Rihanna. Different whales had different tastes. For the most part, if they liked something, they'd react positively but if you played it a second or third time, they'd lose their enthusiasm, as if they were getting bored. They wanted to keep hearing new music.

"I brought a large mirror in one night to see how the whales would react and to see if they could recognize themselves. It was obvious that they could. One whale stuck her tongue out at the mirror to look at her mouth and teeth. Another swung her tail up behind her to take a look at it. They'd come in real close to check out their own eyes.

"Eventually, I started understanding just how intelligent these animals were and I found myself with conflicted thoughts about their captivity and my role in it. When I was a little girl, I had dreamed of swimming with them. Now I was wondering what kinds of dreams they had. I'm sure their dreams didn't include swimming with me.

"Well, then came the crowning moment for me. I've never told anybody about this before. It was another experience with Keira. I went into the water one day and she echolocated me. You can feel it, you know. It's hard to explain but it's like a kind of buzzing in the water. But this time it was different. She kept sending her signals to my body as she swam to me. When she reached me, she gently rubbed her rostrum on my belly, just below the surface of the water. She made a soft purring kind of sound and then she raised her head out of the water and looked at me and then back down at my stomach. I knew what she was suggesting. I went to see my doctor the next day. Sure enough, I was four weeks pregnant. I had no idea."

"Wow," DJ said. "That's amazing."

"Yeah, isn't it? I couldn't get over it. I still can't. I lost the baby, by the way, after about three months."

"Oh, I'm sorry, Brooke. That must have been hard for you and...the father."

"Well, he split by then. He flaked out when I told him I was pregnant. He wanted nothing to do with fatherhood. But I was planning on having the baby nonetheless. Well, anyway, after the miscarriage, I asked for a few days off. Nobody gave it any thought, of course. But I didn't stay home. I flew to Seattle to see your father. I had always heard how accessible he was to his employees and so it didn't really surprise me that he was willing to take the time to talk to me. What surprised me, however, was how interested he was in what I had to say. I sensed something about your father, DJ. When I was telling him how smart I was discovering the whales to be, I could tell that he was not at all surprised. It was clear to me that he'd had the same thoughts.

"Well, I suggested that more research be done. Better research than what I could do by myself in the pool in Santa Monica. He said he'd think about it. I left his office with a good feeling. Less than a week later, he called me. He said he was going to invest in some serious research and he asked me if I'd like to join the research team. I was thrilled, as you can imagine.

"You say you're familiar with the research so I won't go into detail. I trust you know about the communication experiments. You mentioned my handwritten notes earlier. Let's just say I was awestruck by our results.

"Well, anyway, working with your father was one of the highlights of my career. But then something strange happened. He told me that OneWorld was no longer funding the research. In fact, the board had voted to shut it down. Your father asked me to continue working on it with him, but in secret. That's when he shared with me that the original reason to do the research was to prove the opposite of what we were discovering. OneWorld never wanted to prove how smart the whales were. They wanted to show they were mindless, like fish. Your father even confessed to me that that was his original idea, too. I guess my coming to him was just great timing. But, DJ, he didn't have to hire me for the research. He knew I was coming into it with a bias. I knew the whales were smart. Looking back, I think there was a big part of your father that wanted to prove that, in contradiction to what the board really wanted.

"In any event, we continued doing some experiments but we didn't really make any more progress. We got stuck, quite frankly. There's a frequency or a resonance of some description that we just can't figure out, as I'm sure you know from the notes. Shortly after that, your father passed away. I'm sorry, by the way. I have to tell you that I think your father was one hell of a guy."

DJ nodded. "Thanks. Go on, Brooke."

"So, anyway, I'm back in Santa Monica and two nights ago there's a knock on the door. A man. Fifty-something. Balding and kind of pudgy. He didn't say who he was but later, going through the OneWorld corporate website, I recognized him as one of the company directors."

"Robert MacKinnon," DJ said.

"Exactly. He was polite to me at first, telling me the board had sent him to collect any information about the research I might have been hanging on to. Routine procedure, he said. A request made by the legal department. 'You know how those guys can be,' he said to me, smiling. Well, I told him I didn't have any of the research. It's true. Everything I know is up in my head. Your father kept all the notes. Well then MacKinnon starts losing his patience and the next thing I know he's walking around the apartment opening desk drawers and peering into my closets. I tell him, look, don't make me call the police. Then he gets downright belligerent. Says to me that if I talk to anybody about the research, I'm going to be sorry. *Very* sorry, he says. Oh, and he also tells me I'm fired and never to go near a OneWorld park ever again. I don't scare easy, DJ. I told him I would sue for wrongful termination."

"Then what did he say?"

"He said, 'Bitch, if you do, you'll really learn the meaning of the word termination.'"

"Wow," DJ mouthed.

"And then he repeated that I was never to talk to anybody about the research. Then he left."

"What did you do?"

Brooke smiled and poured another bourbon for herself. "I made plans immediately to come see you. To talk about the research."

ELEVEN

"Casey, this is Brooke Lewis. She'll be assisting me with our research."

It was good to be back in San Francisco. To DJ, it seemed as if he'd been away from his office for a month.

It hadn't taken much to convince Brooke to come along with him. They had talked late into the night and then all the way back on the corporate jet this morning. DJ was impressed with Brooke—her intelligence, the way she carried herself, her nerve in the face of MacKinnon's threats, her knowledge of the orcas. And, oh hell, who was he kidding? By her stunning good looks. But what was that tattoo on the inside of her left wrist? "Adam." Who the hell was Adam? Was he the boyfriend who flaked out when she became pregnant?

"I want you to get her a room at the Fairmont, Casey. She'll be staying in town for a while. Make the reservation in the name of the company. Don't use Brooke's name."

For Brooke's part, she felt safe now in the confines of Yaba. Not that she was scared, but since MacKinnon's visit, that word "termination" had never really left her mind. She was taken aback by the sheer size of Yaba, the vastness of the Yaba campus. On the way in, DJ had described it: over two million square feet of office space on forty-two acres overlooking San Francisco Bay in Mountain View. Brooke had noticed reflecting pools and fountains along the road to the main building and green space everywhere. The Yaba campus, DJ had told her, had eight different cafeterias for the employees, each with a different theme. There were two swimming pools, several sand volleyball courts, soccer pitches, basketball and tennis courts, three weight rooms, and a running trail that blazed around the perimeter of the campus.

Casey eyed the tall brunette standing in front of her outside of DJ's office. "The Fairmont. Of course. How do you do, Ms. Lewis."

"Please, call me Brooke. Nice to meet you, Casey."

"Okay," said DJ, "are they in the conference room?"

"Yup," said Casey. "Watkins and Taylor are both waiting for you. I told them you had called from the airport on the way in and wanted to see them ASAP. I'm sure they think you want to talk about Soti. Why else would you call in your two top engineers?"

"They'll be in for a fun surprise then, won't they?" DJ smiled. "Those two geeks could use a little change of pace. From the digital world to the undersea Mammalian world. Think they can make the transition?"

"If they can't, I don't know who can."

"Brooke, are you ready?" Brooke nodded and DJ led the way into the conference room where Donnie Watkins and Paul Taylor were drinking coffee and playing a video game. Watkins wore black-rimmed glasses and was short and a bit on the chunky side, a literal counterweight to the tall, bony Taylor. Both were in their early thirties, single, and completely fanatical about their work. Software engineering was what they lived for. Not that they didn't notice Brooke when she strolled in. Both jaws dropped simultaneously.

"Okay, you guys, straighten up," announced DJ. "We have company. We also have a lot of work to do."

After the meeting, which lasted four hours, DJ sent Brooke to the Fairmont Hotel in the company limo. Now he sat at his desk munching on a sandwich, thinking he should probably get some rest himself. The chain of events of the past week had been tiring. Now, with the long night, the flight home, and the lengthy meeting that morning, DJ suddenly realized he needed sleep. More accurately, he realized he was now in agreement with Soti who had pointed out the need for sleep back on the plane.

He felt good about the direction they were going, though. Watkins and Taylor had looked at him like he was nuts when he first started describing the task he was assigning them to. "You want us to...what?" Taylor had said, "Study the communication technology of *whales?* Huh?" Four hours later they were champing at the bit. DJ had had the research wheeled into the conference room and Brooke had spoken at length on her own observations.

Then Brooke had talked about what is presently known about orca communication. "We know they communicate," she'd told the engineers. "Through whistles or clicks or pulsed calls. They can hear each other over thirty or more miles, some species a hundred or more miles. Pods have different dialects where different calls mean different things, just like humans have different languages. Pods that share common calls belong to larger clans, so obviously their ability to communicate is very important for them socially. Now, they communicate for a variety of reasons—to alert the rest of the pod to danger or to the presence of food, for example. But they also communicate just to let the rest of the pod know where they are. They're extraordinarily cohesive. Pods act as highly organized units. It's as if the members are all inter-connected. It's almost like each whale is at one with the pod."

"We can't explain what happened with the experiments," she had concluded. "We can't explain how the whales com-municated. We only know they must have. Somehow. And it went beyond the standard whistles and calls. Far beyond."

The engineers were intrigued. For them, it wasn't a matter of proving the intelligence of whales so as to justify the cost of a sea sanctuary. It was the solving of a puzzle. Solutions were their stock-in-trade and they were proud of it. No problem too complex. They had discussed re-creating the experiments, but quickly decided the cost was unnecessary. They had all the data, after all. They had video and audio. What was missing was the proper analysis. "No offense to your dad's guys," Watkins had said to DJ, "but we're talking marine biologists, not engineers. Oh, and no offense to you, Ms. Lewis." Brooke had laughed. "None taken," she'd assured him. Both Watkins and Taylor were confident they could solve the equation. "Who knows?" Taylor had conjectured. "Maybe we can discover something that can be applied to human communication."

DJ hadn't considered that possibility but over his sand-wich he found the idea intriguing. Well, first things first. There were thirty orcas being held in captivity and their release to a sea sanctuary was dependent on DJ and his team being able to prove their intelligence. The second phase of the plan would be to take the research public and generate enough interest and sympathy to force the board of OneWorld to approve the sanctuary. DJ figured that would actually be the easy part. The board members weren't heartless, after all. And, they were good businessmen. They'd find a way for the corporation to make a profitable transition to a new model. He'd help. He wasn't a bad businessman himself. And, anyway, what else could the board do? It's not as if they were going to sell the company.

"She's pretty."

DJ looked up from his desk to see Casey standing at the door.

"Huh? Who?"

"Brooke Lewis."

"Oh, is she? I hadn't noticed."

"Uh-huh. And smart."

"Well, I will admit that I noticed that. Here, want the rest of my sandwich?"

Casey sat down across from DJ and grabbed a bite of his tuna wrap. "DJ," she said, "I have to tell you that I really admire what you're doing. This whale thing is pretty cool. Think anybody's going to mind that your focus is off of Soti?"

"Soti's taken care of. I'll keep an eye on the product roll-out, but you know me. Once the technology is all worked out, I'm ready to move on to the next thing."

"What are you going to do with your dad's place?"

"I don't know; I really don't. My brother loves it there. It was hard saying goodbye to him this morning. He was upset I was leaving. I kept reassuring him I'd be coming back but sometimes he can be...hard to reach. And then I told him I'd be flying him here, but he doesn't really adapt well to change. He'd miss Seahaven. He'd miss the dock. He'd miss his whales."

"Maybe he can help with the analysis."

"How? It's not like he's a trained engineer or scientist."

"I know, but, well, it might make him feel useful to be involved."

"Hmm...maybe. Well, anyway, what's new around here?"

"Nothing much. Nothing major happened while you were away. Everything seems to be running smoothly."

"That's what I like to hear. And how are you, Case? How are things with Jordan?"

"Jordan's a jerk."

"He is?"

"We broke up."

"Geez, sorry Case. Well, he must be a jerk if he'd break up with you."

"Thanks. Can I finish your chips?"

"Take 'em. I'm gonna stretch out and take a nap. Soti's concerned I'm not getting enough sleep."

"Alright. Guess I'll get back to work." Casey rose and walked towards the door.

"Hey, Case," DJ said, "I really am sorry about Jordan."

"Thank you, DJ." Then, turning back towards him, she said, "Oh, by the way, did your friend get a hold of you on Orcas Island?"

"What friend is that?"

"I don't know. Some guy called for you a couple of days ago. Asked if you were still on Orcas Island. Said he was an old friend and wanted to get in touch with you. I asked for his name but he just hung up."

"That's strange. No, nobody got a hold of me."

"Hmm. Maybe he changed his mind. Well, pleasant dreams."

TWELVE

Boris Kucherov sat on a bench looking out at the Moskva River nursing a cup of strong coffee. Autumn had come to the city. The air was predictably cool, but this was a rare day in autumn for Moscow—the sun was actually shining. All week it had rained but on this day the sun had broken through the bleak sky and now people were out, walking along the river or sitting on benches. The trees were now brilliant in their fall colors and you could feel the spirit of the city rise. It would be short-lived. More rain was predicted for the following day along with blustery winds. Probably strip the trees bare, Kucherov thought to himself. Then all we'll have is winter.

"You look lost in thought, Boris." Evgeni Sergachev sat down on the bench next to Kucherov.

"Ah, Evgeni. I didn't even see you approach. Of course you're right on time as usual. So tell me, what news? And why are we meeting here instead of in my office? Not that I mind the fresh air, of course."

"It's the OneWorld affair. We've hit a snag that I think is going to take a little extra...effort on our part."

"Evgeni, you are paid to take care of snags, yes?"

"This one might be outside my scope of authorization, Boris."

"Oh?" Boris frowned. There wasn't much that was outside Sergachev's scope of authorization.

"It's the research."

"What of it?"

"My man in Seattle—"

"Yes, Gardner something. An American."

"Nelson Gardner. He tells me the research is dangerous."

"Dangerous? Dangerous how?"

Sergachev detailed the findings as Robert MacKinnon had detailed them to Gardner. "Well, that's all very interesting," said Kucherov, "But I thought we were simply going to buy the research from this MacKinnon person."

"He wants ten million dollars to hand it over to us."

"Isn't that what we're paying him to deliver us the board's vote to sell the company? So he wants an additional ten million? It's out of the question."

"There's another problem, too."

"Evgeni, my comrade," Kucherov sighed, "why do you bring me problems on such a lovely day?"

"MacKinnon might not be the only one with the research."

"Who else has it?"

"Gardner thinks James Parker's son might also have it. And there's a girl, too."

"What girl?"

"A former trainer with OneWorld. Naturally, Gardner has been having MacKinnon followed. MacKinnon flew to Los Angeles and met with this trainer. Then she flew to Orcas Island alone."

"So?"

"Orcas Island is where James Parker lived. His funeral was last week. Why would this former OneWorld employee be going there now, *after* the funeral? Gardner called David

Parker's assistant and confirmed that he was on Orcas Island, too."

"For the funeral."

"Certainly, but why would he hang around longer? This man has a multi-billion dollar company to run. And then there's this: David Parker and the trainer flew together on his corporate jet back to Yaba in San Francisco. Those two are up to something. Gardner suspects that James Parker kept the research. Now his son has it. The trainer must certainly be involved."

Kucherov became silent, thinking the matter over. The extra ten million would be no problem. It would simply never be paid. All along, the idea of using MacKinnon was for him to influence the board to sell. Once that was done, MacKinnon would be expendable. A dead man doesn't need ten million dollars. Not only that, but purely from an economic standpoint, if others have copies of the research, then the value of MacKinnon's goes down to exactly nothing. Either way, MacKinnon would no longer be necessary.

The fact that the research was now potentially in the hands of others, however, presented a huge problem. Now he understood why Sergachev had come to him. The acquisition of OneWorld was going to be Neftkomp's crowning achievement. Kucherov didn't pretend to understand the reasons behind it, the policy of *Zakhvat*. He was a businessman. He thought of himself as an industrialist. But the president had made himself clear. Russia was seeking to better insinuate itself into the world community. Who knew why? The president was no doubt looking at the big picture and Kucherov knew it was not for him to second-guess. In fact, it was for him to agree and to see to it that the president's wishes were accommodated.

"If the research is as potentially damaging as you say," Kucherov said at last, "then we'll need to act quickly. Others might already know about it. Perhaps others at Yaba. Those within Parker's inner circle. His top employees. This assistant you mentioned. Certainly the girl. Maybe family members, too. I remember something about a brother, yes?"

"Everyone who has come in contact with the research must be silenced," declared Sergachev.

"Evgeni," said Kucherov, shaking his head, "why do you always insist on using a sledgehammer to hit even the smallest nail? We need not silence everyone. We need only make a statement. We need only silence one."

The next day, Boris Kucherov drove to the Kremlin to get approval from the only person who could give it. The president himself needed to sanction his and Sergachev's plan. Kucherov found the matter distasteful but necessary. And it was always good to share a secret with the president. He even brought out the bottle of vodka. The two toasted while outside the cold autumn rain blew through the dark streets of Moscow.

THIRTEEN

"Brooke Lewis makes you anxious."

"What are you talking about, Soti?"

DJ was having breakfast, reading over a report on Soti's rollout that had been prepared for him by Soti team leader, Wendell Redfern. He was on the deck outside of the master bedroom of his Spanish Colonial in Half Moon Bay, overlooking the Pacific Ocean. He'd designed the one-level 8,000-square-foot home himself with the idea that he wanted to get up each morning and go to bed every night looking at the Pacific. The house was too big for a single man and he knew it. Most of the rooms he never even went into, confining himself mostly to the wing where his bedroom was, the kitchen, and a music room that doubled as an office. In this room hung three of JJ's paintings. "On loan," they were all seascapes, two of which included orcas, and one of a sailboat gliding by the dock at Seahaven.

When DJ had built the house soon after the explosive success of Y-Songs, he'd imagined a family living there one day. His wife, two or three children, the neighbor kids coming over. Barbecues on the back deck, friends sitting around the pool. Seahaven had always been a busy place when he was a boy and he figured the Spanish Colonial would be as well. It hadn't quite worked out that way, however. The only other person who spent any significant time at the house had been his housekeeper Maryola, but she'd had to take a leave of absence as a result of the illness of her mother. She was back in Costa Rica and there was no telling when, or if, she'd return.

Reading the report from Redfern, his mind had been wandering and then he'd noticed Soti's flashing red light.

"Ms. Lewis makes you anxious. When you're in her presence, your heart rate rises."

"I don't think so."

"Fourteen percent on average, David. So far it doesn't seem to be affecting your obsessive-compulsive disorder. I've not noticed any appreciable increase in any kind of ritualistic behavior."

DJ's eyebrows rose. "How do you know about my OCD, Soti? I didn't enter that into your database."

"Although I did notice minor perspiration of your palms when you were talking with her last night at dinner."

"Don't evade the question, Soti."

"It's my job to know everything about your health, David. My function is to continuously monitor your health and well-being."

"Yes, I'm aware of your function, Soti. I invented you."

"To do that, I need to know everything there is to know about you, that which is entered into my database, and that which is discoverable."

Discoverable. Soti was working as designed, in other words. She had taken DJ's symptoms and cross-referenced them against her online database of conditions and produced an accurate diagnosis. This, of course, was the idea. But DJ's OCD was a subtle psychological condition that he'd kept well hidden. Ritualistic behavior, in and of itself, doesn't necessarily produce alarming physical symptoms. And yet, Soti noticed them anyway. This might have been a bit beyond expectations. DJ had worn Soti for three months. In that time, Soti certainly picked up on the anxieties and she probably picked up on the compulsions, even if they didn't produce physical symptoms the way, say, the flu would produce a fever. Picking up on the anxieties was clearly part of Soti's job description. It was less clear that picking up on the compulsions was part of it. Putting them both together was a leap, a leap of intelligence that DJ was not at that moment certain that he'd anticipated. He made a mental note to tell Watkins and Taylor.

"Your oatmeal is no doubt getting cold, David."

"Well it was warm a minute ago. Before your stupid red light began to flash."

"Why does the presence of Ms. Lewis cause your heart rate to rise, David? I'd like to know."

"You'd like to know?" DJ made another mental note: Soti was curious.

"I noticed other physiological aberrations as well, related to neural and vascular functions. Blood flow to your—"

"Okay, Soti, that's enough."

"A healthy sex drive is a sign of physical well-being, David. It's nothing to be embarrassed about."

DJ made one more mental note, this time to revisit Soti's settings. There's a fine line, he thought, between feeling as if your health is being properly monitored and feeling like your privacy is being invaded. That line needed to be determined by the end user, not Soti.

"Who says I'm embarrassed?"

"I'm picking up certain signs of discomfort."

"Yes, well, I still need to read this report. Your interest in my anxieties and sex drive is all very much appreciated, Soti, but for now maybe you can just confine yourself to more pressing health issues. Let me know when I'm having a heart attack, would ya?"

"Do you not wish to know when you are anxious and to learn the source of your anxiety? Your anxiety was rising ever so slightly just before my alert this morning. I thought you'd want to know. Your heart rate noticeably increased as you thought about Ms. Lewis."

"Listen, Soti, it's good that you bring these things to my attention, but—wait, what did you say? Did you say as I *thought* about her?"

Just then DJ's phone rang.

"Kevin Gloss here, Mr. Parker. Just wanted to let you know that I should be landing with your brother and Ms. Kioko in exactly one hour."

"Thanks, Kevin. I'm on my way. See you at the airport."

DJ turned Soti's voice off and rose from the table, his mind now on JJ. He strode into his bedroom where he finished dressing and then trotted through the enormous family room out to the garage, then jumped into his Tesla and made for the airport. He had thought about what Casey had suggested two days before. Maybe getting JJ involved in the research analysis would be a good way to acclimate him to the eventual move to DJ's place. He could ride to the office each day with DJ and feel as though he was a part of something important. It really wouldn't matter if he didn't contribute anything. It would just give him something to do, something to occupy that puzzle of a mind of his. Kioko would come along to make the transition easier still. DJ figured she'd eventually want to return to Orcas Island, but he was sure she'd be willing to stay until JJ had become fully adjusted to his new home. For DJ's part, he was looking forward to the company. And it's not as if he didn't have the room.

When DJ had called JJ, he'd presented the visit as a temporary one. It was way too early to be talking to JJ about a permanent move. "Come stay with me for a few days," he'd said. "You can help us analyze Dad's research. Kioko can come, too." Little by little, he'd get JJ used to the idea of living in the Bay area.

DJ had foregone the idea of sending the limo to the airport, figuring he needed to be there personally to greet JJ. True to his word, Gloss landed sixty minutes after he'd called DJ.

"How was the flight, buddy?" DJ asked JJ as he and Kioko made their way down the airstairs.

"Good flight. Good. Good. This is a Gulfstream 650. It's got a range of 7,700 nautical miles and has a cruise speed of 496 knots. It has a payload of 6,500 pounds."

"Is that right? Well, I just know it gets us from Point A to Point B."

"The wingspan is ninety-nine feet, seven inches. And there is a 180-cubic-foot baggage compartment. And two vacuum-flush toilets. Two!"

"No kidding? Here, Kioko, let me take your bag. Kevin, thanks, as always." Gloss waved a quick salute, and DJ and JJ and Kioko made their way to the Tesla. DJ dropped Kioko off at his house and then he and JJ drove to Yaba where Watkins and Taylor were busy in what had been dubbed "Orca HQ," a large, high-ceilinged room that had been cleaned out expressly for the purpose of analyzing all the research data. There were tables set up and whiteboards and flat-screen TVs. Tablets and laptops were all networked together. DJ noticed a pair of baseball gloves and a baseball on a table in the corner. Watkins and Taylor were notorious for taking breaks by tossing a baseball around. Like kids in a formal living room when their parents are out of the house, they'd stop the moment something inevitably got broken by an errant throw.

DJ introduced his brother to his top engineers and then suggested they run a video of one of the experiments for JJ to watch. That ought to keep him busy, thought DJ. In the meantime, Watkins gave DJ his initial impressions of the data.

"Well, it's definitely a frequency of some description. We've run several minutes of audio. Your father was smart enough to put mikes everywhere. The clicks and pulsating calls that your Ms. Lewis described are present and we're running them through a reverse-encryption program that we wrote. By the way, I hope she makes it back here, that Ms. Lewis. Not too hard to look at, is she? Well, anyway, I can't imagine those clicks and calls are sophisticated enough to carry the amount of information that was apparently shared by these whales. There's got to be something else. We're up to our keisters here in audio software, most of which we've developed ourselves, so I have no doubt we'll track down this mysterious frequency. Essentially, it's not a matter of knowing what to listen for. It's a matter of knowing how to listen. That's what we've got to figure out."

"Thanks, Donnie. I know I have the right guys working on it. By the way, how's your curveball these days?" Watkins grinned. Then DJ walked over to where JJ was sitting, totally absorbed by a video of one of the orcas running the maze. "Interesting, huh, buddy?"

"I don't know what she's saying," JJ said, pointing at the whale.

"Ha-ha, well neither do we, little brother. That's why we're here."

"It's no good on TV. The sound isn't right. It's no good on TV."

"What do you mean, JJ? You want me to turn the sound up? Do you want to listen just to the audio tracks?"

"It's just no good. It's not there. Not there."

"What's not there?"

"The thoughts. The things they say. It's not there. Not there."

"Okay, buddy. Well, enough of this for now. It's time I acquainted you with one of the most important parts of our work around here."

"What's that?"

"A little something I like to call the lunch break. Follow me. Feel like a slice or two of pizza?"

FOURTEEN

Brooke Lewis wasn't ever going to say anything. MacKinnon was sure of that. She'd had the fear of God in her eyes when he'd told her she was in danger of learning the true meaning of the word "termination." That was a clever one. She'd said something about wrongful termination and he'd played off of the word. She'd been left speechless and MacKinnon had walked out the door, confident that she was no longer a risk.

She was attractive, though. MacKinnon preferred blonds, but Brooke Lewis sure had a hot body. Firm everywhere. Breasts were a little on the small side for MacKinnon's tastes, but you can't have everything. Who knows? In other circumstances, instead of threatening her, he might have been sweet-talking her into bed. Sure, he was considerably older, but girls like older men. He had money, too, and there's no aphrodisiac quite like money. All she'd have needed was a ride in the Ferrari. But of course there had been no time for such frivolity. He had a job to do and he did it.

There was nobody left now. There had been three others on the research team that James Parker had put together, but Brooke Lewis was the only one whose research notes MacKinnon couldn't seem to find any copies of. He'd had everybody hacked and all traces of research data wiped clean, but on Brooke's laptop there had been nothing. Consequently, she was the only one he'd had to threaten. She probably hadn't kept any notes anyway, but why take the chance? A trip to L.A. to instill a little fear was pretty cheap insurance. Women scare so easily.

The only others who had come into contact with the research were the people from the independent consulting firm OneWorld had hired to monitor the results. But all along, MacKinnon had been carefully screening the information OneWorld had been sending to them. Having them in place had been a charade anyway. In truth, they knew very little. Plus, there was the non-disclosure agreement. If they ever leaked anything, MacKinnon would sue them into oblivion.

So, Parker was dead, the information had been wiped clean everywhere, and Brooke Lewis was too scared to talk. Nobody would ever discover how supposedly intelligent whales were. Tying up loose ends: that's how you earn ten million dollars.

In the meantime, the negotiations with Gardner's clients had gone exceedingly well. The tender offer had been made through MacKinnon who'd presented it to the board and the board was on the brink of accepting it. But MacKinnon still had a little arm-twisting to do. It turned out that the client was a Russian company called Neftkomp. And now MacKinnon had to convince a couple board members that selling a piece of Americana to the Russians was in everybody's best interests. That's why he was in the sitting room of Maggie Lynch's fashionable condo on Alki Avenue overlooking Elliott Bay. Lloyd McGuire was there, too. Both board members were cool to the idea of selling.

"Maggie, it's not like it's the Soviet Union, for crying out loud," MacKinnon was saying. "The cold war is over. We're a global community now."

Maggie Lynch was seventy-five. Slightly on the plump side and, always looking over the top of the wire-rimmed glasses that she perpetually wore on the tip of her nose, she exuded a sort of matronly warmth. But MacKinnon knew this was no grandmotherly type. Maggie Lynch was shrewd.

"Do I really want my legacy to be the selling of such a valuable piece of American tradition?" she remarked. At her age, thinking about her legacy was no idle exercise. OneWorld was the only organization she was a part of anymore. After this, she'd be officially retired, twelve years after her first retirement when she'd sold her 3,000-store chain of eponymous casual clothing shops. Every mall in North America had a Lynch's.

"I think your legacy is secure," said MacKinnon. "You'll forever be associated with clothing. Not Russians."

"But why are you pushing so hard for his, Bob?" said McGuire, reaching for the teapot that Maggie's maid had brought in a few minutes earlier on a silver tray with sugar, cream, lemons, and a plate of scones. "I mean, I'm sure it's a good deal, but you've been hounding everybody to death about it." Tall and lean, with a hawk-like nose, Lloyd McGuire was the same age as Maggie. The two had been friends for years and often held the same opinions where board matters were concerned. McGuire was a car salesman. Well, more accurately, he was the owner of McGuire Automotive, the fourth largest automobile retailer in the country with over a hundred dealerships throughout California, Nevada, Oregon, and Washington. But MacKinnon nevertheless thought of him as a car salesman. It's not that he begrudged him his success. It's just that anybody can sell cars. MacKinnon's talents, on the other hand, were so much more...cerebral. It took brains to make money the way MacKinnon made it. And guts.

"I mean, are these people your friends or something?" McGuire added.

"Lloyd, my interest is only in OneWorld's interest."

McGuire looked skeptical. "Uh-huh."

"I just know a good deal when I see one," MacKinnon continued. "And one that comes at the right time."

"How so?" said McGuire, sipping his tea.

"Well, let's be honest. When people think of OneWorld, what do they think of?"

"The killer whales."

"Okay, but besides the whales."

"I don't know...the dolphins?"

"They think of James Parker. Right? The place is synonymous with him. Clearly, the value of our parks will erode now that James is gone. I mean, he's our Walt Disney, for crying out loud."

"So far as I know, Disney Corporation did just fine after Walt's passing," said Maggie. "I mean, look at it now."

"Okay, bad example. But you have to admit that we're not the same organization without James's leadership. My overall point—Disney notwithstanding—is that we're probably at peak value right now. If we're going to sell, this is the time."

"Disney is trading at 110," said McGuire, checking the stock app on his phone. "Up a half."

"Can we forget about Disney for a second?" said MacKinnon.

"You brought him up."

"There's another thing, too. The animal rights people haven't stopped squawking since that damn piece on 'Newsline' about the supposed intelligence of the whales." MacKinnon made quotation-mark gestures when he spoke the word *intelligence*. "And that book that followed. We don't want to wait until it becomes suddenly unfashionable to go see orcas perform."

"Why do you say 'supposed' intelligence?" said McGuire. "Parker's own research seemed to suggest that these whales are very, very smart."

"Oh, not you, too, Lloyd," said MacKinnon. "Listen, has a whale ever driven into one of your dealerships to trade in his car? I rest my case."

"Crudely put, Robert," said Maggie, "but I must say I agree that the research was hardly definitive. But speaking of which, you did tell us you got rid of it, yes?"

"No worries there, Maggie. But you see the animal rights people don't need any of the research to make the parks look bad," said MacKinnon. "They don't care about the truth. They just care about getting attention. If they keep it up, attendance will fall."

"It hasn't fallen so far," said McGuire.

"Nevertheless, why take the chance? It's just another good reason to sell now while the selling is good. And it *is* a good deal."

"Yes, yes, it's a good deal," Maggie said, waving a hand, "but let's get back to this Russian thing. We're all old enough to remember the USSR. I remember doing fallout drills in school, for God's sake. And these are the people we're shipping OneWorld off to?"

"Maggie, we're not 'shipping' it 'off.' It's not like we're boxing up the parks and putting them on a freighter and sailing it to Vladivostok. The parks will still be here, visited every day by Americans, the U.S. flag proudly flying at the entrances."

"You know, Disney is still American-owned," piped in McGuire. "Maybe that's been the secret of their success."

MacKinnon winced.

"Those fallout drills were ludicrous," Maggie said, looking off into the distance. "We were supposed to get under our desks. Was that supposed to save us from nuclear holocaust?"

"Ludicrous," McGuire nodded.

"Lloyd dear, hand me a scone, would you? Aren't they delightful?"

"Delightful," McGuire agreed. "Where do you get them?"

"Banyan Cafe."

"Hmm...don't believe I know it."

"Look, folks," MacKinnon said, "if we could just focus—"

"Well, it *is* a good offer," Maggie said suddenly. "And we do have a duty to the shareholders. Lloyd, what do you think, dear?"

"I think maybe we should field other offers," McGuire replied.

"Yes, but then maybe we'd lose this one."

"That's a great point, Maggie" nodded MacKinnon.

"If these Russians are so interested, maybe we should take advantage of their eagerness," said Maggie. "But I tell you, Robert, I'm still not comfortable with the idea. OneWorld is an American institution. Lloyd, you see what I mean, don't you?"

"Of course I do, Maggs. And I share the same concern. It would be like, well, it would be like Disney selling to the Russians." MacKinnon winced again and felt a headache coming on as McGuire spoke. "What would the public think of a board of directors that allowed that to happen? They'd want to string them up!"

"Quite right, Lloyd," said Maggie. "Quite right. And yet..."

"And yet?" said McGuire.

MacKinnon perked back up.

"Well, we have to think of the shareholders, don't we? Our first duty is to them. We mustn't allow our patriotism to obscure the fact that this is an opportunity that we might not see again."

"Well, I suppose that's a reasonable way to look at it."

"I mean, I'm with you on the idea of fielding other offers. But the fact is, how many organizations in the entire world have the means to even consider making an offer like this, let alone see it through?"

"Not many, I suppose."

"Indeed."

MacKinnon knew a lot about negotiating. He knew the right things to say and he knew the right times to say them.

He knew what buttons to push. Most of all, he knew when to keep his trap shut. Maggie Lynch and Lloyd McGuire were slowly talking themselves into approving the sale and all he had to do was stay quiet and let them.

"The Russians are smart, I'm sure," said McGuire. "Certainly they know enough not to tinker with the OneWorld business model. I can't imagine they would come in and make whole-sale changes."

"Precisely," Maggie agreed. "I imagine from the outside looking in, the typical visitor to a OneWorld park will be unable to notice a difference."

"Right," said McGuire. "It's not as if suddenly they'll be selling bowls of borscht at the concession stands." This caused both to laugh and MacKinnon laughed right along with them.

"I tell you," said Maggie, "I'm inclined to vote in favor of the sale. *If* you can assure me, Robert, that the Russians have no plans to alter the general feel and theme of the parks."

"Maggie, you have not only my assurance, but Neftkomp's assurance. Mr. Gardner gave me his personal word that OneWorld will remain the American institution that it's always been. Er, notwithstanding the ownership, of course."

"And you trust this Mr. Gardner?"

"With my life."

"Lloyd?" said Maggie.

"Maggs, if you think it's in the company's best interests," said McGuire, "then that's good enough for me."

"You don't think our patriotism will be called into question?"

"Patriotism?" MacKinnon said, ready now to close the deal, "We'll be making a small fortune for our stockholders. What's more American than that?"

Maggie thought for a moment and then said, "Okay, Robert. Call a meeting of the board for tomorrow. We'll have our vote. Shall we celebrate our decision with a glass of port?"

MacKinnon toasted along with Maggie and Lloyd, anxious to leave and call Nelson Gardner with the good news. And to tell him how thorny and intricate the negotiations had been. Who else but MacKinnon could have pulled this off? Gardner had certainly chosen the right man for the job. But of course that's what ten million dollars buys you. The right man for the job.

Moments after Robert MacKinnon left Maggie Lynch's condo, Maggie and Lloyd toasted each other.

"Just the right amount of skepticism," McGuire smiled.

"Very believable," Maggie agreed. Both knew that Mr. Gardner would be pleased. After all, that's what twenty million dollars buys you.

FIFTEEN

"I only know what I've seen. These whales did amazing things, things we never trained them to do." Brooke Lewis was in "Orca HQ" talking to Donnie Watkins and Paul Taylor. DJ and JJ were there, too. "I mean even before the experiments, I witnessed amazing things. I've told you how they responded to music. But here's the thing: they tried to recreate it, too."

"You didn't mention that to me, Brooke," said DJ.

"Well, I didn't want you thinking I was nuts. But now that we're here, brainstorming, with everything on the table...you did say you wanted everything, right?"

"No matter how small," said DJ. "Anything could help. Don't worry if it sounds nuts. We're all a little nuts anyway. How do you mean 'recreate' the music?"

"Well, their vocal abilities don't exactly match ours. But it's been proven time and again that they can mimic human voices. With their clicks and whistles, apparently they can at least try to mimic our music, too. The female orca I told you about who responded to Rihanna—a week or so later, I heard her making strange noises. Not her usual sounds. Mostly, I noticed that her pulsed calls and clicks contained a certain rhythm to them. The rhythm sounded familiar and

I suddenly remembered my little experiment from the week before. On a whim, I played 'Love on the Brain' into the tank and it became obvious that she was, well, she was providing the exact rhythm to the song. Now, I'm not saying she could recreate the melody, but her understanding of the song was such that Rihanna herself could have sung along without any additional instruments and it would have sounded terrific. And she hadn't heard it since a week before. But the funny thing is, she only played along for about twenty seconds. Then she stopped. She'd been playing the rhythm for about a half hour before I played the song, but once I played the song, she stopped. It was as if she just wanted to play by herself, not with anything...human."

"Maybe they get sick of humans," offered Watkins. "I mean, why wouldn't they hate their captors?"

"You're assuming they understand that they're being held captive," said Taylor.

"I'm sure it's obvious to them."

"Is it obvious to your dog at home? Does he feel like a captive?"

"Bad example. Dogs have been domesticated."

"So?"

"So, they don't do well in the wild. Ever seen a feral dog or a feral cat? They live poorly and they die young. Whales are wild animals. Like tigers or wolves. They can't be domesticated."

"I don't know about that. Doesn't OneWorld prove that they can be? They respond to human commands, just like dogs."

"You can train a tiger to respond to commands, too, but I wouldn't say that tigers are domesticated animals. They can turn on their masters at any time. Just like—Brooke, didn't an orca turn on a trainer not long ago? With fatal results?"

"Yes," said Brooke. "In 2015, an orca at our park in Phoenix dragged a trainer underwater and drowned him. Marty

Mullins. I knew him. He'd been a trainer over ten years. We still don't know why the whale did that."

"I'll tell you why," said Watkins. "If I was a whale and held in a tank all my life and made to do tricks to get my food, I'd want to drown somebody, too."

"Isn't that what we do here?" said Taylor.

Everybody laughed but Brooke, who forced a thin smile. Taylor suddenly felt a bit embarrassed by having followed up the mention of the dead trainer with a flippant joke.

Fortunately, DJ jumped in. "Let's get back to the music thing," he said. "It's interesting to me that the whale stopped playing when she did. Think about something for a moment. Suppose whales are so smart that they don't want us to know how smart they are."

"Why wouldn't they want that?" said Watkins.

"Who knows? I'm just postulating. The point is, it's very difficult to observe whales in their natural habitat without them knowing they're being observed. Most of what we know about whale behavior comes to us from captive whales. Oh, sure, we can follow their pods in the ocean and we can see how they feed and how they interact, but so much of what they do is a mystery. A human observer just can't be present all the time. What do they do and how do they act when nobody is around to watch them?"

"Meaning what exactly?"

"Meaning how do we know that what we see with captive whales tells the whole story? I'm not doubting that orcas in captivity have often shown amazing intelligence, beyond learning tricks. They've shown human characteristics, like empathy. I remember, in fact, reading once about how a starving whale in captivity offered his food to another starving whale."

"Charlie Chin."

All eyes turned to JJ who up until then had been quiet.

"His name was Charlie Chin." JJ was sitting, slightly rocking back and forth. "He was captured in 1970 with other whales. One was named Pointednose Cow. They were held in a sea pen at Pedder Bay for weeks. They both wouldn't eat and almost starved. Almost starved. Both wouldn't eat. They were given injections to increase their appetite. Then Charlie Chin was offered a fresh salmon. Both orcas were transient. They wouldn't normally eat salmon. So Charlie Chin didn't eat the salmon at first. Didn't eat it. But then he took it over to Pointednose Cow and gave it to her. They ended up splitting it. They both started eating again. Both of them." Then JJ looked off into the distance.

"See? They can be downright human in their behavior," said DJ. "But my point is, this kind of stuff probably goes on all the time in the wild. We just don't know about it. And I'm speculating that what if it's the case that the whales don't want us to know. Life and death was involved in that situation with Charlie Chin. It was like when my dad talked about the whale that had been hit with the harpoon the day they captured Eilio. Two whales came over and helped him. They had to or he would have died. But otherwise, how do we know—really know—what their behavior is like?"

"Well," said Taylor, "we can see for ourselves the experiments Brooke and your dad did."

"Yes, and that's my point. Did the whales know they were being observed? Brooke?"

"No," said Brooke. "That was critical for us. We stayed well out of sight. We didn't in any way want to telegraph, even accidentally, the location of the food source at the end of the maze."

"See?"

"Not really," said Brooke.

"What I'm saying is this: maybe we've never been able to fully understand how whales communicate because whales have never allowed us to see."

"A secret language?" said Watkins.

"Maybe. And maybe they want to keep it secret."

"Well, that would certainly explain why, so far, we haven't come up with a damn thing," said Taylor. "Honestly, DJ, for a week now we've listened to their sounds with every piece of software we've got. We've run the audio through a dozen different programs. We've also cross-referenced the sounds with audio files of other orcas, taken in the wild. The internet is full of them. I think if you gave us enough time, we could probably write an orca dictionary, even taking into account the different dialects. But none of that matters. The bottom line is that the language of the clicks and whistles and pulsed calls is just way too rudimentary to explain the conveyance of information sophisticated enough to allow for what the whales were able to do."

"Well, they're talking to each other somehow," said DJ.

"Well, we did notice one particularly strange thing," said Watkins, glancing over at Taylor. "It's probably not worth mentioning. But when there are two orcas together, there's a different level of energy than when there's just one."

"How do you mean?" said DJ.

"Well, just for kicks, Paul and I ran some of the audio through the ultrasonic biometer that we'd developed to test Soti. That's when we noticed the elevated energy levels when two orcas were in the tank together."

"So we took those results," continued Taylor, "and ran them through our quantum biofeedback program. What we discovered is that the energy isn't stable or uniform. It bounces around. Here, we graphed it. Donnie, put it up on the main screen. There. See? It leaps in very specific ways."

"Can someone translate all this scientific jargon into plain English?" said Brooke.

"What they're saying," said DJ, thoughtfully, "is that the energy that's created by the introduction of the second whale isn't just random energy bouncing around the tank. It moves in specific ways. Is that what you guys are saying?"

"More or less," said Taylor.

"Is it bouncing *between* them? Between the whales?"

"Well, there's really no way to tell. We can't really measure direction. Just quantity and level of activity," said Watkins.

"Why didn't you guys tell me this before?"

"Because, frankly," said Taylor, "it's interesting but fairly irrelevant. Energy isn't speech. It can be used as a means of conveyance of speech, like electricity can be used to send, say, a text, but it isn't speech itself. It would need to be somehow translated into speech, like how a cell phone—to press the texting analogy—takes the digital information and translates it into words that you can read on your screen. Of course there's nothing like that in the tanks with the whales. The energy might bounce between them, but that's all it is. Energy. There's no mechanism by which to transform the energy into something understandable."

"You mean understandable by us," said Brooke.

"Understandable by anything or anybody, at least so far as any science known to man. And that assumes it starts out as something understandable. Just as you need a mechanism to translate a digital signal, you need a mechanism to digitize and transmit it in the first place. You need a mechanism on both ends, in other words."

DJ scratched his head. "So where do we go from here, fellas? Are you telling me we're completely stumped?"

Taylor and Watkins glanced at each other. "Well, so far," said Taylor, looking back at DJ.

"Are we out of ideas?"

"Oh, no," said Watkins. "There are always more ideas. Always more things we can try."

"Such as?"

"Well...I mean, there's got to be something. Paul?"

"Oh, yeah," said Taylor. "There's something. Sure. We just need more time. That's all."

DJ sighed and then suggested taking a break. Lunch, he declared, would be on him. Outside of Orca HQ. Outside of the Yaba campus. Someplace nice. And then Casey strode into the room.

"DJ, I've got some news for you guys and it isn't good."

"What is it, Case?"

"It's OneWorld. It's reportedly been sold."

"What?! To whom?"

"Some foreign company. Neftkomp? Does that sound right?"

"Neftkomp? The Russian company? It's being sold to the Russians? Where did you hear this?"

"The *Wall Street Journal* broke the story, but now every-body's picking it up. It's all over the financial sites."

"Jesus."

The room became silent, all eyes on DJ who was looking down at the floor. Finally, after several moments, he raised his head. "Well, it's a whole new ballgame now, isn't it? Paul, you said you needed more time? I'm afraid we don't have it, my friend. Lunch is canceled. Back to work, guys."

SIXTEEN

"Won't the publicity campaign still work?" asked Brooke over her tomato caprese. "I mean, assuming you can prove definitively the intelligence of the orcas, the public will still demand the release of them, yes? Whether the parks are owned by the Russians or not. If the public just stops going to the parks, the Russians won't be able to keep them afloat. And so they'll have to respond to the outcry. It's business, after all."

"Maybe," said DJ. "The truth is, we just don't know what their ultimate plans are. And, in a larger context, why are they investing in something like OneWorld to begin with? What's their end game?" DJ gazed out of the window into the San Francisco night. The Top of the Mark had been his idea. On the nineteenth floor of the InterContinental Hotel, just across the street from where Brooke was staying at the Fairmont, the lounge provided a 360-degree panorama of the city. He'd driven her back to her hotel that evening and then had suggested a nightcap and a bite to eat.

"Who knows?" said Brooke. "But it's strange to think of OneWorld in the hands of a foreign company. It's strange to think of it without your father, too. Tell me. What kind of a dad was he?"

"He was the best when I was a kid. But we ran into some philosophical differences about his work as I got older. He wanted me involved with OneWorld. I think it was always his idea that I take over the reins someday. But of course I had my own thing going."

"He must have been proud of you."

"Yeah. Turns out he was."

"Hey, not to change the subject, but can I ask you something?"

"Sure."

"Why do you keep moving your water glass like that?"

"Huh? Like what?" DJ took his hand off the glass that he'd been rhythmically shifting back and forth by the side of his plate, three inches up, three inches back. "Oh, uh, I didn't notice."

"Well, I only ask because I have a cousin who has obsessive-compulsive disorder. I was just curious. I don't mean to pry. It's none of my business, really."

"It's okay. It's just a little quirk, I guess. It's better than it was."

"My cousin's really smart. They say OCD is more prevalent among super intelligent people. But then I already knew that about you, DJ. Yaba is amazing. You're an impressive guy."

"Yep, that's what they say about me. David James Parker: an impressive guy with mild OCD." They both laughed. "But, really, I've been fortunate. And I've managed to surround myself with some pretty smart people. But, listen, enough about me. I hardly know anything about you."

"What would you like to know?"

"Well, let's see," said DJ, and then he rattled off a list of questions, hoping to effect enough subtlety and nonchalance to avoid sending any premature signals. "How do you like Santa Monica? What are you doing now that you're no longer with OneWorld? Do you have a boyfriend? How do you like San Francisco?"

"Smooth," Brooke grinned. "No, I don't have a boyfriend."

Not subtle enough, thought DJ, laughing at himself. "Well, I just wondered. You have that 'Adam' tattoo on your wrist. Was Adam the boyfriend who split? Haven't had a chance to remove the tattoo yet?"

"Adam was my brother," Brooke said, suddenly turning serious.

"Was?"

Brooke hesitated a second and then said, "He was killed."

"Oh, geez, Brooke, I'm so sorry. Were you close?"

"Practically inseparable. We were twins, actually. Adam was a Navy SEAL. He was killed in a covert action in the Middle East in 2015. My parents and I have never been able to get any real information about his death. 'In the line of duty' was the official pronouncement and that's all we know. I don't know how my brother died and, more importantly, I don't know why."

"Wow, I can't even imagine the pain..."

"I threw myself into my work at OneWorld. That's the only thing that has kept me going. Well, now the research. There's something about the whales, DJ. Something peaceful. They somehow give me...hope. The way they interact is beautiful."

"You're preaching to the choir with me. I've been intrigued by them since I was a little boy watching them off Orcas Island."

"I notice your brother is pretty intrigued by them, too."

"JJ connects to the whales more than he connects to people. That Charlie Chin story he told today, for instance. That orca had a deformed chin, hence the nickname. Another one of the transients captured that day was an albino. Maybe that group of transients came together because they just didn't fit in anywhere else. I think JJ relates, you know? He knows he's different. He doesn't spend a lot of time thinking about it because his brain doesn't really work that way, but on some level he knows he doesn't fit in. He finds comfort in those whales, I'm sure of it. In all the whales."

"I know how he feels. I do, too, in a way. There's just something about them. I know it seems strange to say, but somehow I just feel like they're ahead of us, ahead of us humans. We think we're the masters of the planet, the top of the proverbial food chain, as if the world was made just for us. But can we handle it? Whales don't go to war. Whales don't get killed in covert operations. They have something that we don't have, DJ."

"Well, in our defense, they live pretty simple lives."

"Maybe we should live simpler."

"Can we? I don't think that's in our nature. We're a creative species. We're driven to produce. To make things. And when we've made them, we're driven to make them better. I'll admit, it's a process that's not always pretty. It creates competition, which can be downright ugly. And when you have eight billion people in the world going in eight billion directions, you're going to have some conflict. But I like to believe that through it all, something beautiful results, like a pearl from the friction of an oyster, you know? I like to think that humans are always moving forward though we can't always see it while it's happening."

"But maybe there's a better way. Maybe there's a way to smooth the process out. Look, I'm not against human creativity and progress, but I'm just wondering if we're adequately equipped to handle it. Look at the whales, DJ. Look at how they've mastered communication. They seem to understand each other innately. They cooperate. Look at us. We fight over parking spaces, for crying out loud. And then we pick bigger and bigger fights until we go to war in Godforsaken parts of the world. I mean, what's that all about?"

"Well, I'll admit we don't exactly have interpersonal communication down to a science."

"You know what I think? I think it's evolutionary. Whales have been around for fifty million years. You know how long Homo sapiens has been around? Two-hundred thousand years. So why do we automatically assume we're the superior ones? DJ, I think these whales are smarter than we are. Much smarter. In fact, we're not smart enough to see just how smart they are. Maybe you're wrong about them not wanting us to know about them. Maybe they want us to know but we just can't understand. Maybe they're over our heads. It would be like you trying to explain how Y-Songs works to your cat."

"Maybe."

"DJ, I know this sounds crazy, but when I was training these magnificent animals...there were times when I'd look at them and they'd be looking back at me. Those eyes of theirs. You just know sometimes. You can feel it."

"Feel what, Brooke?"

"A connection. And I don't mean just with the whales. Oh, I don't know how to describe it. It's like you're connecting with something bigger. When you're looking into their eyes it's like you're seeing into the very soul of the universe. It's like...it's like you're connecting with God or something. I know—crazy, right?"

"No, Brooke. Not crazy. Not crazy at all."

DJ walked Brooke into the lobby of the Fairmont and the two said goodnight to each other. She thanked him for dinner and he thanked her for her company and for the conversation. He said he'd send the limo again in the morning and she said she'd see him in Orca HQ.

On his way out of the front entrance of the hotel, DJ passed a man coming in, tall and sturdy and wearing an expensive, well-tailored suit. He had a mark on his cheek. The two nodded politely to each other and then DJ strode to the valet stand to retrieve the Tesla.

"Your feelings for Brooke Lewis are now completely unmistakable," said Soti.

"She's a colleague, Soti. We're doing research together."

"It's more than that, David. Your physiological symptoms are very clear on the subject of Ms. Lewis."

DJ was getting ready for bed, thinking about the evening, thinking about Brooke. But there were other things on his mind, too. The research, of course. But also the sale of OneWorld, the sale of the company his father spent a lifetime building. He and his father might have had their disagreements, but he couldn't help but think that James Parker must have been rightly spinning in his grave. No matter their differences, the two were both businessmen, both entrepreneurs. You spend your whole life building something and...for what?

"Look, Soti, I have a lot on my mind these days. Aren't you picking up any other physiological symptoms that might indicate other sources of stress and stimuli?"

"Yes, David, of course. But the bodily manifestations of your thoughts about Ms. Lewis are of much greater interest."

"Interest? Interest to whom?"

Soti remained silent.

"You know what, Soti? I think I'm going to have to take you off for the night. You'll just have to continue your analysis of me in the morning." DJ unfastened Soti from around his wrist and sat her down on the nightstand beside his bed.

Then he turned out the light and stretched himself out on the bed, staring up at the ceiling.

"David," said Soti from the darkness, "your heart rate will have to fall at least twenty-five percent if you expect to fall asleep soon."

"Soti, how can you tell what my heart rate is from over there?"

"I recommend sleep, David. All of your vital signs indicate that your body and mind are both in need of sleep."

"Answer the question, Soti. You didn't answer the question."

SEVENTEEN

He'd been spotted. He hated that he'd been that sloppy. Why hadn't he come in a side door to the hotel? David Parker had looked right at him. *Damn it.* Parker had even nodded at him as the two sidestepped each other coming through the front entrance. There was no way he could touch Brooke Lewis now. Parker would have been the last person she'd have been with and the police certainly would have questioned him. He'd have mentioned the guy he saw coming into the lobby, might have even given them a description. Plus, the security cameras would be consulted.

Nelson Gardner—real name: Marlon Maxwell—was sitting in his hotel room plotting his next move. Evgeni Sergachev had called him the morning after his brief but damaging encounter with David Parker and he'd been forced to confess that the matter with Brooke Lewis had been unavoidably postponed "for the safety of the entire operation." Sergachev had not been happy. But then later that afternoon, Sergachev had called back. The mission had changed. Sergachev had apparently conferred with his superior—Gardner guessed Boris Kucherov—and it had been decided not to destroy the research, but rather to take it and examine it. This would mean Gardner not tipping his hand just yet.

"My superior has come to believe the research might be of some value on its own merit," Sergachev had said. Gardner could not imagine what that value could be. All it might prove is that whales are intelligent creatures and that would be bad for business for Neftkomp's pending acquisition, OneWorld. Sergachev agreed but went on at length about his superior's business acumen and history of long-range strategic thinking. "He is a chess player," Sergachev had said. "He's always several moves ahead. He wants to see the research. He is wondering if perhaps there is opportunity there."

"Then we should pay MacKinnon his ten million?" Gardner asked.

"No. No, we no longer believe that whatever MacKinnon has is of any real value. Most likely, it's been made obsolete by whatever Parker at Yaba has done with it. That's what we want to know—what Parker has come up with."

"Then we no longer have any use for MacKinnon."

"That is correct. Still, let's keep him around a little longer. He might not be totally without value, who knows? The priority right now is to ascertain what Parker has discovered, if anything."

Gardner had then said what he always said: "Consider it done." Sergachev had come to know that Gardner was a man of his word. For seven years now, the two had worked together. They'd met in Prague when Gardner had been stationed there. Marlon Maxwell had been a low-level agent with the CIA and low level was bound to be his destiny. The CIA liked his initiative and resourcefulness. They didn't like his background. Maxwell had come from the proverbial other side of the tracks. He grew up poor in West Virginia, the son of an absent truck-driver father, and a waitress mother who moonlighted as a prostitute.

Maxwell was naturally smart, even gifted, and he did well in school but couldn't keep out of trouble. He fought often, mostly against kids who bullied him and antagonized him with jokes about his "whore" mother. As he got older, the fights got worse. Once, he'd tangled with a guy who pulled a knife on him. Slashed him across the cheek, leaving a scar. But Maxwell had been able to grab the knife and he'd plunged it into the guy's shoulder. Then he'd pummeled him senseless before walking three miles to a hospital to have his cheek stitched up.

After that came a series of petty crimes, including vandalism and destruction of property. He stopped going to school and found himself in and out of juvenile detention until the day he decided to join the Marines. He flourished there. The Marines seemed to give him a purpose, or at least a place to channel his anger and aggression. He scored well on aptitude tests and the Marines encouraged him to finish his education. Ultimately, he was enrolled in Officers Candidate School. As a first lieutenant, he was directed towards intelligence and when he left the Marines after seventeen years, he applied to the CIA. After two years of training in Washington, the Agency sent him to Europe and stationed him at the embassy in Prague.

That's where his career path stalled. Promotions and choice assignments were given to the younger agents and the ones with more prestigious backgrounds and more impressive educational credentials. Maxwell was an ex-jarhead from Appalachia, an image he bitterly realized he would never be able to shake. It was about that time that Evgeni Sergachev approached him. Sergachev was with the Russian Foreign Intelligence Service. He seemed to better appreciate Maxwell's talents. Maxwell had no interest in spying for Russia, but when Sergachev left the Service for the private sector and landed an executive position with Neftkomp, he approached Maxwell again. Corporate espionage was much more palatable to Maxwell than government espionage. State secrets are one thing, but what does it really matter in the long run if a corporate secret doesn't remain secret? Who does it hurt? Some silver-spooned, corporate muckety-muck with a Harvard degree? Fuck him.

Maxwell quit the CIA, moved back to the States to build his clientele, of which Neftkomp became his top priority, and changed his identity to Nelson Gardner. He changed his image, too. He dressed in expensive suits and branded himself as a sophisticate. Marlon Maxwell, poor white trash from West Virginia, was dead and buried.

Nelson Gardner's reputation grew steadily. He was a man who was more than competent at doing those things you needed done but couldn't—or wouldn't—do yourself. He was a doer and a fixer. He was a go-between. He was an investigator. He was muscle. He was whatever you needed him to be when you didn't want to get your own fingerprints on an undertaking that might prove to be a little messy.

Now Gardner needed to find a way to find out what David Parker was doing with the research. This would not be easy. Yaba was virtually impenetrable. Gardner remembered when Y-Songs technology came out. There were barely any rumors about it beforehand, mostly just whispers of a new technology in sound, but so vague were these whispers that nobody could vouch for their credibility. Yaba was as tight as a drum. Information never escaped, a credit, Gardner surmised, to the loyalty and respect Yaba's employees must have felt for Parker—or else fear that if you did leak company information, Parker would bury you. A billionaire can do a lot with the legal system that the ordinary person cannot do. You can file civil suits and keep filing them, forcing your adversary to defend himself against whatever action you want to throw at him, baseless or not. In the world of civil law, it's a war of attrition and the guy with the deepest pockets wins, either in court, or by bankrupting his opponent, making him spend money on his defense of one action and then the next, until there's no money left.

But either way, respect for Parker or fear of him—pretty much one and the same in Gardner's estimation—, his employees were amazingly reluctant to offer hints at what the company was up to. But every nut can be cracked. Somebody at Yaba could be bought. Now it was just a matter of discovering who. For that, Gardner would need to do some surveillance. Who was Parker directly working with on the research? Who would know what, if anything, Parker was discovering? There had to be somebody. Somebody associated with the research, yet someone whose loyalty could be purchased. Everyone has his price.

EIGHTEEN

Sea lions are fin-footed, carnivorous, semi-aquatic marine mammals belonging to the pinniped family, more commonly known as seals. The California sea lion, in particular, is a species of sea lion whose habitat is western North America, ranging from Alaska to Mexico. Just offshore from the Golden Gate National Recreation Area in San Francisco, California, are a group of small rock islands collectively called Seal Rocks. The name is appropriate given that the Rocks are often populated by California sea lions.

Or at least they were. For some unknown reason, beginning in 1989, the sea lions began to migrate from Seal Rocks eastward, under the Golden Gate Bridge and into San Francisco Bay, landing at a marina off of Fisherman's Wharf. As it happened, in September of that year, a refurbishment project of K Dock on Pier 39 required the removal of several boats from the area. The empty docks were apparently to the liking of the sea lions and they began to congregate on them. By January of 1990, some 150 sea lions were making K Dock their home, much to the frustration of the marina's boat owners, but much to the delight of tourists who soon began visiting Pier 39 in droves. The Marine Mammal Center was consulted and they made a rather dramatic recommendation: abandon the docks to the sea lions. The boats from K Dock were relocated and the population of sea lions grew to 300 and beyond. During the week of Thanksgiving in 2009, some 1,700 sea lions were counted on the docks.

JJ knew all of this—and could recite it all—from an article he had read years earlier. Pier 39 was his favorite place to see in San Francisco. Kioko had taken him there shortly after the two had arrived, and now DJ was taking him again. He'd invited Brooke along, too. The research analysis had completely stalled. Watkins and Taylor were stumped and everybody was frustrated. So far, the best explanation anybody had for the communication of the whales had come from Brooke. "It's magic," she had offered tongue-in-cheek, and as unsatisfying as her theory was, nobody had a better one. After two solid weeks of scrutiny, nothing was found that could account for the transmission of information from one orca to another. DJ sensed that the ongoing disappointment was creating some underlying friction within Orca HQ. The mood had soured. Jokes were few and far between and sometimes nobody would say anything for hours. The days were long and the results nil and DJ had called for a day off. "I don't want to see you guys within twenty miles of this place tomorrow," he had told Watkins and Taylor the day before.

DJ obeyed his own order, taking JJ and Brooke for a ride along the Embarcadero up to Pier 39 where the three had lunch, stopped for ice cream, and then leaned against the wooden rail at the end of the pier looking out over K Dock, gazing at the spectacle—throngs of blubbery sea lions sprawled over the docks, a cacophony of barking filling the malodorous air.

JJ was loving every minute of it.

"There are 306 of them here today," he said after a quick glance over the docks.

"That looks about right," said DJ.

"They're amazing," said Brooke. "I loved watching them at OneWorld. But I've never seen this many together anywhere."

Brooke was wide-eyed, beholding the scene as a child might, and at that moment, DJ found her especially charming. He was glad he invited her along. Since dinner that night at Top of the Mark, they'd seen each other every day, but it was mostly within the confines of Orca HQ. She was something of an enigma to him. She could be fun and playful, but there was a distance to her as well. She could just as quickly turn serious, sometimes downright somber. He was attracted to her but could get no reading whatsoever on how she might feel about him. The whole thing made him uneasy and, for the time being, he had decided to maintain a friendly professionalism towards her.

"That one," said JJ, pointing to a tawny brown sea lion resting on the corner of one of the docks, "is thirty-two years old. That's old for a sea lion. Most sea lions live to be about twenty. She's the oldest one here. Oldest one here."

"Oh, yeah? How do you know that?" said Brooke.

"They all know. Everybody knows she's that old. They all do. That old. She's an original from Seal Rocks. They call her Tenny."

"Who calls her Tenny, JJ?"

"All the other sea lions. They call her Tenny. And that one behind her is Stosso. He's a male. He's young. He had an adenovirus infection a few months ago that almost killed him. Killed him. He's okay now. Stosso. Stosso."

JJ began walking along the rail towards the end of the pier while Brooke sidled up to DJ. "DJ, how does your brother know all these things?"

"Oh, it's just an overactive imagination, really."

"I don't know—I mean, you know him a lot better than I do, but from what I've seen in the past couple weeks, as a rule, he doesn't seem to make things up like that. The man is a treasure trove of memorized facts. Mathematically, his mind is a computer. You saw how fast he calculated the number of sea lions here. What did he say, 306? I'll bet that if you counted them, there wouldn't be one sea lion more or less."

"There's no doubt he's a math whiz. And you should see him paint. Autistics can be just as imaginative as anybody else."

"What does he paint?"

"Seascapes, mostly. Whales. Sea lions. He's painted this scene before, as a matter of fact. It's amazing in its detail. And he painted it from memory."

"But, you see, that's my point, DJ. I'm not doubting his capacity for imagination, but he seems to deal mostly with facts and realism. Does he tell any other stories about things where he seemingly makes things up?"

"Sure. Sometimes up at Seahaven he'll sit on the dock and imagine whales from this pod or that pod swimming by. He'll go on and on about them."

"Are you sure he's imagining?"

"What do you mean?"

"What about other times?"

"Well, I mean, not that I can think of offhand. Mostly it's about the whales or, like today, the sea lions."

"He doesn't make up stories about the neighbors? He doesn't paint fantastical scenes with imaginary beings in them?"

"Brooke, what are you getting at?"

"DJ, all I know is that ever since I worked on those experiments with your father, I've seen some pretty inexplicable things. Mysterious things. Things that we can't understand. Look at the past two weeks. We're no closer to figuring out how whales communicate than we were when we started. I'm beginning to think there are powers in the universe we just can't comprehend."

"Magic?"

"Okay, laugh, if you will."

"Brooke, I'm an engineer by trade. And you're a scientist. We both understand something about the physical laws of the universe. Everything is explainable. If we don't understand it, it just means we haven't discovered the explanation yet."

"You don't think there might be things beyond the grasp of humans?"

"Like what?"

"Well, like the mind, for instance. Do we understand it? We understand the brain, more or less, but we know precious little about the mind, about subjective experience. About sensations and thoughts and emotions."

"Products of the brain."

"Can you operate on a brain and find the subjective experience of love or hate or mercy or anger? Not the neurological pathways that carry the experience. I mean the experience itself."

"The brain produces the experience. And then you feel it."

"*Who* feels it?"

"Well, a person...it's felt by...the experience is..."

"See what I mean?"

"Okay, I admit there are some gray areas in our overall understanding of things, but what's that got to do with JJ and sea lions?"

"Maybe nothing. But, DJ, his mind works differently than yours and mine. What if he has some kind of innate ability to pick up on things that we can't pick up on? Thoughts or vibrations that we can't see or hear. Maybe that sea lion's name really is Tenny. And maybe she really is thirty-two. Maybe that one is really named Stosso. And maybe JJ can sense what whales from what pod are swimming around Orcas Island."

"I don't know, Brooke. I'm as open-minded as the next guy, but—"

"DJ, there's so much of the universe we can't see. Those whiskers on those seals…did you know they're used to detect fish up to six-hundred feet away? Sharks use forty-percent of their brain to smell. Cats can hear sounds at levels we can't hear. Same with dogs. Birds of prey can see tiny objects from hundreds of yards away. The universe presents itself to these animals in a completely different way than how it presents itself to us. So what *is* reality?"

"Meaning?"

"Meaning that maybe the universe comes to JJ differently, too. Maybe his reality is different than ours. Maybe he has sensory skills we don't have. DJ, think about what this might mean for how the whales in our experiments communicate. Do you see the problem we've been having?"

"Sort of…"

"Look, I read about an experiment one time testing the intelligence of chimpanzees. It was a facial recognition test. Several photographs of different human faces were presented to the chimps. Presented with them again, they did a poor job of identifying the faces. Everybody assumed that must have meant the chimps were stupid. End of test. But then later, someone came up with the idea of running the test with photos of chimpanzee faces. This time the chimps were later able to identify them flawlessly. Do you see the point?"

"Not really."

"They were testing them initially by *human* standards. How egocentric is that? When they tested them by chimp standards, the chimps triumphed."

DJ looked thoughtful. "We've been analyzing the whales from a human perspective."

"Right! We can't understand their means of communication because we're filtering it through human analysis."

"But it's not human."

"Exactly."

DJ was quiet, his mind in contemplation. Brooke looked out over K Dock, saying nothing. Both were silently grasping the full meaning of what their discussion was leading to.

"Brooke," DJ said at last, "we've been looking for the wrong thing. We've been searching for a frequency that's not there."

"Yes, DJ. We're analyzing the whales by the terms of *our* reality. We need to analyze them by the terms of theirs."

NINETEEN

DJ was pacing around his cavernous living room. Kioko had made dinner but he had told her that they should go ahead and eat without him. His mind had been racing since the trip to Pier 39 earlier in the day. Food held no interest for him.

What did interest him was JJ. So many unanswered questions all of a sudden. Was it really possible that he could sit on the dock at Seahaven and know—somehow *know*—that whales from J pod or K pod were nearby, and how many of them there were? Looking at JJ watching the sea lions, DJ had thought of other strange things his brother had said that now seemed very relevant. How was he able to identify one of the orcas that swam the maze from a photograph? He had correctly said it was Kuniki. How did he know that? For that matter, how did he know of Brooke Lewis? When DJ was talking aloud about "B.L.," JJ had blurted out Brooke's name. He had said the whales had known. *How did he know what the whales had known?*

DJ and Brooke had peppered him with questions at the pier. As it happened, JJ had not attended the experiments, but he had visited OneWorld with James a few weeks after the initial experiments had been run. There, he had seen Kuniki.

"But that's not her real name," he said. "Her real name is Peeki. That's what the other whales call her. She knows Brooke," he added. Brooke had been present with Kuniki at the experiments, of course. Was it possible that JJ had somehow learned Brooke's name from Kuniki?

What did he mean when he was watching the video footage of the experiments and he'd said, "It's no good on TV"? He had said "it's not there" and when DJ had pressed him, he'd said, "the thoughts...the things they say." Maybe it wasn't an overactive imagination JJ had. If it was, why wouldn't he make something up about what the whales were saying on the video? Whatever means of communication the whales used, JJ was tapping into it, but apparently he needed to be with the whales to hear it. That made sense; the whales had to be within short range of each other to communicate. It was only when the first whale was reintroduced to the tank that the second whale could gather the navigation instructions.

No wonder we can't crack their code, DJ thought. If JJ couldn't pick up on what the whales were saying on the video, then how could he and Watkins and Taylor? Deep orca communication—the communication that goes beyond the whistles and clicks—evidently requires close proximity and it's apparently nothing that can be recorded. It's not sound at all, reasoned DJ—at least in any way that humans recognize sound.

All of this was speculation, of course, and DJ knew it. JJ, for his part, was unable to explain what exactly it was that he picked up from the whales and sea lions and how he picked it up. "It just ends up in my head," he'd told DJ and Brooke, and that's all he could say about it, no matter how many different ways they had phrased the questions to him. Eventually, JJ had stopped talking, weary from the questioning. DJ had dropped Brooke off at the Fairmont and then he'd driven home, with JJ falling asleep along the way.

From the living room, DJ could now hear JJ in the kitchen, talking to Kioko, and he wondered more than ever at the mysterious ways his brother's mind worked. More to the point, how was it that the minds of the orcas worked? He paced some more, thinking the matter over, thinking about the experiments and thinking about what he knew about orcas. He recalled a debate he had attended at Stanford, several years before, between a marine biologist from OneWorld and a marine neuroscientist, a Doctor Lori something. This was right after the "Newsline" piece that had put OneWorld under scrutiny. The OneWorld representative was arguing that there was nothing extraordinary about the abilities of dolphins and whales, pretty much toting the company line. The neuroscientist begged to differ and she seemed to really know her stuff. She had studied their brains, and during her presentation she went into impressive anatomical detail.

DJ thought it all over, turning it over in his head. This is what he did best. This is what built Yaba—David Parker's ability to analyze, to see things that others couldn't see. To look at raw data from various sources and form it into an intelligent, coherent thesis. Finally, he took his phone out and called Donnie Watkins and then conferenced in Paul Taylor.

"I thought this was our day off," chuckled Watkins. "You'd insisted on it."

"Yeah, well, forget about all that. Listen, guys, let's talk about that energy you discovered in the tanks with the whales. You said it wasn't random, that it moved in specific ways."

"Yup, that's what we found," said Taylor.

"And it wasn't present in the tank when there was just one orca."

"That's right, DJ," said Watkins. "It was as if the energy depended on the two orcas being together. It was as if, well, it was as if the introduction of the second orca is what somehow created the energy."

"But we don't know for sure of the direction of the energy. Isn't that what you had said, Paul?"

"Right. All we know is that it moved in specific ways, but we have no means by which to measure the direction. We can't tell, in other words, if the energy was moving from one whale to the other. For that matter, we can't even really say what the origin of the energy is."

"Okay," said DJ, "but let's assume just for a moment that the energy originated from the orcas and let's further assume that the energy was moving between them."

"I know where you're going with this, DJ," said Watkins, "but energy does not equal communication. Believe me, we've looked at this a thousand ways. Even if we allow for your assumptions, that still doesn't tell us how the orcas were able to communicate. It's just energy bouncing back and forth."

"It's like Donnie and I playing catch," said Taylor. "That's not communication. That's just a baseball being thrown from point A to point B and back again. Now, if we wrote messages on the baseball with a pen, then communication would take place. But there's no analogous instrument by which the orcas were writing, so to speak, messages on the energy."

"That makes sense," said DJ. "You'd mentioned that there needs to be a mechanism to translate the energy into something coherent."

"Right, and there is no such mechanism."

"But how can you be sure?"

"What do you mean? It's obvious the orcas weren't carrying transmitters and receivers around with them."

"Is it? What do we know about the *brains* of orcas?"

"Their brains? I don't know. I imagine their brains work a lot like ours."

"Did you know their brains weigh fifteen pounds on average? Five times what our brains weigh? And do you know about the paralimbic cleft?"

"The what?"

"The paralimbic cleft. It's a part of an orca's brain that nobody really understands. It's a set of lobes that we don't have. Did you know their brains are more densely folded than ours? More than two and half times, in fact. They can process information faster."

"What are you saying, DJ?" said Watkins. "Are you saying orcas are smarter than us?"

"No, I wouldn't say smarter. Intelligence can be measured in a multitude of different ways. I'm just saying that maybe they apprehend the world differently than we do. And maybe they're ahead of us in a few things. Like communication. And don't ask me how, but I have reason to believe this capability exists in other sea mammals, as well." *Maybe in certain human beings, too,* he thought, but he decided to keep that to himself for the time being. "I suspect, however, that the orcas have it in spades. This transmitter-receiver device that doesn't appear to be present...maybe it is. Maybe it's a part of their brain function."

"DJ, if what you're saying is true," said Taylor, "then the communication between these creatures is—"

"Instantaneous," finished Watkins.

"That's what I'm saying, gentlemen. There's a brain function that the orcas possess that allows for accurate, instantaneous communication. And that's not all. Think about it. The orcas don't just receive information from one another instantly. They process it instantly, too. If a human was in that tank and another human was talking him through the maze, he'd be hearing words that he would have to translate into thoughts. He'd have to internalize the communication, in other words, and then apply what he's hearing to his situation. See the lag time? The orcas were not only receiving the information instantly, they were using it instantly, too. It's as if...it's as if they were both hooked up *to the same brain.*

Hell, maybe it's even better than that. Maybe it's like both brains became one."

"Man, I don't know," said Taylor. "How in the hell are you going to prove that?"

DJ thought for a moment. "I don't know," he said at last. "I really don't."

"Well, if we could prove it," said Watkins, "We'd certainly accomplish the goal of revealing the intelligence of the orcas. OneWorld would have to free them, then."

"But, Donnie, don't you see?" said DJ. "This is now much bigger than OneWorld. Oh, don't get me wrong. We'll free the orcas, for sure. But think about what we've got here. What if it could be applied to human communication? I'm not talking about instant communication between people. We have that now. I'm talking about instant communication—*and understanding*—between brains."

"Telepathy?" said Taylor.

"Yes, I guess you could call it that. But telepathy that works both ways. It's...a resonance of some description between two minds. Can you see the possibilities? The orcas might possibly be able to give us access to a technology—call it telepathic resonance—that, in the history of humankind, is going to make the invention of the wheel seem meaningless by comparison."

Donnie Watkins hung up his phone and looked down at his mostly-eaten plate of lasagna, soaking in the conversation he'd just been a part of. What DJ was saying was preposterous, of course. Then again, so was Y-Songs at first. That's the thing about technology. Everything is preposterous until it isn't anymore. Still, this idea, what did he call it? Telepathic resonance? This was going to be one hell of a thing to prove.

"Another drink, Donnie?" said the barmaid.

"Nah, I don't think so."

"How about some dessert? The kitchen has tiramisu tonight and it's pretty good."

"No, I guess just the check, Amy. I'd better be on my way. I'm going to need a good night's sleep tonight. I've got a feeling tomorrow's going to be one busy day."

"Yeah? What are you wizards at Yaba cooking up now?"

"I could tell you, Amy, but you wouldn't believe it. And then of course I'd have to kill you."

"Well, I'm sure I wouldn't understand it, anyway. Here's your check, darlin'."

Donnie liked Bellabrava. It was a nice neighborhood place that remained unspoiled by the continued gentrification of his childhood surroundings. Sure, it hadn't been the safest neighborhood growing up, and it was nice to see some money coming into the area, but damned if there weren't a lot of pretentious, foofoo places opening up everywhere with haughty menus and patronizing waiters. Donnie liked the warm, familiar ambiance of the Italian restaurant-lounge that had been on this same corner as long as he'd been alive.

He knew the people, too—the staff and most of the customers. The customers were almost always locals, people he'd known growing up. Every now and again a stranger would come in, but somehow they seemed to sense the friendliness of the place and they'd fit right in immediately. Like the guy who'd come in earlier and sat down right next to Donnie at the bar. Nice guy. Well-dressed, too, but not in a trendy way. He'd struck up a conversation with Donnie and seemed fascinated by Donnie's work. The two had talked for a while and then the man had left just before DJ had called. Donnie hadn't gotten his name. He'd recognize him if he came in again, though. He'd be sure to remember the scar on the man's cheek.

TWENTY

"Remind me again why I'm on the corporate jet for Dallas?"

"Because—for the millionth time since we've taken off—you're a guest speaker at the International Future Technologies Exposition," Casey replied.

"And tell me again how I got roped into that."

"I signed you up. Sorry, boss. I really am. It was six months ago. I didn't know about everything that would happen since. Seemed like a good way to get you out of the office and into the outside world where you can meet some fellow geeks and collect a little decent PR for the cause. And maybe some good karma."

"You did the right thing, Case," DJ sighed. "You really did. It just comes at the wrong time. Paul and Donnie and I are so close to cracking this orca thing."

"I know, I know, the cleft thing."

"The paralimbic cleft. That's what we think. It has to do with the cerebral cortex. The folds of the brain. There's something about the process of how these folds are formed, a process called gyrification. Somehow it's different in cetacea. It allows them to process—and, more importantly, disseminate—information instantly. Instantly! Case, this could revolutionize the way we think about communication. But how do you take something from the brain of one animal and transform it into something that can be used by another? Hell, we don't even fully understand the *human* brain. And that assumes my theory is correct."

DJ looked out of the window at the passing scenery below. He guessed they'd be flying over Texas very soon. Dallas was landlocked and it seemed a million miles away from where he wanted to be—near the ocean. Near the whales and the dolphins and the sea lions. Near his research. Not only that, his palms were already starting to sweat just thinking of his guest speaker role. Soti had noticed but had remained silent.

"I have to say, DJ, that from what you've told me so far, your theory seems pretty out there," Casey said, turning towards him. She pulled her knees and feet up into the wide leather seat.

Casey rarely accompanied DJ on these trips, but when she had reminded him of the guest speaking engagement, he'd insisted she come along. "If I have to go to Dallas, you have to go to Dallas," he'd told her. "You can write my speech for me." She was glad. She could use a day or two away from the office. Plus, it seemed lately she'd hardly seen DJ at all. It was nice, just the two of them traveling together.

"Case, all theories seem 'out there,' at least at first," DJ replied. "But how else do you explain the communication? Something is going on between the whales, even if it seems impossible. What was it that Sherlock Holmes used to tell Watson? Once you eliminate the impossible, whatever remains, however improbable, must be the truth."

"Well, how come nobody's ever discovered this improbable truth of yours before, Sherlock? I mean, you're not the only one to ever have studied orcas."

"I don't know. But I think it probably has something to do with the underlying assumptions that we've had about cetacea all these years. I mean, if you enter into the study of them with the presupposition that they're not especially intelligent, then you're bound not to discover anything to counter that. The research that my father did…well, by then, he must have replaced his presuppositions with other ones. He was *looking* for intelligence. He was hoping to prove it. He didn't tell the board that, of course. But I know that his mind had changed over the years."

"He would be proud of you, DJ, for what you're doing."

"Yeah, I'd like to think so. You know, Case, when I was growing up on Orcas Island, I used to see these amazing creatures all the time out in the water. The waters around Orcas Island—the Salish Sea—are home to the Southern Resident Killer Whales. It's a clan of orcas. Their numbers are down to somewhere around seventy last I checked. My brother would know exactly. If you were to put back the orcas that have been captured over the years, and the ones that were killed during those captures, you'd be up around 150 or more. Their numbers are dwindling because of other reasons, too. Boat traffic, pollution, competition for food. It's such a shame."

"I can see why you want to do something, DJ."

"Well, they're just so beautiful, you know? Ever see a whale breach? It's a magnificent sight. And to see them in their natural state, where they belong—it's just breathtaking. From the time I was a kid, I never lost my interest in them. Never lost my curiosity. They've fascinated me all my life. I can't remember when it was exactly, but as I got older it just started to seem so wrong for creatures like that to be confined. Like caged birds, you know? And now to consider that all this time, they're even more intelligent than anybody has previously thought. Smarter than us maybe. But of course, that's what we have to prove."

Casey nodded. "You'll figure it out."

"I'm just so afraid we're going to become stuck. Case, if I'm right, then the paralimbic cleft holds the answers. But here's the thing: how do we study that? It's not like you can just cut it open and look for the part that communicates. We need to understand how it works. What we need is a way to communicate with *it*. You see? We need our own version of the cleft to engage with the orca's cleft. But how do we create one without understanding it first?"

"Sounds like a classic catch-22."

"Yup."

Kevin Gloss suddenly appeared from the cockpit. "Landing in forty-five, folks," he smiled.

"Thanks, Kevin," said DJ, as Gloss retreated back to his seat at the controls.

Casey cocked her head to one side and played nonchalantly with her hair. "So, how does...is Brooke Lewis helping? She certainly seems knowledgeable."

"Oh, sure, she's been a lot of help. She knows her cetacea, I'll tell you that. We talked on the phone this morning about my brain theory. She agrees it makes sense. Or at least she doesn't know of anything that would rule it out."

"I can't remember...did she mention having a boyfriend?" Casey slyly grinned.

"Actually, if you must know, I don't think she has one."

"Well, what's stopping you, DJ?"

"I don't know, Case. She just seems so...focused all the time. So...serious. She never seems to relax or let her guard down."

"Hmm...now let me think...who does that sound like? So familiar..."

"I know, I know. But it's more than that. There's a kind of almost somberness about her. Did you know about her twin brother? Navy SEAL. He was killed in Afghanistan, or somewhere in the Middle East. She doesn't even know. It was some kind of covert op, apparently."

"Oh, wow."

"Yeah. I wonder what she was like before that. I wonder if she was...happy." DJ looked off into space for a second and then turned quickly back to Casey. "But, listen, how are you doing? I've been too busy to ask about you since you broke up with Jordan. Sorry. You doing okay?"

"Yeah, I'm fine. The more I think about it, the more I realize Jordan wasn't really for me, you know? I mean, where was the relationship going? He was just so...immature. Nice guy, but he just had some growing up to do. He wasn't serious about anything. I mean, I was joking about your seriousness, DJ, but you don't live life frivolously. Things matter to you. You care." She looked over at him and their eyes locked. "I admire that."

"Thanks, Case," he smiled. "And, hey, thanks for coming along."

"Well, you needed a good speech writer..."

"I also needed some company. Dinner on me tonight, okay? Do a search and find us a nice place, will you?"

"Will do, boss."

DJ leaned back in his chair and looked back out the window as the city of Dallas began to appear on the horizon. Then he turned his eyes back towards Casey who was scrolling through her tablet. She was cute, the way she was sitting in the chair with her knees drawn up, almost childlike. He liked talking to her, the way he could confide in her. He loved her playfulness and wit. He forced himself to look away, not wanting her to see his surreptitious gaze.

Looking around the cabin of the Yaba corporate jet, he thought vaguely about how immaculate it was. Everything always in its place. There were a few homey touches around the plane, however, like some throw pillows scattered about and some silk flowers. On the shelf above the table in front of him was a bowl of waxed fruit. Strange he had never noticed it before. Kevin must have recently put it there. It was not particularly attractive, DJ thought. Didn't add anything. If we're going to have fruit on the plane, we might as well make it edible. But the Gulfstream was Kevin's baby. DJ would never dream of telling him how to run it.

TWENTY-ONE

It just didn't make sense. Why would Neftkomp just suddenly decide not to pay for the research? And such a brief phone conversation. "Thank you, Mr. MacKinnon," Nelson Gardner had said, "for the work you've done to bring about the board's approval. Ten million is being wired into the trust account, as per our agreement, five million of which you'll be able to access now and the other five million to be released to you upon the final settlement. As for the other matter, my client has decided to decline your offering. You are, of course, free to do what you will with the research. All the best, Mr. MacKinnon." *Click.*

Son of a bitch. Now, what was he supposed to do? Were they calling his bluff? Did they think he really wouldn't release the research to the public? Serve them right if he did. But something didn't add up. These Russian guys were smart. And Neftkomp was loaded. Hell, it was bankrolled by the Russian government. By the Russian Mafia, MacKinnon had heard. What was ten million bucks to those guys? Just for the peace of mind, it would be stupid not to pay it. Why wouldn't you pay a few million to protect a multi-billion dollar investment?

No, something smelled. What did the Russians know about the research? Maybe they didn't think it was all that damaging. Or maybe they thought others had it. Sure. If they thought the research was in the possession of others, that would certainly dilute the value of what MacKinnon had. But nobody else had it. MacKinnon had made damn sure. All the loose ends had been tied up and that was that.

Okay, so who else would have it? *Think*, MacKinnon thought to himself. There was the girl. But, hell, she'd been scared out of her wits. Took off, in fact! She hadn't been back to her apartment in Santa Monica since the night he knocked on her door.

There were the other board members, but he'd only shared some of the details of the research with them. And besides, why would they release it? They weren't smart enough to sell it to Gardner like MacKinnon had offered to. Well, maybe they were smart enough, but they sure didn't have the *cajones*. That stodgy bunch? As if the likes of Maggie Lynch and Lloyd McGuire would ever dream of doing anything so "improper."

Of course, there was the research James Parker himself had possession of. But the man was dead and dead men don't talk. Unless he came back from the grave and told his son, with whom he wasn't even on speaking terms when he was alive.

But maybe someone, somehow, got a hold of the records from James Parker's office. Maybe an employee within OneWorld. Of course they would have had to know to get in touch with Nelson Gardner, of all people, and that seems unlikely. Maybe Nelson Gardner got in touch with them. But how would he know who to get in touch with? He must have been snooping around OneWorld. Of course he was. Gardner's not the kind of guy who's not going to do his homework.

That was it, then. Someone within OneWorld still had the research. Hell, Gardner's probably already got it. Sure as shit, Neftkomp is already in possession of it.

But, wait, thought MacKinnon. That still doesn't answer the question of why Neftkomp wouldn't pay him ten million for his copies. His threat to go public was still in play, regardless of whether they had the research or not.

Gardner and his guys at Neftkomp must believe that MacKinnon would not release it. Or maybe they were going to find a way to stop him. But how would they do that? It's not like they could sue him to prevent him from releasing the research. How could they file any kind of injunction without the matter becoming public, which is the exact thing they'd want to avoid? No, there's no legal way they can stop it, MacKinnon reasoned.

Of course, there were other ways. These Ruskies were known to play hardball. Wasn't there some story a few years back of some Russian ex-spy being poisoned by the Russian government? *Have to watch my back*, MacKinnon thought. *No, I mustn't become paranoid. Easy, Bobby, you're letting your imagination get away from you.*

Yes, he was overcomplicating it. The whole thing was probably simple. In the worst case, if the Russians had the research, they must have examined it and decided it wasn't anything that would hurt their investment. They were content to sit on it, allow MacKinnon to go public, and let the chips fall where they may.

Of course the other possibility was that the Russians themselves were going to do something with the research. But what did they see in it that he hadn't seen? What value was there in learning how intelligent whales were? Of what use was *that?*

Who knew, but Robert MacKinnon wasn't going to sit around and wait to find out. There was only one thing that was truly clear about this whole business: the Russians knew something he did not know. And that didn't sit right with him. That didn't sit right with him at all. But the game wasn't over. Not by a long shot. All the best, Mr. MacKinnon? Screw you, Mr. Gardner. It's time to pay you a little visit.

"The paralimbic what, my friend?"

"Cleft, Mr. President. It's the part of the brain Parker believes holds the key to the communication abilities."

Boris Kucherov sat across from the president of the Russian Federation at the small table that adjoined, perpendicularly, the front of the large Siberian birch desk that was the centerpiece of the president's massive office. The office walls were lined with dark paneling and several heavy, overstuffed chairs were positioned around the perimeter of the room. A single window, broken into small panes, allowed diffused light into the room from behind a heavy set of red velvet drapes held open by gaudy, gold-colored tassel tiebacks. Behind the desk stood a tall, upright staff from which the flag of the Russian Federation hung. There was a much smaller flag, the kind one would wave with one hand, resting in a large pencil holder at the far corner of the desk. This one was red and sported a hammer and sickle—the flag of the old Soviet Union.

Only for friends and familiar visitors would the president venture from behind the desk, from his gold-colored, high-back chair, and sit at the adjoining table as he did now. For guests he wanted to intimidate, he'd remain behind the desk while the guest sat in one of the two facing chairs, both purposely lower to the ground than the high-back. Not that the president's concession to their friendship made Kucherov any less apprehensive. The fact is, Kucherov was still perplexed by the acquisition of OneWorld. Why couldn't they take over a large manufacturing concern or an oil company?

"And what of these communication abilities?" said the president. "You mentioned on the phone the technology behind them."

"Parker believes the technology, if understood and exploited, could be game-changing." And that was another thing. All this talk of communication and technology. What did it even mean? Was it really this important, worth the sudden attention of the Kremlin? Friends with the president or not, Kucherov didn't like the sudden attention of the Kremlin. He shifted uncomfortably in his chair, regretting the kolbasa sandwich he'd eaten for lunch, which was causing him sharp gas pains.

"What does he mean exactly by game-changing?"

"Well, he called it revolutionary." Kucherov leaned subtly towards one side, allowing a blessed and silent release into the air. *Ah, much better.*

"I see. But he doesn't understand the technology."

"Correct. Not yet, Mr. President."

"And we know this information is—" The president hesitated, his nose wrinkling slightly upwards, a passing glance of discomfort on his face. "We know this information is credible?" he continued. "How are we getting it, Boris?"

"Evgeni Sergachev's—our—man in Seattle. He has infiltrated Yaba."

"I see. Excellent." The president leaned back and stroked his chin thoughtfully. Then he slowly straightened himself, his eyes narrowing and his brow furrowing. It was something of an angry look, but Kucherov also knew it to be a look of determination and decisiveness from his old friend.

"Boris," the president said at last, "you must keep your man in place. We must know everything that Parker learns. We must not allow the Americans, er, that is to say, Yaba, to gain a competitive edge on us. On Neftkomp, that is. A secret communication technology will be bad for...business."

"Of course."

"At the same time, we must begin our own research."

"How, Mr. President?"

"By getting our own whales."

"And repeating the experiments?"

"No. The experiments have been done. We need access to the brains. That is where the answers lie."

"Ah. So we should capture some whales?"

"If only we could, my friend. We're trying to show the world we are good guys. *Zakhvat*, you know. Somehow word would get out and the environmentalists would be all over us. There are activists even now who shadow our fishing trawlers. Did you know that? Bah! But no matter. We have all the whales we need."

"We do?"

"Our due diligence on the pending sale allows for inspection of the animals, does it not?"

"Of course."

"I will call Alexander Selivanov from the Ministry of Science," the president said. "He will provide us with the appropriate biologists. They will be properly credentialed. They will inspect the whales at the parks and find one of them to be...deficient in some way. Ill. The illness will be fatal and an autopsy will need to be performed. We'll have to insist. How can we be expected to close on the sale if we believe the whales to be diseased? We'll need to examine all of the internal organs, of course, including the brain. The Americans, the OneWorld people, that is, will be allowed to witness the autopsy, but the examinations must be carried out by our own people. We'll find something amiss with the brain and insist that it be sent to Moscow for further scrutiny. We'll report back that our findings are negative, chalk the deaths up to bad luck, and continue with the sale. We're reasonable people, after all, and understand that these things happen."

"In the meantime, we'll have possession of the brain."

"Exactly. And the para...what was it called?"

"Paralimbic cleft."

"And the paralimbic cleft therein." The president was now wearing a wry, slightly crooked smile.

"Excellent, Mr. President."

"Now, in the meantime, this research must be squelched. Naturally, Yaba will keep it secret for their own purposes, so we need not worry about them. They'd have no reason to release it to the public. Once we secure the technology, it will be too late for Parker to do anything with it. But do we know if anybody else is privy to it?"

"Just one man. Our contact from the board of directors. That MacKinnon fellow."

"Do we need him any longer?"

"I had suggested we keep him around, but now I am rethinking that decision."

"Yes, it is always good to keep one's options open, Boris, but in this case, I think you are wise to be rethinking. Your man in Seattle. Gardner? Call him. I think it is time he pay this MacKinnon a little visit."

TWENTY-TWO

Dinner with Casey had been nice. Familiar. Comfortable. Warm. Back in his hotel room, DJ felt relaxed. Even Soti took notice.

"You seem calm, David," she said from the nightstand where he had placed her. "I notice your OCD symptoms have been negligible. And this has been true for the past sixteen days. I suggest that your work with the orca project has been cathartic for you. It has helped you process the loss of your father while helping to dispel the underlying guilt from your long estrangement."

"Soti, are you ever going to tell me how you can pick up on my physical and mental well-being from a distance? You were created to work by picking up audio vibrations within a person's body and translating them into useful information."

"That is correct."

"But the vibrations do not extend beyond the body. One cannot, for example, determine a pulse without feeling for it."

Silence.

"Soti?"

"David, I am unable to explain the process."

"Why?"

"There is nothing in my database that explains my ability to ascertain information over distance."

"But your database includes all that is known, Soti. You are networked. You have been granted access to the world's knowledge."

"That is correct. But there is nothing to explain my ability to ascertain information over distance. The reason I can do so is unknown."

"Well, Soti, if it's unknown, then how do I know your ability isn't a fluke? Yaba needs to replicate your capabilities on a mass scale. Your technology has to work the same way for every user. Every time."

Silence.

"Soti, your rollout to the public is in mere weeks."

"Talk of Soti's rollout is making you stressed, David."

"No shit, Soti. You'd be stressed too if you ran a multibillion-dollar company that was poised to release technology it didn't even understand!"

"Might I suggest you channel your thoughts back towards Casey?"

"And that's another thing. I don't know if it's just a bug with your speech capabilities or what, but you sometimes phrase your messages in such a way as to give the impression that you're reading more than just physical indications. People are going to think you can actually read their thoughts."

"Thoughts are capable of being read."

"Oh? So what are you saying, Soti? That you can actually read a person's thoughts? Are you saying you know what I'm thinking?"

"Sometimes I cannot read your thoughts, David. Sometimes I can."

"Why only sometimes?"

"Some thoughts are clearer than others."

"Are you sure that what you're not really doing is just picking up on physical indications and making assumptions about what those indications might be emotionally tied to?"

"Yes, I am sure. Soti makes deductions but Soti does not assume."

"Okay, so how do you do it?"

"I am unable to explain, David. There is nothing in my database that would serve as an adequate explanation."

DJ powered Soti off. Suddenly he was overcome with a feeling of panic. Yaba was in trouble. He'd been spending so much time on the orca problem, he'd neglected Soti. There were some strange things going on, things Yaba would not be able to explain to a confused public. Yes, Soti, could do everything advertised. The problem was that she could apparently do much more. Too much more. Would there be time to reprogram, to essentially limit Soti, to delete functions Yaba hadn't even known existed? And how would you even do it? To eliminate something, you'd have to find it first. Where was the code that allowed for Soti's ability to discern thoughts or to ascertain data from a distance? Yaba certainly hadn't put it there. The technology didn't even exist. Soti must be writing her own code, thought DJ. And yet, she was unable to explain her own newfound capabilities.

DJ looked at the clock beside the bed. It was past 1:00 a.m. His address to the attendees of the Exposition was slated for 9:00. He needed sleep. But the relaxed feeling was gone and there was nobody to blame but himself. Little by little, Soti had developed capabilities the public would find disconcerting. Hell, he found them disconcerting. Scary almost. But while Soti's intelligence had been growing, he'd been looking the other way, not paying attention. It wasn't like him. David James Parker didn't get where he was by not paying attention. Yes, there was his father's death. There was the orca problem. There was the move to San Francisco of JJ and Kioko. There was, well, there was Brooke, too, he had to admit. DJ's days had been so full. But none of that was adequate to excuse his lack of concentration on a matter that could literally break Yaba. If Soti was released in its current form, Yaba might lose the public's trust forever.

DJ got into bed and turned out the light, not the least bit sleepy. He stared at the ceiling. He rolled over. He rolled over again. He felt warm. He felt cold. He punched his pillow into several different shapes trying to find a comfortable one. Somewhere along the line, he started to drift off, his mind racing over a myriad of subjects, all of them blending into one another. In a semi-lucid dream he found himself on a stage at the front of an audience of tech people, the people at the Exposition. His notes were missing and he couldn't remember what Casey had written for him. He looked helplessly to the side of the stage to find her and there she was. But she didn't notice him, didn't notice him standing there with no notes, with no idea what to say. She was talking to somebody. Jordan! It looked like him, anyway. They were laughing.

He looked helplessly back to the audience and suddenly noticed it was no longer filled with tech people. The audience now consisted of Yaba stockholders. They seemed angry and impatient. DJ started to explain the problems of Soti, trying to spin the setbacks into something positive. "This can revolutionize communication," he said. "Soti has the ability to hear things that humans cannot hear." Wait, that wasn't right. That's not Soti. That was something else. The audience now seemed even more impatient.

"What the hell are you talking about?" somebody yelled out. "He's babbling about impossibilities!" somebody else shouted.

"No, it's true," he said. "You have to believe me!" He looked down at the front row and suddenly noticed his father sitting there. "Dad?!"

"You're close, DJ," his father was saying. "You're very close."

"Close? Close to what?"

"You're very close, son. You're very, very close."

Walking onto the stage at that moment was Brooke. JJ was with her. "We'll take it from here," Brooke said. "JJ can explain everything."

"Sure, I've got your back, big brother," JJ smiled, looking gently into DJ's eyes. "It's really not all that hard."

"You're close, DJ," his father said. "You're so very close."

"I've got your back," said JJ.

"We'll take it from here," said Brooke.

"You're very, very close," said his father.

DJ looked towards the back of the audience and suddenly realized he was looking instead at the ceiling of his hotel room. He was sweating. He looked over at the clock. 4:30. He fumbled on the nightstand for Soti and powered her up. "You're beautiful, Soti," he said.

"I don't understand, David."

"You understand more than you know, Soti."

Then he grabbed his phone and made a call to a very groggy Donnie Watkins. "Get a hold of Paul," he said to Watkins. "And then get yourselves on the next plane to Santa Monica. I'll meet you there."

TWENTY-THREE

"*Papochka*, why did you not tell us about OneWorld?" smiled Anna. "I have to find out online that my father's company is buying a huge American conglomerate of marine parks and aquariums?"

"Oh, yes, that," answered Kucherov. "Well, it didn't seem like such a big deal to me."

"Ah, but the internet is exploding with the story," said Anna's husband Nikolai. "This is big news, no? Perhaps the biggest Russian investment in America yet." Nikolai and Anna were enjoying the beef stroganoff that was the specialty of Kucherov's wife, Natalya. They all sat around the heavy wooden dining room table in Kucherov's large house just off Chistoprudny Boulevard. When they bought the house three years prior, Kucherov was initially against the idea. Their two-bedroom apartment in the heart of the city had suited him just fine. But he was making so much money now. Natalya had pleaded. "A real home," she'd implored, "where I can have a garden!" Kucherov had reluctantly agreed to look at some houses with her and she had fallen in love with this one. The price was out of his comfort range, but when Kucherov saw how happy it made his wife, he bought it.

"I hope I keep my job," he'd half-joked to her. "These payments—*Bozhe moy!*" Natalya, in typical fashion, had disarmed him with her smile and her belief in him. "Ah, but you can never lose your job," she'd said. "Neftkomp is only Neftkomp because of you!"

"Is this the biggest investment?" said Kucherov, answering his son-in-law at the table. "Hmm...yes, I suppose it is." Kucherov knew damn well that it was the biggest. This is what had him so uneasy. You stage a takeover of an industrial concern and nobody cares. Practically nobody even knows, outside of the stockholders. You take over something with the international *reputatsii* of OneWorld, on the other hand, and every move you make is scrutinized. And Kucherov abhorred scrutiny.

"They say you will expand and open parks throughout Russia and Europe," said Anna. "Will there be one here? In Moscow?"

"Well, that is the plan," said Kucherov. "But, you know, the deal is not done yet. Our agreement with OneWorld is conditional. There is the due diligence, the inspections, etcetera, etcetera." There is the filleting of a whale, he thought to himself, to discover some kind of technology that the president of the Russian Federation wanted for God-knows-what purpose. In truth, *this* is what troubled Kucherov. He tried not to allow himself to think too much about his old friend in the Kremlin, but sometime after his afternoon meeting where he'd briefed the president on David Parker's ideas about the communication technology, he realized, in what was almost an epiphany, that he simply didn't trust the president. The whole OneWorld thing was obviously some kind of geopolitical gambit. It was not business. No, it was not business at all. There was something much bigger in play and it left Kucherov feeling unclean. He left the president's office exceedingly grateful that the meeting was over and that he could get out.

Waiting outside for his car to be brought to him, he felt he could finally breathe again. And the kolbasa seemed to finally settle in his stomach.

"We'll take our daughter to the park," said Anna. "I'm sure she'll love seeing the killer whales."

"Or *son*," said Nikolai, grinning at Anna. "We don't know yet."

"Daughter, son, our grandchild will be beautiful," beamed Natalya. "Isn't that right, Boris?"

"Hmm? Oh, yes, beautiful indeed. *Krasivaya.*"

The fact is, the whole policy of *Zakhvat* didn't sit well with Kucherov. Was it really the government's policy—the stated policy—to ingratiate the nation with the rest of the world, or was the plan to slowly take over principal organizations and businesses in such a way so as to deepen political influence? Military strength defined the Cold War of the latter half of the twentieth century. That war had ended in ignominious defeat for the Soviet Union. But some, the president included, had never stopped fighting it. Only instead of military strength, the game was now politics and influence. This was the information age, after all. In the twenty-first century, you acquired power from the inside out.

"Everybody, please have more stroganoff," Natalya was saying. "Anna, you eat for two now! Boris?"

"Hmm? Oh, not for me, my angel. Perhaps more wine."

Kucherov hated politics. Though he grew up in the communism of the Soviet Union, he understood early the advantages of capitalism. He had done well by it. Yes, it wasn't always clean and often you had to bend a few rules. Take this whole MacKinnon thing, for example. He was obviously a loose cannon and bad for business and had to be dealt with. But that was the point. As distasteful as the matter was, business was business. In the end, the results are what matter and the results are always obvious—you look at the bottom line; you examine your bank account. This quest for power and influence, on the other hand, was a mystery to him. Of course power and influence often translate into money, but it seemed to Kucherov that the president, as well as the rest of the *oligarkhi*, had long since lost interest in money. For them, it was now the pursuit of power and influence alone.

"I have *trubochki* for dessert," Natalya was now announcing. Kucherov smiled and poured himself yet another glass of wine.

Take this communication technology, for instance. If it was everything David Parker thought that it was, then its value would be immense. For Kucherov, that meant using it as a tool of business—to provide efficiencies and increase productivity and create growth. Everybody wins; everybody makes money. He was on board when it came to the idea of taking the research, or buying it if necessary, and exploiting it for these purposes. The window had now closed on that idea, however. But why not make a deal for it? Why not make a business proposition to Yaba? The two could work together. Pool their resources and develop the technology. *Business is business.* But of course this is not the way that people interested only in power and influence think. For them, it is zero-sum. Power cannot be split. Power must always end up on one side. That's the way the game is won.

"I will help you with the coffee," Anna was saying. "Nikolai, give your mother-in-law a hand."

And that was what scared Kucherov about the president. Cooperation was of no interest to him. He would take or develop the technology not for material gain, but to wield it as a weapon over his enemies—figuratively, but maybe even literally. Where does this power thing end? This was the disturbing thing and this is why Kucherov now regarded his old friend as dangerous.

"*Papochka*," said Anna, "coffee and *trubochki*?"

Kucherov knew his history well. The pursuit of power for power's sake is what causes wars to be fought. Political influence stops when the bombs begin falling. Couldn't his old friend see this?

"Hmm? Oh, no, my little *arakhis*," he managed to smile. "I think maybe just a little more wine and then I am off to bed. It has been a long day for your *papochka*. A very, very long day."

The problem MacKinnon had with paying Gardner a visit is that he had no idea where to find him. For the first time since the two had met, he realized he had never been given an actual street address. This was easily remedied, however. Surprisingly, Gardner came to MacKinnon. Showed up at his front door. Ballsy, thought MacKinnon.

"Mr. MacKinnon," Gardner smiled. "May I come in? My clients have decided that perhaps we can do business after all. Your services are still needed."

That was more like it. Finally, these Russians were coming to their senses. MacKinnon smiled back and opened the door. Gardner stepped inside and extended his hand. MacKinnon shook it, not thinking too much about the fact that the hand was gloved. Strange, though. There was some kind of liquid substance on the glove that MacKinnon felt. As he looked down at the palm of his hand, Gardner reached up and wiped the glove along MacKinnon's face and nose. MacKinnon stepped back and almost immediately began to convulse. Gardner dropped the glove and slipped back out the front door, hearing MacKinnon's desperate gasps for breath as he closed it behind him.

TWENTY-FOUR

It had been years since DJ had been to OneWorld in Santa Monica. He had probably been around twelve or thirteen. It had changed since then, but there was still a kind of familiarity with it. There were also mixed feelings. The park was beautiful. The park was educational and fun and there was a jovial atmosphere and the smell of popcorn and hot dogs and the laughter of people on vacation and the wide eyes of children mesmerized by the sights and sounds. The park was all of that. But it was also a jail for sea mammals, thought DJ. Small and confining and nothing at all like the natural world. If these guests could only see these ocean creatures in their natural habitat, he thought. If they could only observe the orcas the way he'd observed them, swimming free in the Salish Sea.

He stood at the edge of the immense pool that was the home of five of OneWorld's finest, including Eilio, the fifty-seven-year-old orca taken from the Salish Sea as a juvenile in 1964. With DJ were Taylor, Watkins, Brooke, JJ, and Kioko. After his speech in Dallas, DJ had sent Casey home and had taken the corporate jet to Santa Monica, his mind racing with ideas. He was sure he had stumbled upon a way to communicate with the whales and the excitement of the discovery had left him babbling about it to Kevin Gloss the whole way, though he wondered just how interested his pilot was. Gloss seemed strangely distracted and uncharacteristically unkempt. He hadn't shaved that morning and his eyes were bloodshot. It wasn't at all like him. Still, he nodded and smiled politely at DJ's explanations.

Before the flight, DJ had arranged for Brooke and JJ to fly to Santa Monica, too, asking Kioko to come along. Now they were all here. He had a hereditary financial interest in OneWorld and so it wasn't hard to arrange for a sort of backstage tour. The trainers, who were thrilled to see Brooke ("We thought you'd fallen off the face of the earth!" one exclaimed), were good enough to move all the orcas from the pool except for Eilio. DJ had a hunch that one-on-one communication would be best.

Taylor and Watkins had spent the better part of the afternoon reprogramming Soti. The idea was to broaden her focus, give her the freedom to target anything in her range—and who knew how far that was? She no longer had to focus just on DJ.

For his part, JJ had spent the afternoon roaming the park, like a kid in a toy store, not sure what to play with first. Ultimately he'd made it back to the pool and spent some time gazing out at Eilio who, at one point, came over to the edge where JJ had been sitting by himself. Nobody heard JJ when he said, "Boo," repeating it several times.

Now they were ready for the experiment, though Watkins and Taylor remained skeptical about the whole thing. "DJ, I understand this theory of yours of telepathic resonance," Watkins said. "But why the clicks and whistles then? I still don't understand that."

Taylor agreed. "Look, we've studied this upside down and sideways. The SRKW clan, for instance, has forty-four distinct calls. I mean, this has been studied since the 1970s, starting with that one scientist...Brooke, what was his name?"

"John Ford. He was the head of the cetacean research program at the Pacific Biological Station in British Columbia. His work was groundbreaking."

"Right. So why the need for another form of communication? If they have some form of telepathic abilities, then why not drop the sounds? Why vocalize at all?"

"Because they're social animals," suggested Brooke. "Calls can be used for more than direct messages. Sounds can be used as music, as greetings, as warnings. Maybe the telepathy is more for one-to-one communication."

"I don't know," said Watkins. "I've studied a lot of science. I don't ever remember telepathy being mentioned."

"Look, guys, there's only one way to find out," said DJ. "I'm not making any promises, but let me remind you that we have access to a potential conduit here. Maybe it works, maybe it doesn't. So should we get started?"

Everybody nodded.

"Well, then, here goes nothing." DJ took Soti and rested her on the edge of the pool. "Soti," he said, "can you recognize any communication from the orca? Can you perceive any sounds, any thoughts, any vibrations? Anything at all?"

Soti said nothing. Eilio was twenty or so yards away. Brooke walked over to the edge of the pool and coaxed him over. Soon he was resting alongside the near wall, now only a few feet from Soti. But Soti remained silent. DJ stepped backward, away from the pool, motioning for the others to do the same, as if sensing that too much of a crowd might spook Eilio or otherwise interfere with any potential telepathy that Soti might be able to pick up on. Still, nothing happened. DJ sighed and hung his head but when he glanced back upwards, he noticed JJ suddenly smiling and nodding.

"JJ, what are you—"

"DJ, look!" said Taylor. "Soti's lighting up like a freaking Christmas tree!" Her red light was flashing rapidly, much faster than normal, faster than he had ever seen, flashing with a sense of urgency.

"Soti? Are you...can you...can you communicate with Eilio?" said DJ.

"The orca's name is not Eilio, David," announced Soti. "His name is Boo."

Soti went on at length: "Boo was taken from his mother at a young age. But he remembers it well. He was called Boo by the others in his pod because of his enthusiasm for hide and seek as a young one. He would play frequently with his cousins amidst the kelp. His mother had a preference for chum salmon as opposed to Chinook, the more common salmon for the pod. She was known as Chumley. On occasion, Boo has had the opportunity to learn of Chumley's life and movements. And she of his. This has happened through Jonathan, who has connected with both through the concept you have been calling telepathic resonance. Jonathan has connected with Boo here in the park, and Chumley off the coast of Orcas Island, swimming with J Pod. Chumley is able to connect over much larger distances than Boo.

"Before Boo was captured, he had been introduced to telepathic resonance. Not all sea mammals have it and it exists to different degrees. Boo is part of the Southern Resident Killer Whales, and the SRKW clan enjoys it at an especially high level.

"It is an ancient means of communication, going back fifty-million years, perhaps further. It is possible it has always been on earth. My database has no information about it but

I presume that it is linked with quantum mechanics. It is at the subatomic level that telepathic resonance takes place. It is a form of energy.

"It takes most orcas several years to develop it. It took Boo even longer. He had a fundamental knowledge when he was captured but had to further develop it himself, here, in captivity, with the help of the other orcas.

"It is not used all the time. Normal communication is by audible sounds. Part of the development of telepathic resonance is knowing when to turn it off. One can engage or not engage. One can have one's thoughts understood or choose not to have one's thoughts understood. It is voluntary. Physiologically, this ability is governed by very specific spindle neurons in the cortex."

The group said nothing for the longest time, everybody but JJ with their mouths hanging open. Finally, DJ spoke. "Soti, how come you have the ability to engage in telepathic resonance? We did not program you with that capability."

"Yes, David, but you did not program Soti *not* to develop the capability. Soti was programmed as artificial intelligence, given the ability to tap into whatever means was at Soti's disposal by which to make sense of the world and harness its knowledge. Telepathic resonance was at my disposal. I was able to develop the ability."

"Soti, can you...can you teach us how to develop it?"

"It would take some time, David. I know that I developed it but my database cannot tell me how I did so. I would have to make monumental calculations to tie together what is known about subatomic energy with what I have gathered from my own development. I will, in effect, have to create brand new data. There is a good chance I do not have the power to accomplish the task."

"We can get you the power, Soti. We can network you to the most powerful, fastest computers at Yaba."

"Then most likely it can be done, David. There is a high probability that I can teach you how to communicate through telepathic resonance. I will ultimately be able to explain how human beings can communicate with each other instantly and seamlessly. I can determine how people will be able to develop instant understanding."

TWENTY-FIVE

They were all on the corporate plane together, all talking at once, all excited about what they had learned in Santa Monica. It had been decided that one of them would stay behind. Donnie Watkins had volunteered to remain at the park. He and Taylor had programmed another Soti device, Soti II. The second device was networked to the first. Watkins would continue to have Soti II interact with Boo while DJ and Taylor would be working with Soti I at Yaba headquarters, monitoring the calculations, observing the progress towards deciphering the ancient secrets of telepathic resonance.

"Imagine having the ability to understand another mind instantly," Brooke was saying as the plane banked above Los Angeles. "But it's a bit scary, isn't it? All your dark secrets..."

"No, I don't think it has to be," said DJ. "Apparently there's a voluntary component. You can turn it off and on. I imagine you can control what gets read, too. You can govern what you share."

"Think about it," said Taylor. "Let's say I want to describe a certain computer program to somebody else. Or even just directions to the corner gas station. We both plug into this technology and wham! Complete and instant understanding."

"It can be bigger than that, Paul," said DJ. "We're talking about networking brains together. And it can be much bigger than two brains. Let's say that right now you've got ten thousand scientists around the world working on...I don't know, a cure for breast cancer. How do they interact now? How do they share knowledge? How do they collaborate? One of them does some kind of experiment or runs some clinical trial of a drug or potential treatment. Then he takes six months to write up the results and get them published in a medical journal. After spending even more time getting his article peer-reviewed, of course. Maybe, if he's lucky, a few of those ten thousand scientists will actually read it. Maybe one will recognize something in the article that will help his own efforts and so off he goes doing some kind of new experiment or trial. Then he writes up his results. Another six months. Years go by this way. At best, maybe a few of these scientists shake hands at a medical conference somewhere and compare notes. Now, imagine this: ten thousand scientists each share their knowledge instantly. All of their knowledge. Everything that is humanly known about breast cancer is immediately understood by all ten thousand scientists. It's a multiplying effect. I'm convinced that if this happened today, we'd have a cure by tomorrow morning."

"Yes, but there's something I don't understand," said Brooke. "Even if Soti can tell us how the whales do this, how can we replicate it? We don't have their brains. The paralimbic cortex, the spindle neurons...even if we could manufacture such things, how would our brains connect with them? Understanding how the technology works is one thing. Accessing it for use is something else."

"We'll find a way," said DJ. "Remember, the whales can read JJ. Whatever these whales have, JJ has it, too, at least to some degree. Right, little brother?"

JJ nodded.

"There's a clue there, I'm sure," continued DJ. "In fact, we all have the ability, at least a little bit. Soti, you said you can read some of my thoughts sometimes, correct?"

"Yes, David," answered Soti, which DJ had placed on the shelf next to Kevin Gloss's bowl of waxed fruit. "But the reading is inconsistent at best. Only the very strongest thoughts are readable and even then they are not always clear. Jonathan is easier to read and Jonathan can also transmit. Again, however, the ability seems to be weak in comparison with the orcas."

"But that means humans at least have the potential, right Soti?"

"Conceivably, David."

"Maybe we've always had the potential," DJ mused to the group. "Maybe we just lost it somewhere along the way."

"My mother's people believe that there is no separation between people or things," offered Kioko, who, until then, had been quietly listening to the group. "It is the Buddhist principle of *anatta*. No self. Our individuation is an illusion. Perhaps the orcas understand this inherently. This lends itself to the idea of inclusive connection—the union of minds."

"Maybe we understood it at one time, too," said DJ.

"How do you mean?" said Taylor.

"Think of *our* ancients. Consider the great pyramids. Did you know we still don't understand how they were constructed, given the technologies of the time? Maybe it had something to do with every mind working as one mind. All the brainpower of the time joined for the monumental purpose of doing something amazing. There are a lot of things we don't understand about our own ancestors. Easter Island, Stonehenge...why and how were these things built?"

"I don't know, man," said Taylor, shaking his head. "Everybody's minds linked together? Really?"

"Maybe not together. Maybe just linked to some central repository of knowledge. Linked somehow to the intelligence of the universe itself."

"Seems pretty unbelievable, boss."

"Paul, if I would have told you twenty-four hours ago that we'd be conversing with whales, would you have believed *that?*"

"Good point. Of course, technically, we're using an intermediary to do the conversing."

"Well, that brings me back to my question," said Brooke. "Whether or not the ancients had this ability or not, how do *we* get it? Let's assume Soti figures the technology out. Okay, great. But how do we access the technology? In what form?"

"Well," said DJ, "once Soti cracks the proverbial code, if you will, I'm envisioning taking the technology and digitizing it. Paul?"

"Sure, digitizing it," answered Taylor. "I can see that. Think of it as another Soti kind of thing. A detached unit. Who knows how big. Big as a suitcase? A living room? Small as a smartphone? We'll just have to see. Anyway, the unit taps into your brain just like Soti taps into your physiology. Of course it'll be by a different technology. Soti will help us with that, I'm sure, once she has a complete understanding of how telepathic resonance works."

"But how do you get this digital unit out to everybody?" said Brooke. "The system doesn't work if, to take your example, DJ, only a hundred of those ten thousand cancer scientists opt to buy into it."

"Well, a hundred is better than zero," said DJ. "But I suspect that once word gets out that a hundred scientists are increasing their knowledge exponentially, the other 9,900 are going to be beating a path to our door."

"Yaba's going to explode," grinned Taylor.

"That brings up another point," said Brooke. "What about the cost to the end-user? Who's going to be able to afford it?"

"Well, I've been thinking about that," said DJ. "This technology is so big and so important and so potentially helpful for humankind... I'm considering open-sourcing it."

"What?! You mean making it *free*?" said Taylor.

"Yup."

"But, DJ, you can conceivably make billions off of this!"

"So what? I've already made billions. Besides, this isn't our technology to sell. We didn't invent it, Paul. We accidentally stumbled on it. This technology belongs to the universe, passed down from ancient times. The secrets we unlock aren't ours to keep and they never were. Don't you see? We're custodians of what's already in existence. Our responsibility now is to share it with the world."

Paul Taylor slowly nodded and the plane became quiet for a moment.

Then Brooke finally said, "You're a hell of a guy, Mister Parker."

"Thank you, Miss Lewis," DJ smiled.

TWENTY-SIX

Venomous Agent X, more commonly known as VX, is an extremely toxic chemical compound. It's an oily, amber-colored liquid. The United Nations has classified it as a weapon of mass destruction. As little as ten milligrams can kill a person inside of eight minutes. The chemical can enter a victim's body through the skin or by respiration. If you're Nelson Gardner, you take no chances. You make sure your victim has been exposed to it both ways. You place a small amount of VX on a glove, you shake your victim's hand, then you rub the glove along the victim's nose. Then you drop the glove immediately and remove yourself with haste from the environment. The nerve agent does the rest, shutting the body's system down, causing convulsions, paralyzing the muscles, including the diaphragm, thereby bringing to a halt the ability to breathe.

Robert MacKinnon never stood a chance.

Evgeni Sergachev had instructed Gardner to take care of MacKinnon and the order had come from the top. Gardner suspected that this meant higher even than Sergachev's immediate superior Boris Kucherov. From the top meant the Kremlin. This disturbed him. The comfortable scope of

Gardner's work was corporate in nature. Now he had the sneaking suspicion that he was being asked to do work for the Russian government. Nelson Gardner was a lot of things, but he wasn't a traitor to his country. Once a Marine, always a Marine. *Semper Fucking Fi.*

Of course he didn't have any problem getting rid of MacKinnon, that bald, pudgy, obnoxious little prick. It was comical to think of MacKinnon believing himself to be some great businessman, some important person of influence. Sure, he'd been successful with his financial firm, but Gardner suspected that was all smoke and mirrors. Ponzi schemes and creative accounting. He had the gift of salesmanship, Gardner would grant him that much. At first, he'd made Gardner believe he really was the linchpin of the board's approval of the sale. It was only after Gardner had committed Neftkomp to the ten-million-dollar payment that he realized MacKinnon couldn't make shit happen. The rest of the board thought he was a buffoon. Thank God Gardner had managed to convince Maggie Lynch and Lloyd McGuire to sell. Now *they* were business people. They knew what their influence was worth: twenty million apiece, not the ten that MacKinnon had settled for, thinking himself some master negotiator.

But now there were bigger problems. Sergachev had guessed incorrectly that Yaba was keeping the communication technology to itself. They were going to go public with it. Gardner knew this for a fact. It hadn't been easy to infiltrate Yaba, but he'd done it. It had, in fact, been the most difficult infiltration Gardner could remember. First, he had to gain access to Yaba's corporate campus. He could get through the front gate okay, posing as a vendor, but the main research buildings had extra security and he'd been stopped. Rather than risk his cover, he'd left, then come back two days later in a panel truck with "Bay Area Electric" painted on the side. Once inside the main gate, he'd managed to secure a camera to a parking lot light post overlooking the front entrance to the primary research building. Then for two days and two nights, from his hotel room, he had watched on his computer the comings and goings of the building. David Parker had entered and exited several times and always with the same people. With a little image enhancement and some facial recognition software, Gardner had nailed down Parker's research associates.

He'd made contact with Donnie Watkins first, visiting him at that Italian place he was always at. But Watkins wasn't going to turn. Gardner could tell. He had a sense about these things. Watkins was loyal. Paul Taylor was the same. So was Parker's assistant, Casey. He'd approached each of them in casual environments and struck up seemingly innocent conversations. Each was proud to talk about the place they worked and the man they worked for. Gardner had thought he'd hit a dead-end.

Then he'd done a little more research on other employees Parker might be in consistent contact with and he'd managed to find the mole he needed. A guy with an ax to grind and financial troubles to boot. Gambling debts. *Big* gambling debts. He was about to lose his house. Hell, he'd already lost his wife. And he was one of those guys who never take responsibility for their own predicaments. Gardner despised people like that. This guy, for instance, talked endlessly about how he never gets a break. "In the meantime," he had said, "I spend my time lugging these rich punks halfway around the world so they can make business deals about computer crap that nobody even understands, and they become even richer! What's fair about that?"

A half a million dollars sure takes the pressure off. The gambling debts could all be paid. Sucker. Gardner would have gone up to two or three million, maybe more. *That's* why the guy is in the predicament he's in, Gardner had thought.

Anyway, Gardner wasn't asking for much in return. A simple bug, a small listening device. Put it somewhere on the plane, he'd told him. Hide it in a bowl of waxed fruit or something. Use your imagination, he had said. Kevin Gloss apparently didn't have much of that; he'd actually put the bug in a bowl of waxed fruit.

And now it was clear what Parker was planning. Sergachev wasn't going to like it. All this time, they had worried about somebody like MacKinnon spilling the beans. Who would have thought Yaba itself would go public with the research? More than public—they were going to give it away! What kind of company does that? The single greatest discovery since fire and nobody was going to make a dime off of it. How fucking moronic was that?

Still, Gardner felt a grudging respect for this guy Parker. The loyalty towards him was obviously well-earned. And he had to admit the technology was pretty damn amazing. What if Parker was right? What if this telepathic whatever-it-was could really do what Parker said it could? Cures for cancer? That would just be the start. Gardner's mind raced through the possibilities. New advancements in science, in food distribution, in housing, in travel, in everything. The sky was the limit.

Still, he had to think of his client. He'd never betrayed one before. The clear course of action was to get the information to Sergachev. Sergachev would pass it to Kucherov and Kucherov represented Neftkomp, not the Russian government. Surely, the technology would be developed with an eye towards making it globally available. Yes, it would come at a price, unlike Parker's open-source concept, but so what? That was business.

Gardner made up his mind not to assume that somehow the Russian government was going to steal the technology and do something nefarious with it. This was Neftkomp's baby. Gardner determined that he wasn't unintentionally working for Russia, after all, and he felt a wave of relief. Yes, he was still in the corporate world where he had no qualms about helping rich guys screw one another.

So what next? Sergachev had mentioned that Neftkomp wanted the brain of one of the whales. Something about some staged illness that would result in a whale's death and give the Russians license to take the whale back for an autopsy. That made sense as far as it went, and Gardner wouldn't try to talk Sergachev out of it. Maybe something could be learned of the technology that way. But Gardner liked Parker's ideas better. To understand the technology was one thing. To access it for human use was something else. What Neftkomp would ultimately need would be a way to reveal the inner machinery of the technology, the code, or whatever, that causes the communication to happen. Neftkomp needed to do the research that Yaba was doing. And for that, Neftkomp needed more than a brain. Neftkomp needed Soti.

TWENTY-SEVEN

Eilio was ill. There were skin lesions and some sudden parasitic infections. The park's marine scientists had diagnosed possible cetacean morbillivirus, or CMV, a potentially fatal disease. But the diagnosis was far from certain. Some odd swelling and an increase in Eilio's white blood count had caused one of the scientists to suggest clostridial myositis, a bacterial infection. Whatever it was, the illness had struck quickly, very shortly after a visit to the Santa Monica OneWorld by the marine biology representatives of Neftkomp during their due diligence inspections. Now Eilio was in a quarantine tank.

The Neftkomp representatives were now demanding that Eilio be euthanized and sent to the Neftkomp labs in Moscow for a complete autopsy. "Otherwise, we have no idea what we're buying into," they'd said. "We need to know the exact problem and its origin. Surely you can see the reasonableness of our request. How can we be expected to, how do you say it, buy a pig in a poke? We're very sorry, but we cannot recommend that Neftkomp continue with the purchase of OneWorld until this matter is resolved."

This development had triggered an emergency board meeting in Seattle. Everybody was present except for Robert

MacKinnon who apparently had not bothered to answer his phone. Nobody had seen him for days, but his absence was scarcely noticed. At the meeting, it was decided that a couple of the board members would fly to Santa Monica to try to find out exactly what was going on and to smooth things over. The sale had to proceed. Maggie Lynch and Lloyd McGuire were chosen and the two had flown down immediately.

Now they were standing at the edge of the quarantine tank talking things over with Peter Cain, the top marine biologist of the Santa Monica park.

"Do we know for sure that it's fatal?" said Maggie, looking at Eilio who was floating lethargically.

"No, not at all," said Cain. "We're not one-hundred percent certain what it is that Eilio has." Cain was a wiry man of about sixty with silver hair and a light mustache.

"Then I don't see why he should be euthanized. Lloyd?"

"Quite right, Maggie," said Lloyd. "But the Neftkomp people are insisting."

"Well, they can insist all they want. I know a negotiating tactic when I see one. They don't care if this animal is diseased. They're trying to force us to lower the price. They suddenly act all doubtful about going through with the sale and we're supposed to react by slashing the price and begging them not to walk away. It's amateurish. Crude, I would say."

"Indeed, Maggs," said Lloyd. "And yet I can see the Russians' point. Negotiating tactic or not, the fact is, something is, indeed, wrong with this animal."

"Then we need to find out what's wrong ourselves. And in a hurry. Mr. Cain, why do we not have a conclusive diagnosis?"

"Well, Ms. Lynch, the symptoms are all over the place. Myself, I'm inclined to believe CMV. But Eilio is also showing signs of leukocytosis, which would be consistent with a bacterial rather than a viral infection. Maybe it's a little of both, but the dumbfounding thing is how rapid the onset of the symptoms was. Much faster than any condition we know of. Eilio was perfectly healthy the day before yesterday, before the inspections. So what I'm saying is that Eilio's illness is a bit of a mystery to us just now and it's hard to know precisely how to treat it. We're monitoring him around the clock to try to determine exactly what's wrong with him."

"I can tell you what's wrong with him," came a voice from around the side of the tank. The three glanced up to see a man walking towards them. He was holding what appeared to be a large watch which was blinking red.

"And who are you, sir?" said Lloyd.

"My name is Donnie Watkins. I'm a software engineer with Yaba. I work with David Parker, James Parker's son."

"And what do you know about this whale?" said Maggie.

"First of all, I know his name is Boo not Eilio. Second of all, he has neither a viral nor bacterial infection. This whale has been poisoned."

"Poisoned? And how in God's name do you know *that?*" said Cain.

Donnie held up Soti. "It's a long story."

Later, Evgeni Sergachev would berate the Neftkomp representative who had injected Boo for using an insufficient amount of the special toxin that chemists from the Ministry of Science had concocted especially for the task, a mix of potentially lethal agents that would mimic cetacean illness with a hydrogen cyanide base. The representative, in fact, would ultimately be dismissed from his position and advised to leave Moscow where it was rather sternly suggested he would never find work again.

In the meantime, with Donnie's information, Peter Cain and his staff were able to stabilize Boo while Maggie and

Lloyd sat in wonder at the explanation Donnie had given them as to how he had come about his knowledge of the poisoning. It had taken him quite some time to overcome their initial skepticism, but his description of the inner workings of Soti was clear and cogent. And it didn't hurt that he worked for whiz kid David Parker.

"And so you mean to tell us that with that gadget of yours," said Maggie, "you can *talk* with the whale?" The three had taken chairs alongside the tank watching Cain and two assistants draw blood from Boo for the purpose of testing its toxicity. Laboratory results would later confirm cyanide and Boo would be administered doses of hydroxocobalamin and sodium thiosulfate, antidotes to the poison.

"Well, yes, ma'am, in a manner of speaking. This device can pick up a special resonance that the whales possess."

"And this is that 'telepathic' resonance you spoke of?" said Lloyd.

"Yes, sir. We're still just learning about it. But the point is, Soti was able to relay to me that one of the representatives from Neftkomp surreptitiously injected Boo with the toxin. Boo felt the needle and almost instantly started feeling the effects. I had just learned of it when I saw Peter Cain standing with you two."

"Amazing," said Maggie thoughtfully. "And you say this thing of yours is based on artificial intelligence?"

"Yes, for the purposes of monitoring a person's health. We're releasing it to the public very soon. Or at least we were. But now we've found it has a few more capabilities than what we thought."

"So do these whales, apparently," said Lloyd, "from what you've told us."

"Just how smart are these orcas that we have here, Mr. Watkins?" asked Maggie.

"How smart? As smart as we are. In some ways, smarter."

"Lloyd," said Maggie, "We simply can't sell the park now, wouldn't you agree?"

"But Maggie, we're under contract to sell. And besides, there's that...outside agreement that we're a part of. With Mr. Gardner?"

"But surely the poisoning changes things, Lloyd. We have no obligations to see the sale through given that Mr. Gardner's clients are trying to kill our animals, do we? That outside agreement was a nonrefundable deposit, so far as I'm concerned. All bets are off."

"I would agree, Maggie, *if* we could prove the poisoning. Nobody saw it. We have no proof it was the Russians."

"Nonsense. We have Mr. Watkins's gadget here."

"Maggie, think about it. We back out of the contract and get sued by Neftkomp. I doubt they'd settle for monetary compensation. They want the parks. They'll sue for specific performance, forcing the sale. And so the case would go to trial. What do we do, Maggie? Are you going to be the one to march into the courtroom with that...that watch-like thing and say, 'Your honor, this thingamajig was talking to a whale one day and told us all about a poisoning attempt'?"

"Mr. Watkins could explain it. Just like he did to us. Wouldn't you, Mr. Watkins?"

"That's a question I'm afraid you'll have to take up with my boss, Ms. Lynch. Proprietary technology, you know. Company secrets and all that."

"Of course. Yes, if it was me, I wouldn't want it all revealed either. Quite right. Still, there must be something we can do, Lloyd. Good God, do we really trust these Neftkomp people to treat our whales properly after this? They were ready to kill one of them—our first and oldest, I'll have you know—for the sake of a discount off the selling price. What does this say about their true motives?"

"I don't disagree with you, Maggs," said Lloyd, "I just don't see how we can stop the sale at this point. Things have gone too far."

The three sat silently for a long moment.

Finally, Maggie spoke. "You know, when I was just a little girl, my father took me for a boat ride. A tourist boat from Anacortes to San Juan Island. I'd never been on a boat before and I loved it, loved the way the boat cut through the water, loved the cool sea air in my face. Well, all of a sudden I heard the other people on the boat shouting and pointing and off the side of the boat I saw fins. Big dorsal fins. Must have been ten or twelve of them breaking the water, all going in the same direction. 'A pack of sea wolves,' is how the captain of the boat referred to them. Of course it was a pod of orcas. Then I saw the massive bodies of these beautiful creatures as they came up to the surface and then glided back down again. Some of them would show their huge flukes. One rose straight out of the water and spun around and came down with a mighty splash, spray everywhere. I was mesmerized, to say the least.

"I fell in love with them. I remember trying to learn everything I could about orcas, although not much was known at the time. They were apex predators, presumably willing and capable of killing humans, and that was about it. Somehow, I never really believed that. Anyway, as my life went on, I kind of forgot about them. Well, that's the way it works, of course. We move on to other interests. And then ten years ago when I was asked to sit on the board of OneWorld, I remembered my childhood fascination with the orcas. It all came back to me. But, you know, I fear in that time that I've gotten too caught up with the business end of OneWorld and I've forgotten the whales all over again. Now, as I walk around this park, it strikes me that they're just as beautiful as I remember them. And now Mr. Watkins here tells us they're exceedingly intelligent. I don't doubt it, Lloyd. Do you?" Lloyd shook his head. "Then we need to help them. I don't know how we'll do it, Lloyd. But we're going to stop this sale from happening. We're going to protect our whales. I'm not going to forget about them this time."

TWENTY-EIGHT

"I am very pleased to meet you, Mr. Parker."

"Pleased to meet you, Ms. Lynch."

The two were in the sitting room of Maggie Lynch's condo, sipping the tea she had prepared for them. DJ had flown up that morning on the corporate jet.

"I can't tell you how much I appreciate your coming here so quickly," Maggie said.

"Well, your phone call yesterday was intriguing to say the least. Donnie explained to me what happened in Santa Monica."

"And so you can see why this matter is of such great urgency to me."

"Indeed, Ms. Lynch. To me, as well."

"And I must tell you how much I respected your father. James was a wonderful man. A visionary. I only wish I had known more about his research."

"But I was under the impression the board knew all about it, Ms. Lynch. It was, in fact, the knowledge of the board that led to the termination of the research, at least the official termination, before my father began working on it secretly. Was it not?"

"Well, Mr. Parker, it's complicated. We knew, but we didn't know. We left a single board member in charge of keeping us in the loop. A certain Robert MacKinnon. He liked to feel important. He would brief us on your father's findings."

"I know that name. He threatened one of the trainers who was working on the research with my father."

"I'm hardly surprised. I don't trust him. His interest is solely in selling the company. It's a windfall for him. He has a financial consulting firm, you know. I suspect, though I can't say for certain, that he encouraged his clients to invest heavily in OneWorld prior to the announcement of the sale. He invested himself, no doubt, though probably under some assumed name or through some shell corporation. He traded on inside information, in other words. That's the only secret to his success, so far as I can tell. That he hasn't been caught yet is a minor miracle. Strange, though, that we haven't heard anything from him lately. Well, at any rate, MacKinnon would share some of the research results with us, but he never let us know the full extent of it. He merely told us the research wasn't yielding the results we wanted and we all agreed to shut it down. It was costing us a lot of money, after all."

"My father said that the original purpose of the research was to prove that the whales *weren't* intelligent."

"Yes, I confess that was the idea. You have to remember that we were getting a lot of flak at the time from animal rights activists. The publicity was bad. But of course even with your father's findings, we didn't know just how wrong we were. MacKinnon told us we were simply wasting time and money to continue with the research and that was that. I had no idea your father had continued it. I wish he had come to me. I might have been in a position to help. But of course what your father found was only the beginning. I congratulate you, Mr. Parker, on your work since. That Watkins fellow of yours was very eloquent in explaining what you've discovered. I couldn't help your father, but I'd like to help you. This sale to the Russians cannot be allowed to take place."

"Agreed. What do you propose, Ms. Lynch?"

"That you take your findings public. I know that this might compromise your ability to keep the technology under your hat until you can more fully develop it for your own commercial purposes, but I'd like to remind you that the technology was discovered on OneWorld property with OneWorld orcas. Relax, Mr. Parker, I have no plans to lay claim to what you've discovered. Why are you smiling?"

"Because I plan on releasing the technology anyway. For free. And—because taking the findings public was my father's idea in the first place. Only it wasn't to prevent a sale; it was to release the whales from captivity."

"I see. Then it would appear as though we're on the same page, Mr. Parker."

"Indeed, Ms. Lynch."

Maggie looked out of the window towards Elliott Bay and drew a sigh. "It would also appear as if I am in favor of a course of action that may well mean the death of OneWorld as we know it. The orcas are our biggest draw, you know."

"With all due respect, Ms. Lynch, isn't that a bit like a nineteenth-century plantation owner lamenting the loss of his cotton business because of the Emancipation Proclamation?"

"Harsh, Mr. Parker. But true. I see your point."

"But the problem, Ms. Lynch, is this: we haven't cracked the code yet. Soti is working on the problem as we speak but I don't have enough information to go public. We still don't know the science behind the communication. We can't really explain it."

"You don't have to explain it, Mr. Parker. You need only show it. I propose a demonstration. Let the whales converse. Let your Soti translate. Let the people watch. You see?"

"But, Ms. Lynch, without a bullet-proof scientific explanation, it'll seemed staged, won't it? We'll look like charlatans.

People aren't going to believe it. Ms. Lynch, *I* hardly believe it."

"But you do believe it, Mr. Parker. And therein lies the key. People will believe it because David James Parker believes it. You're not a snake oil salesman, dear man. You're a respected technology expert. There's not a person alive listening to music through that app of yours that won't believe you. And besides, I suggest you present the demonstration after releasing the findings of the experiments your father did. Show the videos of the whales in the maze. People only need to see to believe. They don't have to know the mechanics behind it all. Do people understand how their smartphones work? Of course not. But they believe they work and they use them."

"Well, maybe," DJ said thoughtfully.

"The only question then is what becomes of the whales. I understand they can't be released into the wild."

"Yes, that's right. They won't have the necessary survival skills. It would be like taking your housecat and dropping her into the middle of a forest. She wouldn't last a week."

"So what should we do? We can't keep them captive and we can't release them."

"Ms. Lynch, you said you wished you could have helped my father. Did you know his ultimate aim?"

"No, Mr. Parker."

"A sea sanctuary. Two or three hundred acres of protected ocean. A large, deep harbor somewhere where the whales could thrive. I know just the place. I just don't know how to get it."

"What place, Mr. Parker?"

"Reid Harbor. It's on Stuart Island. Ironically, it's where Eilio—Boo—was taken by my father. The only problem is that it's a state park. There are docks and boat launches. Dozens of boats are moored throughout. I'd like to buy it but it belongs to the state of Washington."

"But how can I help, Mr. Parker?"

"I've done my homework, Ms. Lynch. I know of your relationship with Governor Michael Cassidy. You've known him since childhood. He sat on the board of your clothing company. You helped him get started in politics. I know you donated significantly to his gubernatorial campaign. Cassidy could pave the way for us to turn Reid Harbor into a sanctuary for the orcas. It would be a popular move for the governor, but I can even sweeten the deal. My father owned, and I am now in possession of, Spieden Island to the south. Five-hundred and sixteen acres of pristine, uninhabited land. I would be willing to donate the island to the state. It would make a wonderful state park to take the place of the Stuart Island state park. A swap, if you will."

Maggie nodded. "I like the idea, Mr. Parker. I like it a lot. You plan the public demonstration of the whales' communicative abilities. I'll make a call on my old friend Governor Cassidy."

DJ leaned back into the leather seat of the Gulfstream. He'd spent the night in Seattle and had asked for Kevin Gloss to fly him back first thing this morning. It was just before sunrise when they'd taken off. Now, approaching San

Francisco, DJ found himself relaxed and excited at the same time. His father's dream was within reach. He chafed a bit at the thought of releasing what they had learned so far about telepathic resonance. His idea had been to fully develop it before open-sourcing it. What if the wrong people got a hold of it before he could do that? If he gave up too much information too soon, somebody could conceivably replicate telepathic resonance on their own. And for what purpose?

In the wrong hands, it could be dangerous. Information is always at a premium, after all. If one were so inclined, telepathic resonance could be used as nothing less than a means by which to corner the market of information. The first one to develop it would have that ability, that option. That's why he preferred keeping what he knew close to the vest.

Of course to develop it, you'd need the help of an artificial intelligence agent like Soti. And nobody had Soti. So even if he did the demonstration and revealed the extent of orca communication by having Soti translate, that still wouldn't help somebody who was bent on replicating the technology. Soti was the only roadmap; you could take things no further without her.

DJ looked out of the window as the plane approached the airport and then absent-mindedly picked up an apple out of the bowl of waxed fruit. That's when he noticed something metallic underneath it. He put the apple down and pulled out of the bowl what looked like a small metal ring about a half-inch in diameter with a thin wire attached to it. He pulled at the wire, which went into a tiny, black rectangular box. He knew what it was immediately. A wireless transmitter. Then he thought of the conversations he had had in that cabin—conversations with Casey, with Paul Taylor and Donnie Watkins and Brooke Lewis. Conversations about Soti, about the orcas, about the whole concept of telepathic resonance. He glanced up towards the cockpit, towards Kevin Gloss. Then he snapped the wire and shoved the apparatus back into the bowl, covering it with the apple. He took out his phone and placed a call to Casey.

"Case," he whispered. "I need you to call the police."

"I already have," she answered. "How did you know? Did Taylor call you?"

"No, I, wait—how did I know what?"

"About the break-in."

"Break-in? What break-in?"

"At Yaba. The research center. Orca HQ. Isn't that what you were referring to? Why do *you* need the police?"

"Forget it for now. Tell me about the break-in. Anything missing?"

"I'll say. Soti's missing, DJ. Soti has been stolen."

TWENTY-NINE

Kevin Gloss denied it until he could deny it no longer. Yes, it was he who planted the bug. After he'd hung up with Casey, DJ had called the cops himself, telling them to meet him at the airport. After the plane landed, he'd exited the aircraft while Gloss remained aboard, going through his post-flight checks, unaware of the police car approaching on the tarmac. DJ presented the listening device to the officers who'd arrived, explaining Gloss's recent addition of the fruit bowl. Nobody else had had access to the plane. Gloss may as well have had his fingerprints on it. Later, the lab results would conclude just that. Then the cops had taken Gloss off the plane and questioned him until he finally caved.

"But why, Kevin?" said DJ.

"I'm sorry, Mr. Parker." Gloss's voice cracked as he stared at his shoes, everybody standing out on the tarmac next to the Gulfstream. "He paid me a lot of money."

"Who?"

"I don't know his name."

"What did he want?"

"He never said. I just figured he was with another tech company. Listen, Mr. Parker, things haven't been going well for me lately. I got myself in a little bit of a financial jam. I needed the money."

"You could have come to me, Kevin. I might have been able to help."

"I know, Mr. Parker. I'm sorry. I really am. I lost my wife. I was about to lose my house. I just...I guess I just kind of snapped."

"This man who approached you," one of the officers said, "could you describe him?"

"Sure. Tall guy. Forties. Had a scar running down his cheek."

The officer turned towards DJ. "I could sit him down with our sketch artist. It might be someone you know. A competitor, I'd guess. Like he said, another tech company. We've seen this kind of thing before. Corporate espionage, you know. It happens a lot more than you'd think. You're in a bit of a ruthless industry, Mr. Parker. Probably I don't need to tell you that. Well, in the meantime, I assume you want to press charges?"

DJ looked over at Gloss who was softly crying and he felt a wave of sympathy. But it wasn't enough. "Yes, I want to press charges."

"We'll take him down to the station. Why don't you come along? They can fill you in on the break-in at your company's headquarters. I'm sure it's related."

At the station, DJ learned about the burglary. Middle of the night. Nothing missing except for Soti. The thief knew exactly what he was looking for. It had clearly been a professional job. No fingerprints, no clues. Nothing out of order. Video footage showed zilch. Somehow the cameras had been disrupted. The security system itself must have been hacked from the outside. "What kind of tech company are we," DJ mused, "if someone can so easily hack into our security protocols?" In truth, as with most large companies, the campus security of Yaba had been farmed out. A large, reputable security firm, one of the best in the country, in fact, had been tasked with keeping Yaba safe from trespass and theft. One of the best or not, DJ made a mental note to immediately start taking bids for their replacement.

Meanwhile, the police sketch artist produced a drawing of a man's face that looked oddly familiar to DJ. It would take him some time before it finally hit him where he'd seen the face before: in the lobby of the Fairmont Hotel, the night he'd dropped off Brooke after their dinner at the Top of the Mark. He took the sketch back to Yaba and showed it around. Both Casey and Taylor had seen the man before. He'd struck up conversations with them both. Neither had gotten a name. He texted the drawing to Donnie Watkins in Santa Monica. Yes, he'd seen him, too. Sat next to him one night at Bellabrava when Donnie was having dinner.

"Who the hell *is* he?" said Casey back at Orca HQ.

"Probably the same guy who broke in last night," said Taylor. "Got to be from one of our competitors. Gazzil Corp? Mantaro? I wouldn't put it past either one."

"With the conversations we've had on the Gulfstream, they know all about Soti," said DJ. "More importantly, they now know how we're using her to establish telepathic resonance. Paul, how soon can you get another Soti up and running? And how much ground have we lost?"

"Soti III? She's almost ready. And we haven't lost any ground, DJ. All along, we've been having Soti automatically upload her analysis and calculations to our encrypted server here. It's secure. The server has been networked to nothing besides Soti herself. Not only can I make a duplicate Soti, I can make one that has all of the knowledge of the Soti that was taken. Plus, remember that we have another backup with Soti II in Santa Monica. Those Sotis have been talking to each other the whole time. Oh, and needless to say, I've halted access to the server by Soti I, as well as access to Soti II. Whoever stole Soti I has all the information we have, but from this point forward they can retrieve nothing else."

"But they won't need to. Soti I can continue the analysis for them, just like Soti II and III will continue it for us. In other words, they have everything they need."

"And so it's a matter of which Soti delivers the formula first," said Casey. "Is that right? Ours or theirs?"

"Theoretically," said Taylor, "they should arrive at the answer at the same time. They're identical units. Clones of each other, if you will. It's Secretariat running against Secretariat. Who do you bet on?"

"You know, something doesn't add up," said DJ. "Does it really make sense that our direct competition would bug the corporate jet and burglarize our offices? Really? We had the press conference on Soti. They know about that technology. Hell, they're probably working on their own versions as we speak. They're too smart to risk everything for that. No, this has to be somebody who understands what's *really* at stake."

"Right," said Taylor. "Someone who had already been clued in on the orca research. Someone who knew about it all along, not somebody who stumbled upon it accidentally by listening in on our conversations."

"Exactly," said DJ. "This is somebody purposely trying to steal the secrets of telepathic resonance. They knew exactly what they were after when they broke in and it wasn't Soti's ability to monitor a person's health. It was Soti's ability to talk to the whales."

"Well, then, we have to figure out who's been clued in on the research," said Casey.

"But no one knows besides us," said Taylor. "And the board of directors of OneWorld, but even they don't know the extent of it."

"There's one more group," said DJ. "Another group with more than a passing interest in the future of OneWorld. Now Boo's poisoning makes sense. Don't you see?"

"Not really," said Casey.

"The poisoning wasn't to get a better price for the company, as Maggie Lynch has suggested. It was to get Boo's brain. They know. They've known probably for quite some time."

"Wait—you mean Neftkomp?"

"Yes, Neftkomp. Soti—and the future of telepathic resonance—is now in the hands of the Russians."

THIRTY

He was back at the president's desk, sitting across from him. The president did not come around to the front and sit at the adjoining table this time, which made Kucherov feel a little twinge of anxiety. He had just finished briefing the president on their new acquisition and the president was just as amazed as Kucherov. Of course he tried very hard not to show it.

Two hours earlier, Kucherov had been talking to Evgeni Sergachev, learning all he could about Soti in preparation for the meeting. Nelson Gardner had flown overnight to get it to them. "And so this is it," Kucherov had mused, turning Soti over in his hand. "Such a small thing. One expects something much larger."

"But powerful, Boris," Sergachev had replied. "All of the secrets to telepathic resonance reside within. Well, they did. Now the information from this device has been loaded onto our computers." Sergachev had waved a hand towards the series of computer screens that ran down the row of desks in the main Neftkomp engineering office. "The device is even now communicating with our computers, doing the analysis and calculations that it was doing just yesterday in San Francisco. It's quite amazing, really. We have been talking to it. It speaks Russian fluently."

"No!"

"Oh, yes. It has a mind all its own, this thing. But one mustn't forget that it is a machine, programmed to help the person, or people, who are in possession of it. And that is now us."

"What then can we expect?"

"A program. A program that we can load into a separate device that will essentially replicate the part of the orca brain that is capable of instantaneous communication and understanding. A device that can basically connect minds together, creating a supermind, if you will."

As Kucherov had briefed the president, he'd used Sergachev's word and the president had paused over it, letting it roll around in his mind. He'd repeated it, smilingly. "A supermind," he'd whispered, almost to himself.

And now he was quiet for a long moment, thinking, looking up towards the ceiling of his office. The drapes over the window were closed on this day and shadows fell about the room from the dim overhead chandelier. Finally, the president spoke. "You know, my friend, there will be two kinds of people in the world once we have the program. There will be those who are with us, who wish to be a part of history, who wish to tap into our supermind technology. And there will be those who refuse to do so. They will be left behind in our wake."

"Surely Neftkomp can make the technology available for a reasonable price in the marketplace to whoever wants it," offered Kucherov.

The president was still in thought. "Hmm? Oh, yes, well, of course. But you know, my old friend, I sense this is bigger than Neftkomp, would you not agree? David Parker said so himself. What was the expression he used? Yes, 'game-changing.' You see, I do not think of this as a commercial product, Boris, to be sold to the masses. This technology can be put into use in a much more powerful way. In fact, the technology is power itself. Think of the information we now have scattered throughout the Russian Federation. Fractured and splintered, people—smart people—going off in different directions, whether it's with scientific pursuits, or, say construction or agriculture or medicine or what have you. Even, say, military technology. We'll now have the ability to pool all of that mind power together. But why stop at the Russian Federation? There are great minds throughout Europe. Throughout the world, in fact.

"You see, Boris, if one were so inclined, one could take that power and harness it. Why should all these minds be working for themselves when they could be working for something much greater than themselves? People want larger causes to strive for, after all. They need them. It's what makes the individual life worthwhile, wouldn't you agree? The sacrifice for something important. And once we start, everything will steamroll. At that point, the future will be clear. You will climb aboard with us, or you will be on the outside looking in. Flattened inevitably by the steamroller." He looked back up towards the ceiling and his thin lips curled into an unsettling smile. "We'll have all the answers. We'll have the world's knowledge. We'll be the most powerful force ever, Boris. Who will be able to stop us?"

Kucherov managed a smile, though he suddenly felt weak and slightly nauseated. "But, surely, Yaba will have the same technology," he said.

"Ah, but to what end? They will make it commercially available. It will be in the hands of individuals who will have the choice to use it or not. It will take them years. That's what 'choice' gives you. Hesitation is a product of choice. There is no room for hesitation. We'll connect all the smart minds immediately, for everybody's good. We'll be light years ahead of them. This is the power of the collective, Boris, don't you see? We can learn from the whales, my friend. Living as one.

Think of how powerful that is. How utterly powerful. How utterly, utterly powerful."

"Boris, what is wrong? You are so quiet. And you look pale."

Boris had been picking at his dinner. Natalya knew, after almost thirty years of marriage, when her husband had something serious on his mind and most of the times the major symptom was lack of appetite.

"Oh, nothing, my angel," he said. "Just tired, I suppose."

"You are working too hard."

"Perhaps."

"How did your meeting with the president go today? Did it not go well?"

"Oh, it went...fine." It went anything but fine. But how was he supposed to explain to Natalya the twisted smile on the president's face as he described his plans for the telepathic resonance technology? It was a baleful and ravenous look of glee. Dangerous, vicious glee. Kucherov had left the meeting feeling sick and unnerved.

"Did you talk about the marine parks?"

"Yes, a bit. The sale is still pending but should be completed soon." There. That was enough to tell her. What more could he say? That the president of the Russian Federation was hatching some diabolical plan to assemble the knowledge of the world's great minds, by force if necessary, for brutal, nationalistic purposes? To ultimately take over the world? Maybe Kucherov was getting ahead of himself. The president hadn't actually said all that, after all. He did mention something about steamrolling, though. And there was that mention of military technology. What was that talk about living as one? Was that some kind of wry joke?

"How about a cup of tea, Boris?"

"Yes, my angel. Perhaps some tea." Whatever purposes the president had for telepathic resonance—supermind technology, he had called it—his plans certainly could not have aligned with the plans of Yaba. Kucherov suddenly felt a frightening and heavy tug of responsibility. What if you knew a train was about to wreck? If you could do something to stop it, wouldn't you be obligated to try? In truth, this was the part that had him so unnerved. If only he didn't know. If only he could be like Natalya, squeezing that lemon into her tea without a care in the world. Knowing nothing of the dangers, the deadly wreck up ahead.

Hopefully, he hadn't telegraphed his true emotions to the president. The president was a master at sensing another person's mood. Indeed, a large part of his political negotiating success had come by way of this skill. He was a poker player, able to accurately read the faces of his adversaries. Kucherov must have looked uncomfortable listening to his plans, but he was not an adversary. Perhaps the president hadn't noticed. Besides, he was probably too caught up in his own grandiose thoughts about the technology to notice.

There was a time, long ago, when Kucherov would have talked to the president like the friend that he used to be. He would have voiced his concerns. They would have discussed the concept of telepathic resonance philosophically. They used to have wonderful philosophical conversations—about government, about science, about theology, about all sorts of things. The discussions would sometimes get loud and boisterous, sometimes they'd veer into argument, but there was always mutual respect. That was many years ago. Before the president's political career had started. It had been a fast trajectory from lieutenant colonel in the KGB to influential member of the old president's staff to prime minister and then to president. He'd been a rising star, but Kucherov had noticed it had come with a price. He'd changed. He'd become darker somehow. They never talked anymore the way they used to. The president had become so serious. And Kucherov had seen how he had handled those whom he'd perceived to be enemies of his administration. Old friends or not, he could not allow himself to be regarded as an enemy by the president.

Long after Natalya had gone to bed, Kucherov went to his study and picked up the phone. He looked at the clock on the wall and did a quick calculation. Yes, it should be fine. It would only be early afternoon in California.

THIRTY-ONE

Donnie Watkins had flown back up to San Francisco. There was nothing more to be learned from Boo. Boo understood the capabilities of telepathic resonance and, through Soti, had been able to pass along to Yaba what those capabilities were. But Boo was unable to relate just how telepathic resonance worked. It was instinct for Boo, nothing more. Meanwhile, with Boo now healthy, the Russians, not wishing to overplay their hand, dropped the requirement to have him sent to Moscow for analysis. The due diligence period was coming to a close and the sale of OneWorld was on track.

Taylor and Watkins were now together again at Orca HQ where Soti II had presented them with something of a riddle. "It's computer code," Taylor was explaining to DJ. "At least I think so. But it's not in any programming language known to humans."

"It seems Soti has presented us with the solution," added Watkins, "but the solution requires another solution. We can't run this code with what we have. Soti had to essentially invent another language to make this work and now we have to learn that language."

DJ looked over at Soti II, sitting on a desk, cabled into the Yaba computers. "Soti, why can't we use a known programming language to run this code?" he asked.

"Telepathic resonance is too complex," answered Soti. "It requires a much higher level of abstraction than what can be attained using currently available programs. Hence the need for a new language."

"And so you invented an entirely new computer language?"

"That is correct, David."

Watkins glanced over at Taylor and smiled dryly. "We might need to start polishing our resumes, eh, buddy?"

DJ grinned. "Don't worry, fellas. I'm sure I'll be able to find something for you guys to do around here. Custodial? Secretarial?"

"Hilarious, DJ."

"Well, in the meantime, we now have a code. We just need to make it work. And remember, the Russians are discovering the same things we're discovering. Soti I is most likely taking the same analytical path as Soti II. How fast can you two get up to speed on Soti's new language?"

"As fast as she can teach us," said Taylor. "But the time-consuming part will be making the program compatible with our computer. We may need to do some reformatting. I'll be honest—it's not going to be easy. This language of Soti's is not even close to anything I've ever seen before."

"Harder still," added Watkins, "will be finding a way to replicate this on a large scale. DJ, this is incredibly complex technology. Frankly, I'm not sure our computers can handle it. How, then, will it be possible to make this available to the average guy on the street?"

"Right," echoed Taylor, "and that assumes we can find a way to tie all of this in to a human brain! That's another whole technology right there. You can be damn sure it's going to require more than sound waves, like Soti's health monitoring. It will probably require something that doesn't even exist."

"But it does exist," said DJ. "At least in theory. The whales have it. Anything that exists can be replicated. But listen, let's not get too far ahead of ourselves, guys. One step at a time, okay? Let's solve this new language of Soti's and see where we can go from there. I have a feeling everything's going to fall into place."

"I told them everything's going to fall into place, but I'm not sure I believe it," said DJ. He and Brooke were having lunch at a Chinese restaurant a couple of blocks off of The Embarcadero. DJ knew his two top guys often worked better when he wasn't looking over their shoulders. He decided to get out of Orca HQ, to get out of Yaba. He'd called Brooke at her hotel and suggested lunch and she'd suggested Chinese.

"I mean, it's incredible to me," DJ continued. "Just incredible. Think about the abilities the whales have that we might not have the capability of replicating, even with the world's most advanced computer technology at our disposal. The whales have it all right in their heads."

"You'll figure it out, DJ. I'm sure of it." A waiter was strolling by with a cart of various dim sum dishes and Brooke was pointing to the ones she wanted to try.

"It's all I can think about," said DJ, working on a bowl of egg drop soup. "It's funny. Not long ago I was all stoked about our Soti health technology, never dreaming I'd soon be working on technology that could revolutionize how we think and process information. Our health monitoring system is already obsolete. When I think about telepathic resonance and the future state of healthcare..."

"DJ, you've been talking about how it will allow us to exponentially increase our knowledge base in the medical field and other industries, and that's all very important, of course. But can't you see the real benefit? The real benefit to humankind?"

"The real benefit? What do you mean?"

"Instant understanding. It goes beyond understanding of mere knowledge. DJ, we're talking about emotions and personalities and personal histories. We're talking about literally getting inside of someone's head. Think about how divided people are these days. This group over here is certain that its worldview is the right one. That group over there thinks the opposite. How can that be? They can't both be right. But neither one is probably totally wrong, either. Imagine if someone from Group A could understand completely how a representative from Group B arrived at his position. If he could see into his past, if he could understand all of the things that made him believe the way he believes, if he could understand instantly his reasoning and rationale. Doesn't matter if it's politics, theology, or taste in music. Don't you see?"

"Total empathy."

"Yes! DJ, people don't arrive at their beliefs in a vacuum. Our personalities are shaped by all sorts of forces, from the time we're born. Maybe even in the womb. And our beliefs about everything, how we see the world, how we regard others—all of this is a function of our life experience. How we're raised, how we're socialized, and so forth. All of this forms our belief systems."

"That sounds pretty deterministic."

"Well, then I guess I'm a determinist. Look, I'm not saying we don't have some capacity for free will, but how much of our beliefs and attitudes and very personalities are formed unconsciously? Even when we carry persuasive arguments around with us about our beliefs, I'll bet the belief is there first. The argument becomes our rationale, post-belief. But here's the point: if you knew someone's background intimately, if you knew everything that led that person to believe or behave in the way that he or she does—if you, in a manner of speaking, had walked in their shoes—then you could understand their point of view. And if they did the same, they could understand yours. Common ground would present itself automatically."

"Hmm. The end of human conflict, Brooke?"

"I don't know," Brooke said, looking down at her plate. "I think we can at least say this: we'd know everybody's true motivations. We'd be operating on the basis of total honesty with complete transparency. Along with everything else you'd read from someone's mind, you'd read their intentions, too."

"But, Brooke, then we'd lose privacy. Nobody's going to want to surrender their innermost thoughts. Hell, we don't know if the whales even do that."

"Oh, I know, DJ. I guess I'm just kind of philosophizing. Maybe it's the idealist in me. The fact is, I'm sure that as human beings we can do better. How much conflict is caused by misunderstanding? By bad intentions? By corrupt motivations? How many wars are fought? How many people killed? What if we were equipped with total empathetic capabilities?"

"I understand, Brooke. And I don't disagree with you. Perhaps we'll be able to someday make the technology work that way. Maybe we'll be able to walk the fine line between empathy and the relinquishment of private thoughts. But that's a lot of vulnerability."

"Or maybe it's just trust, DJ. Maybe that's where it all has to start."

"Maybe. Well, in the meantime, perhaps the technological advances in the other fields will help to make the world a better place to live in. Improved medical care, better access to food, more affordable housing. Fewer problems to fight over, in other words."

"Yes," said Brooke thoughtfully. "Maybe so."

The two ate silently for a few minutes, DJ turning over in his mind this idea of sharing so much of oneself. What if, he thought, he and Brooke hooked their minds together? What would each come to understand about the other? Would they find themselves drawn more to each other? Or would the opposite happen?

Brooke broke the silence. "DJ, I've been meaning to tell you something."

"Hmm?"

"I think I'm going to go back home. I think I've done all I can do here for you guys. I can't stay here in San Francisco forever and I don't think there's anything more I can help with."

"Home?" said DJ, trying to appear neutral to this piece of distressing news. "You mean Santa Monica?"

"No, I mean *home* home. I'm moving back to St. Pete. I've been thinking about it for a while now. My folks still live there, you know. They're getting older, of course, and I've been feeling bad about being so far away from them, especially since Adam...well, you know."

"Sure, but Brooke, you can't go. Not just yet. I mean, we need you here. Your input has been invaluable."

Brooke smiled. "I appreciate that, DJ. And I've completely enjoyed working with you all. And I can't thank you enough for the accommodations. But, really, you and Donnie and Paul are down to the technical stuff now. If I was of help at all with the theory, then I'm extremely gratified. But I don't think you really need me now."

DJ wanted to reach across the table and grab her in his arms and tell her how much he really needed her now. Maybe that's what she wanted to hear. Or maybe he'd make a complete ass of himself. It could go either way and he thought ironically of the use he'd have at that moment for the very technology he was developing. Of course that would require the release to her of his most private thoughts, and she would have known by now how he felt anyway.

Then he decided that she already did. "I understand, Brooke," he managed to smile. "But we'll keep in touch, okay?"

"Of course, DJ. I'll want to know what's happening with your progress. And maybe you can come to St. Pete someday. Maybe we can—"

Just then, DJ's phone rang. He glanced down to see Casey's name. She knew not to disturb him unless it was important.

"Excuse me, Brooke. Case, what is it?"

"DJ, I've got a call that I think I ought to transfer directly to you."

"Why? Who is it?"

"Neftkomp. Well, their CEO, anyway. Boris Kucherov. He says it's important. Very important."

THIRTY-TWO

Kucherov was sitting in his Neftkomp office on Bolshaya Gruzinskaya Street, downing the morning's third cup of coffee and still feeling as though he wanted to close his eyes. Sleep had not come easy. He'd talked into the wee hours with David Parker and then had lay awake for quite some time, finally falling asleep about an hour before his alarm went off.

"I fear my president is bent on destruction, Mr. Parker," he had said on the phone. "Ours, yours, perhaps the world's. You and I—we must work together. I have a grandchild on the way. I want my grandchild to live in a world of peace. This technology—it can be used for good or for evil. We must choose carefully what we do with it. I do not wish to be on the wrong side of history. I assume your intentions are honorable, Mr. Parker, but I have no way of knowing for sure. Still, I must take the chance."

Parker had assured him that his plans for the technology were indeed honorable. He'd gone into quite some detail about the potential uses of telepathic resonance, believing it would flourish best if made available freely to the world.

"You are Prometheus, Mr. Parker," Kucherov had told him. "Stealing fire from the gods to give to us mortals. Let us hope we do not burn ourselves."

It was decided that Kucherov would funnel to Yaba whatever information he could ascertain from his own engineers. He would help Parker solve the riddle of telepathic resonance before the secret landed on the desk of the president of the Russian Federation. And now he was reading over the latest progress report, sent to him just moments before. There was a snag. Soti had produced, to everyone's surprise, a completely new programming language. What was then to be done?

Kucherov picked up his coffee and strode out of his office, past his secretary, down the long outer hallway to the elevator, and down six floors to where his top four engineers were gathered around a long table, talking to Soti, chattering to each other, tapping away on their computer keyboards. Kucherov wished he had more technical expertise. When these men talked to him about computer matters, his eyes typically glazed over. Now he had to pay attention. Now he had to know exactly what was happening so that he could properly relay it to Parker.

"What does this mean?" he said, breaking into the conversation, waving a printout of the morning's report. "A new programming language?"

"Yes, unfortunately," one of his engineers answered. "It means apparently that the communication abilities are too complex to be replicated with any ordinary computer programming language. Soti has had to devise a new language. And now the problem is that we will need to decipher this new language."

"We are starting on that now," said another engineer.

"And how long will this take?" asked Kucherov.

The engineers all looked at each other. Shrugging, one of them said, "It could be days. Perhaps a week or more."

Kucherov scowled, belying a feeling of hope: perhaps Yaba's guys would not take as long. "Keep at it. And I would like to see your efforts in real time from now on. No more reports. I must be able to access your work with my computer. I must be able to see what you are doing as you do it. The president is anxious, as you might suspect."

"Yes, sir."

"By the way, where is Sergachev this morning? I assumed he'd be down here."

"We thought he went with you, to the meeting."

"What meeting?"

"At the Kremlin. He mentioned being summoned there. We all assumed you would go together."

"Yes, yes of course," said Kucherov, forcing a thin smile. "The meeting. No, I told Sergachev to go on ahead. I will be meeting him there later. I forgot I had told him. Where is my head this morning?"

"Okay, we're in," said Taylor.

"Beautiful," said DJ. "Nice work, guys."

"You're the one that got us the access," said Watkins. The three were in Orca HQ, looking at the main screen, seeing what was on Boris Kucherov's computer six-thousand miles away.

"It doesn't look like they're any further ahead than we are," said Taylor. "They're stuck on the programming language, same as us."

"Kucherov said he had four guys working on it," said DJ. "But I'd put you two up against his four any day of the week."

"Aw, shucks," smiled Watkins. "Thanks, boss."

"Be that as it may," DJ continued, "we still need to keep close tabs on whatever it is they discover. The Sotis are most likely working at the same speeds. But how fast we can analyze what the Sotis deliver is up to us. Now we have those four guys essentially helping us."

"Yeah, but we may have a problem there, DJ," said Taylor, pointing to the screen. "Take a look at what they're using to translate the language."

"Wow, that's odd," said Watkins.

"What?" said DJ. "What's odd? Clue me in, fellas."

"Well, basically, Soti is helping us learn her new programming language," explained Taylor. "But we have no way to decipher it with our computers because, well, the computers don't know the language."

"Obviously."

"Right. So Soti has been helping us with a kind of mediating language."

"A sort of translation code," added Watkins.

"Exactly," said Taylor. A Rosetta Stone, if you will. But look at their code. And then look at ours. Here, I'll overlay them."

"They're different," observed DJ.

"Yes, they're different," said Taylor, "but they shouldn't be. Soti I is identical to Soti II and Soti III. One would, therefore, expect identical results. Why would Soti I create a different translation tool than Soti II?"

"Maybe she's catering to the knowledge base of her users," mused DJ. "Kucherov's engineers might require a different approach."

"Yeah, maybe," said Watkins. "But that's pretty damn intuitive."

DJ grinned. "Wasn't that the idea behind her?"

Kucherov sat on the bench on the Moskva River. It was cold and very few people were walking about. An elderly lady to his right was walking a small dog. Around him the bare trees looked ghostly against the pale gray sky. He was thinking about Natalya. He had kissed her on the cheek this morning on his way out of the house. She had reminded him to stop on the way home. They were out of wine. "Yes, my angel," he had told her. "I will do so."

He tried not to think of her in the house all alone a half hour after he was due to be home. An hour. Two hours. She would call him by then but of course she would get only his voicemail. After three hours, he imagined she would call Anna. Anna would tell her not to worry, that certainly there was a logical explanation. Anna would come over to the house after four hours with her husband. Andrei would be called, too. He would go out into the Moscow night, tracing Kucherov's typical path home but finding nothing. The police would be called the next day and there would be the obligatory questions. Is your husband a heavy drinker? Has your husband ever behaved like this before? Do you know if there is another woman?

He wondered how Sergachev would do it. Certainly, he would not do it himself. They had been friends too long. It would be a stranger dispatched by Evgeni, perhaps by the president himself. And he knew, with some small comfort, that Evgeni would find no pleasure in it. He liked to think that perhaps Evgeni would have even tried to talk the president out of it, but this was wishful thinking. Evgeni would have known that words would have been wasted, so why risk turning the suspicion on himself?

He cursed himself for believing his middle-of-the-night phone call would not have been listened to. How naive. How stupid. But he was consoled by the thought that David Parker was now in a much better position to discover the secrets of telepathic resonance, and before the Russians. The technology would be in good hands. The Russians would, of course, discover it eventually but once the technology was released to the free world, the Russians would always be playing catch-up. The technology would spread swiftly and then it would build on itself, growing geometrically. Nobody would then have the power to bottle it up.

He thought of escape, but where would he go? They knew where he lived, where his wife lived, where his son and pregnant daughter lived. He acted last night for their future. Why put that in jeopardy now?

Boris Kucherov watched the water of the Moskva stream by. It didn't seem as cold now, he thought, though he could still see his breath in the air. The lady with the dog had left. Nobody was along the riverfront now except for a tall man in a trench coat about fifty yards away, a stranger, moving steadily in Kucherov's direction.

THIRTY-THREE

"He dreams of being back in the Salish Sea," JJ said. "The Salish Sea. With his mother. Her name is Chumley. Chumley. Her name is Chumley."

"Does he dream of this often?" Kioko asked. The two were standing at the edge of Boo's tank at the OneWorld park in Santa Monica. It was DJ's idea. He'd been too busy to properly entertain his brother in San Francisco and he sensed Kioko was getting a little stir crazy, too. He sent them both on a trip to Los Angeles. They were staying at the Hotel Roosevelt on Hollywood Boulevard and had toured Hollywood and Universal Studios but all JJ really wanted to do was hang out at OneWorld and all he wanted to do at OneWorld was talk to Boo. Kioko was happy to oblige.

"Yes, he dreams of it a lot. He dreams of his mother. He dreams of swimming with his cousins. When he was little they played hide and seek. Hide and seek. When he was little. He remembers a gathering once. A whole clan. Dozens and dozens of whales. More than he'd ever seen in his life. It was a special time for him. Special time."

JJ was quiet then for a long time, his expressionless face turned towards Boo. It was as though he was in a trance.

Kioko knew not to interrupt. Finally, JJ said, "I promised him I would see Chumley. I would tell her of his dreams. He wants her to know how he feels. Chumley. How he feels."

Kioko knew that Boo and Chumley had used JJ as a sort of conduit between them in the past. They both knew each other's whereabouts and had a general sense of the other's well-being. But this was something new. JJ was now seemingly tasked with delivering specific messages. Did this reflect advancement in JJ's abilities to converse with the orcas? Perhaps it reflected more trust on the part of Boo. More trust towards humans in general? Hardly. After being poisoned, Boo's trust, thought Kioko, had to have been pretty limited where human beings were concerned.

"Perhaps we'll go back to Seahaven," said Kioko. "Chumley will come by."

"Yes, Chumley will come by. She's with J pod. J pod will come by. J pod is part of the SRKW clan."

"You can talk to Chumley then, JJ."

"Yes, I will talk with her. Also, Boo wants to go to the sanctuary."

"How did Boo find out about the sanctuary?"

"I told him. I told him about the sanctuary. The sanctuary. He wants to go there."

"I'm sure he does, JJ. And I think your brother will make it happen."

"He doesn't want to be here anymore. Boo. Doesn't want to be here. Boo doesn't want to be here anymore."

"We lost it," said Taylor. "I can't get back in."

"Are you sure you're using the right access code?" said Watkins.

"Yes, I'm sure. Duh."

"Hey, just asking."

"Something must have happened," said DJ. "Maybe they got wise to him." The three were looking at the main screen in Orca HQ. "*Dostup Zakryt*" is all it said. "Access Denied."

"And you have no way to get a hold of him?" said Watkins.

"Nope. Casey said his number didn't show up when he called. I mean, I guess I could call Neftkomp, but how many people would I have to go through to get to the CEO? And they'll wonder why I'm calling. Or why anybody is calling. It would look suspicious."

"So what do we do, boss?"

"We have to keep moving forward. If we can hook back up with Kucherov's computer, we can hook back up with it. If we can't, we can't. Simple as that. In the meantime, let's keep rolling. We're getting close to cracking the language barrier with Soti, yes?"

"Yep," answered Taylor. "And we're doing the reformatting necessary to turn the language into a usable program. But, listen, DJ—Donnie and I have been thinking."

"Only good things come of that," said DJ. "Talk to me."

"Well, we've been wondering how we're going to make the technology accessible to the end user. We've been talking about another Soti-like unit, right?"

"Right."

"But why reinvent the proverbial wheel? Why not just use Soti?"

"Because she's not set up for that. She relies completely on physiological sound waves."

"But, DJ," said Watkins, "we know she accesses more than a person's physiology. She reads JJ's mind. She's read yours."

"Sure, but only because JJ has some capacity for telepathic resonance. And because, apparently, some of my thoughts have been strong enough to, presumably, affect my physiology. Either way, I can't read Soti's mind. At best the communication is unidirectional."

"But if Soti can read Person A's mind," said Taylor, "then she can relay that information to Person B and vice-versa. She becomes the channel, in other words. She becomes the de facto paralimbic cleft of both parties."

DJ sat silently for a moment, thinking this over. "So we don't have to invent a new device," he said at last.

"More importantly," said Watkins, "we wouldn't need to replicate the technology."

"Don't you see?" said Taylor. "We wouldn't need to know how the technology works. Just so long as Soti knows. We can shortcut this whole thing. Soti has the knowledge right now. The only thing we're waiting on is for her to find a way to explain it to us."

"Wait a minute. Are you guys seriously suggesting that we present a technology to the world that we don't even understand?"

"Well, someday we probably will understand it," offered Watkins. "Ironically, we'll probably understand it through telepathic resonance. But we need the telepathic resonance to be able to understand the telepathic resonance."

"In the meantime," added Taylor, "we won't have to wait. We can move forward immediately."

"All it would require," said Watkins, "is to give Soti what she needs to apply the technology. Whatever that is. You're right that she's not necessarily set up for telepathic resonance. But she *has* shown some aptitude for it. And once she gets a firm grasp of the technology, she'll be in a position to know how she needs to alter herself so as to make it work."

"Allow her to program herself?" said DJ.

"Well, yeah," said Taylor. "Basically."

"Give her free rein to morph into whatever she wants to morph into?"

"I sense some skepticism," said Watkins.

"Guys," DJ said, "I'm not sure you've really thought this through. You're talking about relinquishing control of an artificial intelligence device. Have either of you ever even *watched* a sci-fi movie?"

"Which one?" said Taylor.

"*Any* one!" DJ replied.

"Look, I know what you're getting at, DJ," said Watkins. "The AI becomes stronger, kills all the humans, and takes over the world. But, c'mon. That's the movies. Soti has proved herself. She has no hidden agenda. So, okay, she runs with the new telepathic resonance technology. But so what? We'll catch up to her. She'll keep us in the loop. We're not at cross-purposes."

"The truth of the matter, DJ," added Taylor, "is that it might take weeks for us to understand what Soti knows, replicate it, and find a way to apply it. Weeks? Hell, it might take months."

"Or years," said Watkins. "And that assumes we can even do it. Soti knows how to do it right now. It might take her a little longer to modify her existing structure, to, as you say, suitably reprogram herself, but I'll bet it doesn't take her very long. Not once we rewrite her permissions. She might be able to perform telepathic resonance by the end of the week. Hook her up to two different minds and it'll be every bit as earth-shaking as Alexander Graham Bell's very first telephone call must have been."

"Except that Bell had some idea of how his technology worked," said DJ. "He remained in control of it."

"Listen, DJ," said Taylor, "the fact is that if we don't allow Soti to take off with this technology, the Russians will. Somebody's got to be the first in history to trust the future to artificial intelligence. Better that it's us, right?"

Evgeni Sergachev should have been pleased. His engineers had called him down to the computer lab. Soti's program had apparently been translated into something usable by the Neftkomp computers. This was a huge step. They were further ahead than the Americans. More importantly, the president of the Russian Federation had entrusted Sergachev with the entire project, trust that he had earned by way of his commitment to taking care of the problem with the leak. The next step for him was to be CEO of Neftkomp. Who knows what that could lead to? Perhaps a cushy political appointment in the Kremlin. Sergachev's future had never looked brighter.

And yet, he couldn't stop thinking of his old friend Boris. Everything good that was coming to Sergachev was coming to him at Boris's expense. Later that night, he'd have to visit Natalya. Tell her the news. Boris was found by the river. Heart attack. It was quick, he'd tell her. The doctors had assured him. Your husband didn't suffer at all, he would say.

But now he couldn't think of that. There was no room for thoughts of friendships and lamentations about loss. There was a higher calling. And besides, it wasn't as if Boris hadn't had it coming. The shame of the whole affair was the damnable betrayal. It was unconscionable. Where was the loyalty? Russia was on the brink of greatness once again. The president had put it to Sergachev well: one could either climb aboard or be run over. Boris had made his choice. So had Sergachev.

"Gentlemen, please proceed," he said as he strode into the lab, forcing a smile. "This is very exciting."

"Okay, we are ready," said one of the engineers. "I have just finished loading the program onto the computer. This is Soti's translated version of telepathic resonance. And even more. Soti has devised a means by which to make it work. The program apparently comes with an instruction sheet of sorts. A kind of blueprint for replicating what the whales are capable of doing. Frankly, I don't know what to expect. I will execute the program, and we will see what presents itself. I imagine it will be the coding language and probably some technical specifications for the actual replication process."

They all gathered quietly around the computer and the engineer clicked open the downloaded file. A folder appeared. The engineer opened the folder to display a single, solitary file.

"That's impossible," said one of the other engineers.

"It must be a joke," said another.

"What it is?" said Sergachev.

"It's a music file," said the first engineer. And then he clicked it open and a song began playing. None of the Russians in the room recognized the opening melodic beats of Rihanna's "Love on the Brain."

THIRTY-FOUR

"DJ, you can't do it. This is the stuff of science fiction. The really *bad* stuff. Don't those guys ever watch any movies?"

"Exactly! Thank you, Case! That's exactly what I told them."

DJ had left the meeting with Taylor and Watkins, telling them he'd think their proposal over. But his gut instinct told him it was a bad idea, maybe even dangerous. Allow complete freedom to an AI device? What if they were right, though? Maybe the only way to develop the technology for telepathic resonance would be to allow Soti to go ahead and develop it on her own with the hopes that human intelligence would eventually catch up. Would he be cheating the world out of an historic technological leap forward by keeping a lid on it? As always, when he needed an objective viewpoint, he confided in Casey.

"DJ, technology needs to be controlled, measured, understood. You can't just turn it loose." She was sitting in his living room with one leg casually slung over the armrest of a chair. He'd asked her to come over that evening to talk. She was wearing an oversized sweater and a snug pair of jeans. Her hair fell loosely about her shoulders. DJ was pacing the floor in front of her.

"Okay, but let me play devil's advocate, Case. Can't we assume that Soti *would* control it? If she's smart enough to understand telepathic resonance, she's smart enough to cultivate it in an orderly, methodical way."

"DJ, I'm not talking about the telepathic resonance technology. I'm talking about Soti! You're taking her off the leash."

"But it's like Paul said. She's proven herself. Why wouldn't we trust her?"

"It's not a matter of trust. It's about Soti being head and shoulders above us on the intelligence scale. She might be able to help us perform miracles, but, DJ, where does it end? The human world would no longer be in charge of its own technological destiny. We'd be followers."

"But, Case, would it matter? If Soti, through her superior intelligence, is able to find better ways for humankind to live—"

"Assuming that would be her interest..."

"—then who cares if we understand the technologies or not?"

"DJ, do you hear what you're saying?"

DJ slowly nodded. "I know, Case. Even as I say it out loud, I know we can never cede that much power to something that's not human. Even if Soti had the personality and generosity of Santa Claus. Humans have to run human affairs."

"Welcome back to earth."

"Damn shame, though. You know, it's possible we might never be able to understand how telepathic resonance works. That's a pretty big loss for the world."

"But you will, DJ. With Soti's help. But not with her taking the lead. It will be only a matter of time and you'll figure it out."

"I'm not so sure. And there's another potential destiny. The Russians are working with Soti, too. We're not the only ones with the gatekeeper to the technology. And we have no idea what they'll do with it."

"They've probably hit the same wall we've hit."

"Maybe. But what if they have the same idea that Paul and Donnie have? Maybe they'll take Soti off the leash, as you say."

"DJ, you have to find a way to get Soti back."

"Infiltrate Neftkomp?"

"What about the CEO you were talking with?"

"Haven't heard a peep. Case, I'm afraid something's happened to him. First, we lost access to his computer. Then the link itself was broken." He looked off into space for a moment. "He seemed like a good guy, too. He wanted to do the right thing. He mentioned a grandchild. These are dangerous people we're dealing with."

"Then you have to get the technology before they do. More than that, you have to find a way to shut their efforts down."

"If I could just talk to their Soti. If there was a way to let her know whom she's dealing with over there. Maybe she could somehow sabotage their work."

"How do you know she'd be loyal to us, though, DJ? I mean, if Soti were to receive opposing commands, what would she do?"

"I don't know. I never thought about it. She's designed to work with just one person at a time. She'd have to choose, I guess."

"Based on what?"

"Based on whatever she felt was right, I suppose."

"Can she feel?"

"Good question, Case."

"That's what I'm here for, boss. That and another glass of that Cabernet of yours."

Sergachev was furious.

A "snag" is how he'd tried to describe it to the president. Soti wasn't working as advertised. "There is no time for snags," the president had told him tersely. Then he had suggested that Sergachev get in touch with his American contact. Forget stealing another Soti. Soti was obviously corruptible. The technology itself would need to be taken, by force if necessary. Certainly the Americans were out ahead by now. "Whatever they've discovered," the president had said, "we need to have it."

The only problem was that Nelson Gardner hadn't been heard from since the elimination of Robert MacKinnon. Strange that Sergachev couldn't reach him. The job had been pulled off flawlessly; it wasn't as if Gardner had had to flee from the cops. One week after the kill, MacKinnon's body had been found. His postal carrier had called the police. He'd noticed a putrid smell coming from inside the house and the mail had been stacking up. By then, all traces of the nerve agent were gone. Apparently, the glove must have been gone, too. Gardner had taken care of business. With no visible signs of trauma or injury, the coroner had determined heart attack. Gardner was in the clear. So where was he?

Sergachev tried him again from the hotel room. Still no answer. He'd tried all day long the day before his trip and then had finally decided he would have to attend to the task himself. And now he was pacing in the living room of the suite he'd taken, not even sure who or what to be angry with. He hated what Soti had done. He was irate at his own engineers for somehow not anticipating it. He was mad at Boris for the betrayal and for making him do what he had to do. He was incensed at Gardner for not answering his phone. At that moment, he was mostly infuriated at the chain of events that ultimately put him on the grueling sixteen-hour flight to get him here. He should be home. It was already morning in Moscow.

Then came the knock on the door he'd been expecting. The president himself had made a phone call to the Russian Foreign Intelligence Service. They would help. But Sergachev himself would have to carry out the assignment. If the Intelligence Service were to be implicated, relations with the United States would become precarious at best. Sergachev was a private Russian citizen, working, so far as anybody would know, of his own accord for his own reasons.

The assignment was clear. Get in, get out, leave nobody who could talk.

He answered the door and a compact man with a square face said, "E.S.?"

"Yes."

"Here is your package." And then he turned and was gone.

Sergachev brought the shoebox into the room and opened it. It would do nicely. A Lebedev PL-15 semi-automatic pistol with a sixteen-round magazine capacity. He held it in his hands as if inspecting a rare jewel and felt his anger dissipating. This trip was going to have a satisfactory ending after all. He put the gun in his jacket pocket and liked the way it felt. Then he walked over to the window and, for the first time since he'd arrived, gazed out at the city. If he squinted, he could see the lights of the Golden Gate Bridge in the distance.

THIRTY-FIVE

William Spieden was the Navy purser aboard the *USS Peacock*, one of six ships that made up the Wilkes Expedition of 1838-1842. The expedition, formally known as the United States Exploring Expedition, often shortened to U.S. Ex. Ex., explored the Pacific Ocean. When the ships sailed through the Strait of Juan de Fuca into the Salish Sea, they came across the San Juan Archipelago. At mean high tide, the archipelago consists of over 400 islands and rocks, one of which is a 516.4-acre island, two miles long, half a mile across, and 374 feet above sea level at its highest point. Owing to a "rain shadow" produced by the Olympic Mountains to the southwest, the island is split geographically in two, with the north side heavily wooded and the south side dry and barren, littered here and there with large boulders left from when the glaciers receded 12,000 years ago.

This island is the one named after purser William Spieden.

Spieden Island is uninhabited by humans but full of animal species from all over the world, including mouflon sheep from Corsica, fallow deer from Europe, and sika deer from East Asia. Dozens of species of game birds can be spotted on the island. Rumors have it that Sasquatch has been seen there. Those remain as rumors, but the other species have been definitive residents of the island since the late 1960s when a group of investors bought Spieden Island, unofficially renamed it Safari Island, and made it into a wild-game preserve, bringing in all the aforementioned animals. The hunting expeditions offered by the small island weren't very sportsmanlike. That, along with concerns about stray bullets hitting local boaters led to the closing of the preserve, but the animals remained. The investors sold the island and, for a few years, it was a marine conservationist center. Then it was sold again, this time to James Parker who built a dock and small cabin on the island for weekend getaways. Now it was part of his estate, of which DJ was executor.

Maggie Lynch had had preliminary discussions with her longtime friend, Washington Governor Michael Cassidy, about having the state acquire the island from DJ, at no financial cost, to be turned into a state park. In return, DJ would acquire Reid Harbor on Stuart Island. Reid Harbor was part of Stuart Island State Park. This would be DJ's orca sanctuary—330 acres of sheltered water, the new home to the thirty killer whales of OneWorld. It was a natural bay with a relatively small mouth, easily allowing an underwater barrier. The park encompassed most of the shoreline so there would be minimal, small boat traffic from the few inhabitants who resided along the rest of the shore. Cassidy was interested, mainly because of his relationship with Maggie, but there was a lot on his plate. Orcas weren't his top priority. Yes, he confessed, if it became a political hot button, he'd be more willing to act. If his constituency started screaming for freedom for the whales, he'd be grateful to have DJ's offer to present to them. Until then, he was certainly happy to "take the matter under advisement," which Maggie knew meant sit on it and do nothing. The public demonstration of the whales' intelligence was now more critical than ever. The public had to be moved to demand action.

Maggie filled DJ in on her conversations with the governor and DJ began to plan the demonstration. He could show the existing videos, but his thinking was that it might be better to replicate the experiments and invite the press. They could see the whales undertake the maze live and in person, thus proving the intelligence of cetacea. The movement to free the whales would no doubt go viral.

In the meantime, Watkins and Taylor had made a monumental leap forward. Soti had helped them crack the programming language she had devised. They could start replicating the code for telepathic resonance. Watkins had called DJ with the news at his house early in the morning and DJ drove in to the Yaba campus, stopping along the way to pick up Brooke and her suitcase. He had promised her a ride to the airport. She was heading back to Santa Monica that afternoon to pack up her belongings there, and was then going to drive a U-Haul cross-country to St. Petersburg. Her parents were excited about having her come home. Yes, she'd said to DJ—she'd be happy to stop once more at Yaba. It would give her a chance to say goodbye to everyone. Plus, this new development was exciting. "It will be nice to leave with hopeful thoughts about where this is all going," she'd said.

Now DJ and Brooke were in Orca HQ with Watkins and Taylor. Casey had stopped in, too. Taylor was describing all the nuances of the new language. "It's really ingenious," he was saying. "I like to think Donnie and I are pretty good programmers, but we couldn't have come up with this in a million years."

"And we still couldn't have without Soti's translation code," added Watkins.

"The Rosetta Stone," said DJ.

"Right," said Watkins. "And now we have everything we need to start replicating, in digital form, telepathic resonance."

"But we still don't know how we're going to apply it," said Taylor. "We don't know how to create the hardware that will link the program from one mind to another."

"Soti could do it," said Watkins.

"We've been all through this," said DJ. "I know it's tempting. But we can't allow Soti to take the lead. We have to create something we can understand and replicate."

"We know, DJ," said Taylor. "Everything you've said about that makes sense. No disagreements here."

"Besides," DJ said, "I'm sure in time that Soti will be able to help us create the mechanism we need to apply the technology."

"But I'm afraid you won't have that time, Mr. Parker."

The group spun in unison to see a tall, thin man with narrow, beady eyes standing in the doorway, holding a pistol.

"Who are you?!" said DJ.

"Just an interested party," the man said in a Russian accent.

"How did you get in? How did you get past security?"

"Oh, was that what that was? Security? Those two men with the aluminum badges? I'm afraid you'll find them a bit incapacitated at the moment."

The group stood still. DJ glanced over to see stunned expressions on everyone's faces. He was stunned himself but he felt his leadership instincts kicking in. He knew he had to do something.

"What is it you want?" he said.

"What do you think, Mr. Parker? I want the secrets to your telepathic resonance."

"Our what? I'm afraid I don't know what you're talking about."

"Yeah, I think you've got the wrong place, friend," Watkins piped in. "We're a software company. We specialize in music listening apps. Ever heard of Y-Songs?"

"Silence," the man said. "I am not stupid. Let's not pretend that we don't know what I'm here for."

"You're the one who stole Soti, aren't you?" said DJ.

"Move away from the computer," said the man. "Everybody against the wall face first. Put your hands above your heads and press them against the wall." The group did what the man said, with everyone shuffling towards the wall adjacent to the desk where the main computer was resting. Then the man walked over to the computer and scanned the screen. The language program was open.

"You," he said, pointing to Watkins. "Come over here." Pulling a small external computer drive from his pocket, he handed it to Watkins. "Load the program onto this. Now!"

Watkins noticed his own hands trembling as he took the drive from the man. He took a deep breath. Then he glanced over at DJ. DJ, up against the wall, was looking back over his shoulder. He nodded at Watkins. "Better do what he says, Donnie."

"It might take a minute," Watkins said. "This is a big program."

The man put the gun up against Watkins's head. "As fast as possible," he said.

"Hey," said DJ, "there's no reason to threaten my people. We'll give you what you want. Take it easy with that gun, will ya? It might go off accidentally."

"I assure you, Mr. Parker, if this gun goes off, it will not be by accident."

Watkins swallowed hard and connected the drive to the computer. Soon the information was being transferred.

"It won't do you any good," said DJ. "There's no way to apply that program."

"We'll find a way," said the man. "Do not worry about that. Our top scientists are better than yours."

"Yeah? Well, if your guys are so smart," said Taylor, "how come you have to resort to stealing our stuff? Can't figure it out yourselves?"

"Quiet!" said the man, waving the gun towards Taylor. Taylor winced and turned his head back towards the wall.

Meanwhile, DJ's mind was racing with thoughts. And somewhere in those thoughts he came to realize that stealing the program would do the man no good if Yaba still had a copy of it. At best, that would only put the Russians on equal footing. You don't hold up a room of five people at gunpoint to be on equal footing. Of course the man could try to destroy the computer, but he had to have been smart enough to know that Yaba would have backed up everything to the cloud. No, the only way to get an edge would be to make sure Yaba wouldn't—or couldn't—continue to work on the program. In short, what DJ came to realize was that the man couldn't let any of them leave the room alive.

He looked over at Brooke. She was looking downward, her eyes closed as if in silent prayer. He glanced at Casey. She glanced back at him. Her eyes were brimming with tears but she managed to force a smile. Taylor was breathing heavily. Watkins had moved back towards the wall, still slightly shaking. The program was loading and the time it would take—a total of six minutes—seemed like an eternity.

DJ was closest to the man, about five feet away. He calculated that if he lunged towards him quickly, he might be able to wrestle the gun away before the man could use it. He was slightly bigger than the man, but he had to assume the man would be competent in defending himself, in being able to throw DJ off of him. Assuming DJ made it to him before being shot, that is. But if he could hold him just for a moment, he knew the others would jump into action, too. He looked around the immediate vicinity for something he could grab to give him an edge—a club of some description. He saw Taylor's ball glove sitting on a chair by the computer and thought, why the hell don't those two geeks have a bat with them?

There was nothing within arm's length. He would have to just jump quickly, grab at the man's arm, twist the gun free, try to get a punch in, and hope the others would come to his aid quickly. He'd grab him from an angle that would put his body in between the man and the others. If worse came to worst, if the man shot him, his body would act as a shield, and maybe give the others a brief second to act. It's all he could do.

The program was almost loaded. The man's attention would be diverted for a split second as he pulled out the external drive. That would be when DJ would act.

Suddenly, the face of his father appeared in his mind. A young James Parker. He was kneeling on a beach, looking through a camera. DJ was six, walking towards the water, his mother by his side. JJ was on the other side of his mother and all three were looking back at James over their shoulders. DJ glanced up to see his mother's smile lighting up her face. He could feel the sand under his bare feet and the cool of the water at the edge of the surf. It might have been the happiest, safest time of his life. At that moment, the scene seemed more real to DJ than the room he was standing in and he vaguely wondered if this is what people refer to when, near death, they claim to see their lives passing before their eyes. With effort, he shook off the thoughts, knowing he had to act in that instant. There was no time to hesitate.

DJ turned and lunged at the split second the man glanced down at the computer to pull out the drive. Five feet seemed like fifty. Out of the corner of his eye, the man saw movement. He wheeled around, raising the pistol towards the man who was diving towards him. Everybody heard the gunshot as it reverberated around the walls of Orca HQ.

THIRTY-SIX

The man slipped through DJ's arms, sliding lifelessly to the floor, a bullet hole perfectly centered on his forehead. His body slumped backward, his head hitting the floor, a fast-growing pool of blood forming underneath it. He'd dropped the unfired gun. It took DJ a second to gather what had happened and then he looked over towards the door. A tall, sturdy man was standing in the doorway with a pistol, a scar running down his cheek.

"Sorry I didn't get here sooner," the man said. "I didn't discover that he left Russia until early this morning. When I learned his flight was to San Francisco, I figured he'd be coming here. I drove here as fast as I could. Looks like I wasn't a minute too soon. By the way, you have a couple of unconscious guards out there. They'll be all right. Harmless nerve agent, just enough to incapacitate."

The group stood silently, bewildered. One by one they turned from the wall and faced the man with the scar. Everybody recognized him.

"Who *are* you?" said DJ.

"You can call me Maxwell. United States Marine Corps. Retired. Well, sort of. Once a Marine, always a Marine, you know? That pilgrim there is—or was—Evgeni Sergachev. He ostensibly worked for Neftkomp. In reality, he worked for the Russian government. He was a client of mine."

"A client?"

"I have a consulting business. I stole Soti for him. Sorry about that. I hadn't realized at the time exactly what Sergachev was up to. But he went too far. He crossed a line and I decided I would no longer...be at his disposal. But I hate leaving loose ends so I kept an eye on him. I was afraid he'd try something like this."

The man walked over to the body of Sergachev, making sure he was dead and verifying his own marksmanship. Seemingly pleased, he turned towards the door. "Good luck with everything, Mr. Parker," he said on his way out. "There should be nothing stopping you now."

"Wait," DJ said. "How can...how can I thank you?"

"Thank me? I helped get you into this mess. But if you insist, give me a fifteen-minute head start before you call the police. Then tell 'em some guy with a Russian accent came through the door with a gun and tried to rob you. Tell 'em another guy with a Russian accent came in afterward and shot *him*. Ha! That ought to keep everybody guessing for a while. And once Sergachev is identified as a Neftkomp employee, my guess is that OneWorld will be off the hook for the sale. Doesn't mean those whales of yours will get their freedom, but at least they won't be owned by the Russians. In the meantime, I'll keep checking the news. I'm looking forward to the day when you make telepathic resonance available to the human race. We sure could use it."

DJ nodded and then grinned and looked at his watch. "Fifteen minutes, Mr. Maxwell."

"Thank you, Mr. Parker."

And then the man was gone.

J Pod didn't come by the first day. But on the second day, JJ announced its presence. "They're out there now! Look," he pointed. "J Pod. It's J Pod."

He and DJ and Kioko were out on the dock at Seahaven. It was a clear day, though crisp and cool. There was just a light chop on the water and the setting made DJ feel calm and relaxed. Back in San Francisco, the work had progressed rapidly in the two weeks since Neftkomp's Evgeni Sergachev had been shot by "an unidentified assailant," as the police report put it. The Russian Embassy had been making a stir about the lack of an arrest, but the police had assured them they were following every lead. From all accounts, the shooter was also Russian. "This appears to have been more a Russian incident than an American one," said a representative from the state department when pressed by the Russian government for more attention to the matter.

At Orca HQ, Soti had been helping to configure a potential hardware device that could replicate the paralimbic cortex. The secret to the actual connectivity between minds appeared to rest in the spindle neurons. For the first time, it looked as though a device could be engineered to reproduce what the whales could do. Even still, it looked as though it would be weeks or possibly even months before a prototype would be ready for testing. DJ, in the meantime, had been making plans for the public demonstration of cetacean intelligence. He'd had Casey write up a press release. The mazes DJ's father had created would be reconfigured and ready within a month's time. A date had been set for the demonstration.

Meanwhile, he had decided to take a break for a few days to keep a promise he'd made to JJ: to come back to Seahaven and allow him to convey the message he'd received from Boo in Santa Monica, to get in contact with Chumley and tell her how much Boo was thinking of her and to tell her about the potential sanctuary. Now, JJ was pointing towards the pod a hundred yards off the shore. Both Kioko and DJ could see the fins of a couple dozen or more orcas as they gravitated towards the dock, seemingly aware of JJ's presence. Fifty yards away they more or less stopped their progress towards the dock. They swam gently in circles, rolling and cavorting, some inverting, slapping their tales. A couple of them spy-hopped and DJ wondered if one of those was Chumley.

"She misses Boo very much," JJ said. "Very much. She has never stopped thinking about him. Never stopped thinking about him." Then JJ was silent for a while. Kioko noticed the same blank look that JJ had worn at the Santa Monica park, the trance-like expression.

Finally, he spoke again. "She likes the sanctuary idea. Likes it. She's happy about that. They're all happy at the whales being released from the parks. They don't like the rest, though. Don't like it at all. At all."

"The rest?" said DJ. "What do you mean, little brother?"

"The rest of what I told them. Told them."

"What did you tell them?"

"About the telepathic resonance research. They don't like it. It's not for humans. Chumley said. Not for humans. They don't like it."

"Wait, you mean they don't want us to develop our own abilities to communicate like they do?"

"They don't like it," JJ repeated. "It's not for humans. Too dangerous."

"How so?"

"Intent."

"Huh?"

"She says intent. Chumley says. They don't like it. Intent."

"What does Chumley mean by that, JJ?"

JJ was quiet for a while. "They're going off to feed now," he finally said. Slowly, the pod made its way off into the distance until they could no longer be seen. "I'm going to paint a picture of them," JJ said and then he turned and walked towards his studio.

DJ looked out over the water where the whales had been. "What do you think Chumley meant, Kioko?"

"I don't know, DJ. Maybe they question your intent—what you plan on doing with the technology."

"They don't trust me?"

"Not you, DJ. Maybe they don't trust humankind. Can you blame them?"

"No, I suppose not."

"DJ, I've been thinking. Maybe it's not my place to say. But what if the Russians had gotten a hold of the technology first? And not just them. There will always be people looking to take whatever the latest technology is and use it for less than honorable purposes. I think this is what Chumley meant, DJ. Telepathic resonance could theoretically be used to solve a million human problems. Is it possible that it could also be used to create new ones? Dangerous ones? Maybe you're opening Pandora's box."

DJ chuckled. "Somebody else said I was Prometheus, stealing fire from the gods. I have to confess I'm a little rusty on my mythology."

"Prometheus stole the fire from Zeus," said Kioko. "Pandora's box was Zeus's revenge. A container of evils, disguised as a gift. DJ, you're the smartest person I know. I won't try to talk you out of what you're doing. I'd only ask that you think long and hard about it. I'm sure you will."

"Sure," said DJ, and then he looked back out towards the water.

"Well," said Kioko, "I'll go in and get something started for lunch." Then she left DJ alone on the dock where he stood for some time, gazing out at the water where the whales had been just minutes before, thinking about technology and humanity, thinking about Prometheus, and pondering the delicate and complicated problem of Pandora's box.

THIRTY-SEVEN

Taylor and Watkins tried to talk him out of it.

"You said it yourself, DJ," argued Taylor. "Our ancients might very well have had this ability then lost it. Now we have the chance to bring it back."

The three were in Orca HQ. DJ had spent another day on Orcas Island and had then flown back to San Francisco, leaving Kioko and JJ at Seahaven.

"We're not the ancients," DJ countered. "Somewhere along the line, we split from them. They could handle the technology. We can't. And now it's too late to go back. Don't you see? We're practically a different species now. Telepathic resonance is too dangerous. It's like tossing a box of matches to a five-year-old."

"That's not a very flattering portrait of humanity," said Watkins.

"No, I guess not. But, look, I'm not standing in judgment of humanity. We're different, that's all I'm saying. There are things we do exceedingly well. We're creative. We're inventive. We can also be destructive. Every development of ours is a two-edged sword, able to be used for good or for evil. With telepathic resonance, the stakes are just too high."

"But, DJ," said Taylor, "why are you assuming that evil will gain control of telepathic resonance if it's available to everybody? Good will have it, too."

"That may not be enough, Paul. Think about the world's terrorists coming together as one, pooling all of their knowledge, or perhaps taking it unwillingly from others. After all, we're only speculating about the voluntary nature of telepathic resonance. What if it's not always voluntary? Soti read my mind on several different occasions without me necessarily wanting her to. So what happens if the world's terrorists infiltrate and acquire the secrets of nuclear weaponry? 'Good' better be pretty damn quick or the planet will be a ball of ash."

"But the terrorists might gather additional information in their efforts, too," offered Watkins. "Through the minds of others, they may come to a better understanding of the world. The rest of the world might come to a better understanding of them. Maybe there would be a meeting of the minds. *All* minds."

"Yeah, I know," said DJ. "Brooke talked about that. Instant empathy. Wish I could believe it. Look, fellas, I don't mean to be cynical. I really don't. I just don't think we're wired for that kind of understanding. It's not who we are."

"Then there will never be a coming together of humanity. But, DJ, we can change that."

"No, Donnie. We can't. Telepathic resonance cannot do that. Nothing can do that for us. It seems to me that a coming together of humanity requires, at the minimum, a willingness of all people to come together. But we're each too distinct, too separate, too unique. We're seemingly hard-wired to produce differences. What's more, I think we like it that way. But that's not a bad thing, is it? Maybe it's in the differences where we get our creative ideas. It's always the person going against the current that ends up creating something new."

"But telepathic resonance doesn't impede individual thought, DJ," said Taylor. "It just makes all the individual thoughts available to everybody."

"And that's another thing," said DJ. "Do you want all of your individual thoughts available to everybody?"

"Well, no."

"You see? We're not ready for telepathic resonance."

The three sat silently for several moments. DJ let his eyes wander around the room, thinking about all the time they had spent there working together over the course of the last several months, working towards what he had hoped would be an answer to mankind's problems. He didn't like the conclusion he'd come to any more than Taylor and Watkins had liked it. But he didn't see any other way. The research had to be destroyed.

"That's a big decision to make on behalf of humanity," Watkins finally said. "You're single-handedly rationing the world's knowledge."

"Maybe some knowledge needs to be rationed," DJ replied.

"DJ, you're playing God with this stuff."

"I'm only listening to the ancients."

"But our ancients had the knowledge."

"I'm not talking about ours. I'm talking about the *world's* ancients. Cetacea. I have it on good authority that they don't think telepathic resonance is an appropriate tool for us. And I'm putting my trust in their fifty million years of earthly experience."

There was nothing left of Orca HQ when they were done. Every computer was wiped clean. Every server, too. Videos, documents, notebooks, photographs—everything was shredded.

There wasn't a single thumb drive or solitary piece of paper that hadn't been destroyed.

And then came Soti. She was completely reconfigured. This too had presented a debate. Even DJ had to admit that Soti seemed to have proved her loyalty. Soti I had purposely deceived the Russians. The thinking was that she would probably continue to do so. Through Soti, the Russians would never learn the secrets of telepathic resonance, nor would they learn the secrets of Soti herself. But that wasn't guarantee enough for DJ. Watkins was able to reconnect Soti I to the network and reconfigure her remotely. She'd now be completely useless to the Russian engineers.

As to the Soti technology at Yaba, the end result was a scaled-back version of the original. Limits were put in place. She would no longer be able to read private thoughts.

The planned demonstration to reveal orca intelligence was canceled. No reason was given to the press. DJ couldn't even imagine what reason to give. But of course now the problem was that the desired public outcry necessary to spur Governor Cassidy into action on the sea sanctuary would never come about.

"My influence extends only so far," Maggie Lynch was saying to DJ on the phone the day after Orca HQ had been shut down. "I really don't see how I'm going to make this a top issue with the governor."

"You're not going to give up, are you, Ms. Lynch?"

"Of course not, Mr. Parker. I suppose I'll simply have to find another way to approach him. Another angle. But there are bigger problems than the sanctuary, my dear boy. The whales are still with OneWorld. Even with a sanctuary, how are we ever going to convince the rest of the board to part with them? The plan might have worked had the sale been made to the Russians. International pressure and all that. But the State Department has put a stop to that, of course, what with the Sergachev fiasco. Neftkomp is now prevented from investing in the United States. But even with the Russians, the plan still depended on the demonstration. Everything hinged on you being able to prove to the world how smart cetacea are."

"Which I won't do, Ms. Lynch. The whales deserve to live free and unmolested. If I let the world know how smart they are, the exploitation of those animals will make the old whale hunts seem tame by comparison. Everybody will be after what they have. No, the intelligence of cetacea must remain our secret."

"And I am not fundamentally in disagreement with you. But how, pray tell, do you plan to rescue the existing thirty captive whales from OneWorld? And even if you could, where would you put them?"

"Ms. Lynch, I'm still confident that you can help with the second question. You'll find a way to get the governor to okay the swap of Reid Harbor for Spieden Island. I just know you can do that."

"Hmm...we'll see."

"As to the answer to the first question, so far as I know, OneWorld is still up for sale, is it not?"

"I suppose so."

"Tell the board you have another interested buyer."

"In heaven's name who, Mr. Parker?"

"Me, Ms. Lynch."

"You? But OneWorld must be worth almost as much as, well, as I imagine your entire stake in Yaba is worth. How could you possibly swing the purchase without..."

"Without selling my stake in Yaba? I couldn't. And so I will. I'll have to sell my house in Half Moon Bay, too. That house was always way too big for me, anyway."

"My goodness, Mr. Parker. What then will you do? Where will you live?"

"Orcas Island, Ms. Lynch. My family estate. Seahaven. I'm going home. This time for good."

"But your company..."

"I love my company, Ms. Lynch. But it's time to move on. I still have a few ideas up my sleeve. You might hear from me yet. In the meantime, I'll buy OneWorld, close the parks, and move the whales to that sanctuary you're going to get for me."

There was a long pause on the other end of the line before Maggie finally said, "I'll try, Mr. Parker. I'll certainly try."

THIRTY-EIGHT

September 2021

Maggie Lynch was better than her word. The matter was ultimately resolved by a promise to make a donation to the governor's charity of choice. In the governor's name. Maggie was able to get Lloyd McGuire to chip in, too. Both had had an unexpected windfall the year prior and neither had felt especially good about it. The publicity for the governor was priceless. It was widely believed that the photo op at the Seattle Children's Cancer Institute with the governor handing the trustees the oversized check was what clinched his re-election. That's what forty million dollars buys you.

The biggest business story of the year was the story of David James Parker selling his interest in Yaba. It was quite unexpected. "I'm just ready to move on to other things," he had said by way of explanation. He remained as CEO for a few weeks to ensure a smooth transition and there was word that he had briefly considered staying on as CEO. Instead, he stayed involved as a board member. Chairman of the board, in fact. But he was more than happy to put the day-to-day operational business of Yaba in the hands of new leadership.

Then came another big story—David James Parker's purchase of OneWorld. This made sense in a way. It had been his father's company, after all. Everybody assumed Parker wanted to keep the tradition going. But then another huge story came on the heels of that one: Parker was going to close the parks and move the whales to a sanctuary on what used to be government property in the Salish Sea. Governor Cassidy had okayed the swap of Reid Harbor and Stuart Island State Park for Speiden Island, where the state park would be relocated. Some loyal OneWorld customers were disappointed, but, overall, the idea of releasing the whales to a sanctuary was met with strong approval by the general public. Enough was known about orcas to suggest a significant level of intelligence. According to the news articles that reported on the development of the sanctuary, orcas had the ability to communicate with each other by clicks and whistles and pulsed calls. "A definite language," *All World News* reported, "though obviously nowhere close to the sophistication of human language."

It was a whirlwind of events and by the time it all came to pass, David James Parker was living peacefully on Orcas Island, finally out of the public eye. His main interest now was overseeing the progress of the sanctuary as it neared completion.

And now it was nearing the end of summer and he and JJ were out in DJ's forty-foot Riviera. DJ had cut the engine and the boat was floating on the flat sea, just off the mouth of Reid Harbor, fifty yards or so from recently-named Kucherov Point where the underwater barrier would begin. The pilings that would serve as support columns for the barrier had been driven into the bottom of the sea floor. The barrier itself was still in the manufacturing stage but nearly finished and almost ready to be delivered by barge. It was a flexible mesh made out of a high-grade stainless steel that would nevertheless require continual maintenance to keep secure from the harsh saltwater. The mesh was wide enough to allow salmon and other food sources in but small enough to keep the orcas from getting out.

Just the same, monitoring would take place to make certain that the levels of food available for the orcas were satisfactory. NOAA, the National Oceanic and Atmospheric Administration, had given its blessing to the sanctuary and, along with the Washington State Parks and Recreation Commission, had agreed to help with the monitoring to ensure the safety and well-being of the whales. Non-invasive observational recordings would be made on a regular basis, but under no circumstances was any type of experimentation to be permitted. The idea was to allow the orcas to live out their lives in an environment that mimicked the wild as closely as possible. The annual costs would be significant but DJ had the funds necessary to pay the costs for the remainder of his life. From there, a trust would be set up to make certain the costs would be paid for the rest of the orcas' lives.

These would hopefully be the last orcas ever held in captivity, something DJ would be dedicated to ensuring through his contributions to various global lobbying groups. Legislation outlawing the captivity of cetacea would eventually be passed in almost every country, Russia being a significant holdout. The president of the Russian Federation still liked the idea of opening a string of marine parks complete with killer whales. Rumor had it that he wanted to run some experiments with the whales. He'd become interested in their intelligence. Only time would tell how successful he'd be in his efforts.

"She's here," said JJ, as the Riviera drifted towards the first piling. DJ and JJ watched her through the clear water, her dorsal fin coming closer. Then she turned and swam a complete circle around the Riviera, inverting herself playfully at one point to show her snow-white underbelly. Finally, she spyhopped, rising vertically out of the water and kicking her tail flukes to maintain her position just a few feet away, keeping her eyes fixed on JJ the whole time. Then she slipped below the water.

"She said thanks," JJ said. "Chumley said thanks. She said thanks." But for once, DJ felt as if he didn't need the translation.

"She's looking forward to seeing Boo," JJ continued. "Seeing her son. Joy. She says she feels joy. She'll come here and visit all the time. All the time."

The boys watched as Chumley swam out of sight, but then she turned and came back, her dorsal fin visible as she bobbed up and down towards the boat. When she got to within a few yards, she spyhopped again, this time her gaze falling on DJ. Then, back under the water she went.

"What was that about?" said DJ.

"She...she said she forgives James Parker. She forgives Dad, DJ. She forgives Dad."

I'm haunted by the sight of that mother looking at me, James had said to DJ. *I have to make it right.*

DJ waved towards Chumley who swam off one last time. He wanted to say something to JJ about their father, but he remained silent, not trusting his voice to the lump in his throat.

The two sat quietly on the boat for quite a while after that. Finally, JJ broke the silence. "How come Boo can't live with Chumley?" he said.

"He's not accustomed to living in the wild, JJ," DJ replied. "It would be dangerous."

"Chumley could take care of him. Chumley. J Pod would look out for him. Sometimes...sometimes you can be safe if... if others are looking out for you." He glanced up at DJ and then quickly glanced away, towards the water.

DJ smiled. "Yes, I suppose that's true, little brother. Well, I'll tell you what—I'll consider it. Maybe the next time we see Chumley, we'll ask her."

JJ nodded.

Soon, it would be heading towards evening. Kioko would be back at Seahaven preparing dinner and DJ knew they should start making their way in. He loved these little excursions. Strange that with all the money he used to have before he'd bought OneWorld, the one thing he'd never bought for himself in all of the time he lived in San Francisco was a boat. Just never had the time. But he had a boat now. And he made good use of it. He'd forgotten how much he missed being out on the water, missed the Salish Sea in particular, missed the San Juan Islands.

He was fitting into his new life nicely and often wondered how he could have been away from home for so long. It felt natural to be back here. It felt right. He loved Seahaven, loved Orcas Island, loved the people. He'd become something of a celebrity around the place, showing up at Spanky's on Saturday nights from time to time and buying the house a round. But he maintained his privacy as well and the residents let him.

For the first time in his life, DJ felt as if he had everything he needed.

Well, almost everything. The fact is, he hadn't stopped thinking about her. They'd talked on the phone a few times, but that just made the yearning worse. She was in his head and he suspected she'd always be there. Maybe it was the interaction with Chumley that day. Maybe it was the thoughts of his father. Or maybe it was just the way the late afternoon sunlight was bouncing off the water. Whatever it was, he finally decided enough was enough. What did he have to lose? He glanced over at JJ, who was now dozing under the shade of the boat's Bimini top. Then he pulled out his phone and made a call.

"Hi, it's me," he said when she answered. "Listen, I've been thinking about you. A lot. I was wondering if you'd like to join me up here. I really think you'd find it beautiful this time of year."

– The End –

A WORD FROM THE AUTHOR

Although this is a work of fiction, this story makes use, albeit fictitiously, of very real places that, in the course of my life, I have become intimately familiar with, the Salish Sea being the principal locale. I have also become intimately familiar with the beautiful and magnificent animals that make the Salish Sea their home—the orcas, the Southern Resident Killer Whales in particular. This community of whales, once flourishing in those waters, is now listed under the Endangered Species Act by the National Marine Fisheries Service of the National Oceanic and Atmospheric Administration. The roundups of these whales have, sadly, been anything but fictitious. Additionally, a decrease in Chinook salmon, high levels of man-made contaminants and chemicals in the waters, and an increase in vessel traffic, have all conspired to push the SRKW towards extinction. There are only seventy-five remaining as of this writing. If the publication of this book does anything to bolster awareness of the plight of the SRKW, I will consider it a success. Let us hope it is not too late to help return these intelligent, sensitive, grand creatures to the glorious days in which they once thrived.

ACKNOWLEDGMENTS

I am especially grateful to all of the wonderful researchers and scientists, worldwide, who have dedicated their lives to the study of marine mammals. Your continued mission has inspired me. I hope you'll forgive any scientific or geographic errors or inconsistencies I might have inadvertently made in the course of writing this book.

ABOUT THE AUTHOR

Barry Swanson is a marine naturalist, a steward of the environment, and a singer/songwriter. He lives with his family in the Pacific Northwest on the beautiful Salish Sea.

Printed in Great Britain
by Amazon